'This lovely book wraps yo[...]
A wonderfull[...]
Julietta Henderson, au[...]
About Nor[...]

'A delightful, funny, rom[...]
and romance to b[...]
Ericka Waller, author of *Dog Days*

'A feel-good treat'
i newspaper

'A joyous celebration of female friendship, community,
and the power and freedom found in later life, it will
warm the cockles of your heart'
Sunday Post

'A heartening read'
CultureFly

'This book is all heart and all soul . . . and just
the right amount of humour'
Frost

'A brilliantly fun feminist adventure about
friendship and second chances'
Best

'*The Invisible Women's Club* celebrates brave, bold, tenacious
women who fight for each other and for what they believe in'
Bookanista

'A lovely read about friendship'
Bella

'Funny and joyful'
Woman's Own

'A charming story about finding your voice'
Good Housekeeping

'It's so refreshing to read a story with such
well-drawn mature women at its heart'
Yours

www.penguin.co.uk

Helen Paris worked in the performing arts for two decades, touring internationally with her London-based theatre company, Curious. After several years living in San Francisco and working as a theatre professor at Stanford University, she returned to the UK to focus on writing fiction.

Also by Helen Paris

LOST PROPERTY

THE INVISIBLE WOMEN'S CLUB

HELEN PARIS

PENGUIN BOOKS

TRANSWORLD PUBLISHERS
Penguin Random House, One Embassy Gardens,
8 Viaduct Gardens, London SW11 7BW
www.penguin.co.uk

Transworld is part of the Penguin Random House group of companies
whose addresses can be found at global.penguinrandomhouse.com

Penguin
Random House
UK

First published in Great Britain in 2023 by Doubleday
an imprint of Transworld Publishers
Penguin paperback edition published 2024

A CIP catalogue record for this book
is available from the British Library.

ISBN
9781804991084

Typeset in Sabon LT Pro by Jouve (UK), Milton Keynes.
Printed and bound in Great Britain by Clays Ltd, Elcograf S.p.A.

The authorized representative in the EEA is Penguin Random House Ireland,
Morrison Chambers, 32 Nassau Street, Dublin D02 YH68.

Penguin Random House is committed to a sustainable future
for our business, our readers and our planet. This book is made
from Forest Stewardship Council® certified paper.

MIX
Paper | Supporting
responsible forestry
FSC® C018179

For Juliette Avril Paris, my darling mum

1

Janet Pimm's chance at a new life almost went out with the recycling. She was crouching kerbside, swiftly sorting the paper from the tin before her neighbour Bev could collar her with yet another of her befriend-the-elderly overtures, when something in the newspaper caught her eye. Uncrumpling it, she carefully brushed off a leaf of Assam that hadn't made it into the compost caddy. And there it was. Her finger trembled slightly as she traced under the words.

Are you retired? A keen gardener?

Would you like to share your enthusiasm for horticulture and historic landscapes with others?

If so, this could be the position for you!

That familiar logo, those dear snub-nosed leaves of the oak, seeming almost to . . . reach out to her. Janet read the advert aloud, savoured the words in her mouth, editing them slightly as she did so.

'Share your enthusiasm *and extensive knowledge of* horticulture, *particularly medicinal herbs and evergreens*, with others.'

1

And, of course, those other words, sweet as honeysuckle nectar, which ran along the top of the advert:

National Trust

What a heady rush *those* words left in their wake! What horticultural idylls they conjured! It was Nancy who had first introduced Janet to the National Trust. Janet, brought up to watch her pennies, had baulked at the entry prices, but Nancy waved her protestations away and before long they would regularly round off a weekend's hiking with coffee and a walnut slice at a National Trust garden.

Janet knew the job was for her, knew deep inside. She felt it as a yearning, pulling from her heart up the column of her throat to her lips, which opened slightly in anticipation and let out a small moan. From the moment the longing took up residence in the hollow of her breast, Janet sensed herself moving through her quiet, tapered life with a renewed sense of purpose. She felt a tilt to her shoulders that if not exactly jaunty was at least somewhat spry, and though it might be excessive to say there was a caper in her stride, it would be perfectly acceptable to describe it as a clip.

She telephoned the number on the advert immediately to put her name forward and was told that all applicants would be contacted for an informal interview after submitting a brief online form. The link to the form would be emailed to her in due course. Due course? Why, that could be any moment! Janet raced upstairs to her chilly spare room, pulled the dust cloth off her grey breeze block of a computer, and thenceforth commenced a regular patrol of her inbox, which remained steadfastly empty.

Until today.

Gobbling her breakfast, Janet throws on her old fisherman's jumper, arms herself with a cup of Assam and rushes to the spare room, taking the stairs two at a time despite her knees and the tea slopping into the saucer.

1. Why are you applying for this position?

offers a multiple choice of responses from

To develop my knowledge and interests

to

To make a difference to the natural environment

but what really catches Janet's attention is

To meet like-minded people and make new friends.

Janet lingers for quite a while over that one. 'Like-minded people,' she mutters, gazing through the plume of steam curling from her teacup, lightly stroking the tips of her fingers across her lips.
There are a couple of further options to do with 'time' and 'usefulness' that Janet pretends not to see.

Then she selects 'Other' from the drop-down menu, which opens up a small box allowing her to input her own answer.

She rolls her shoulders, flexes her fingers and gets as far as *to share my extensive knowledge of plants, particularly evergree* – before a warning flashes up informing her that she has reached her 'character limit'.

Janet directs a variety of terse and colourful comments at the computer screen, including the fact that one 'clearly needs to be trained in the art of ruddy haiku!' in order to fill out the form.

Things improve significantly by the time she gets to

2. Can you list any relevant experience and qualifications?

'Now you're talking!' Janet's fingers dance happily over the keys.

Finally, the form is complete, and Janet sits back, reads it through once and then once again, her pulse zipping like a fast-flying pollinator. When has she been flooded with such a sense of vitality? Last May, when her little *Daphne odora* had such a growth spurt?

Is there anything else?

No, try as she might, Janet can't remember the last time she felt such a rush of . . . of . . . oh, what is it, exactly?

Life.

She has, she realizes, been living in the shade, curled over like a fiddlehead fern. But this new calling coaxes her upwards to unfurl towards the light. Perhaps now the blessed rains will come to quench her thirst. Rinse her clean of her sins.

At last.

She presses send, clips downstairs to make her lunch and sets off to the allotments with a spring in her step.

Janet works at her allotment daily, from one p.m. till six p.m. sharp, making it abundantly clear to anyone interested that she has *several* other places to be each morning and every evening. She eats her lunch at midday, chews her cheese-and-tomato sandwich deliberately, sips her tea slowly. Only when the clock strikes the half-hour does she lace her hikers, pick up her Thermos, snap two Bath Olivers into the Lakeland 'Biscuits for One' snack container and set off for her plot at Seaview.

Order and Routine. Her two bookends, essential since retirement. Whip Order and Routine away and you might manage to remain upright for a moment, but it's only a matter of time before the fall comes, toppling you forward into chaos and snapping your spine. Upright and evergreen, that's how Janet likes it.

Once at the allotment she can easily make her tasks last all afternoon. There's always something to do, which is one of the things that is so agreeable about gardening. It keeps you in the present.

Which is precisely where Janet wants to be.

Today her euphorbias keep her busy. As she tends them, she thinks back to the National Trust application and her thoughts rise like sap as she goes over her answers and imagines the interview – when it might be and where.

Across Seaview Allotments, gardeners whizz back and forth, chatting to each other. But not to Janet.

'This weather certainly puts a song in your heart!' the

Power Ballad couple at Plot 35 warble across her plot to the couple at Plot 33.

'And a smile on your face!' the 33s call back over the hedge. 'Spring is in the air!'

Everyone goes gaga for spring, Janet thinks, reaching into her gardening-apron pocket for her secateurs and snapping them open. Fully grown adults paroxysmal about buds and blossom. People with no fidelity to nature suddenly dewy-eyed about 'pops' of colour, endlessly photographing Parma violet panicles of lilac. Anyone who knows anything about gardens knows they aren't about ruddy pops of colour; they're about sex and death. It's not that Janet has anything against spring itself. Not at all; in fact, she appreciates its forthrightness.

One thing she particularly admires is the behaviour of flowers towards their pollinators. Her favourite is the silken-petalled bee orchid who waits, holding it all back, until her pollinator, the dashing carpenter bee, vibrates its wings at a precise middle C frequency. Only when the bee reaches that desired note does the flower succumb, release her shower of golden pollen.

'Brava!' Janet says, pausing from her euphorbias for a moment to imagine the scene. Perhaps it is somewhat similar to making love to Chopin's Nocturne in C Sharp Minor? The ardent, attentive suitor, that quivering, pulsating C . . .

'Janet, quick word?' Patrice, Chair of Seaview Allotments, stands at the grassy border of Janet's plot.

Janet startles, feels her cheeks flush. How long has Patrice been standing there? Patrice is a proper gardener. On occasion Janet finds herself lingering by Patrice's plot, admiring the handsome viridescence of her kale, the generous abundance of her cauliflower and the downright pluck and ambition of her wasabi. Mid-sixties, so a few years younger than Janet, Patrice also dresses like a proper gardener: earthy corduroy trousers, unbleached cotton drill work shirts, a pair of sturdy cracked leather boots. Perhaps Patrice might like to give Janet's *Magnolia grandiflora* a quick once-over? It's looking particularly radiant this afternoon, the coppery underside of its leaves like the lining of a fancy dinner jacket. Janet quickly rakes her gloved hand through her silver hair, hopes she hasn't left a streak of mud on her forehead and strides towards her.

But Patrice's usually friendly face is tense and her eyes – an exact early-autumn sweet chestnut – look anxious.

'We've had a bit of a . . . complaint, I'm afraid. From Nick and Mary.'

Who the heck are Nick and Mary? Janet frowns and Patrice gestures towards Plot 33. Ah, her neighbours to the east.

'Apparently you left a "load of shit" on their plot?'

Janet nods enthusiastically. Indeed she had (and is yet to be thanked!).

'I spotted a hint of early blight on their tomatoes so I brewed up a fresh batch of my steer manure tea for them – thought they might still be able to save the plants if they gave them a good dousing.'

'Right. I see.' Patrice shifts uncomfortably. 'The thing is, did you explain it like that to Nick and Mary? Because they seem to think you did it to . . . get at them.'

'*Get at them?*' Janet's brow furrows. Not only was it a particularly excellent batch of tea – you could tell that by the punch of its aroma alone – but she had neglected several tasks on her own plot in order to concoct it. Also, she had left the manure in her best zinc-galvanized ribbed metal bucket, which, it might be noted, has still not been returned.

'It seems there was a . . . disagreement recently. About the hedge?' Patrice gestures to the hawthorn running between the two plots.

'We didn't come to fisticuffs, I can assure you. I simply informed them that pruning the hedgerow at the start of the nesting season meant that the sparrows would not return to their nests and so . . .' Janet pauses, clenches her gloved hands, clears her throat. 'And so they had, in effect, killed the babies.' An image slashes before her: the baby birds, hungry and alone, crying out for their mother. Their mother who never comes. Janet forces a painful swallow.

'I see.' Patrice nods, her eyes soft. 'It's just that I think they thought the shi— that the manure tea was a sort of . . . revenge. A joke at their expense.'

Janet stares at Patrice. Why would she joke about any of this?

'I know you didn't mean to upset them,' Patrice says, her voice wonderfully warm. 'I do know that.' She reaches her hand out towards Janet.

'Do not touch me!' Janet barks, taking two large steps back. Euphorbia sap – hell to pay if it gets in your eyes. She is shielded by her gloves and goggles; Patrice is not.

Patrice's arm falls to her side and when she speaks her voice has lost its cardigan of warmth. 'The thing is, it's not the first time something like this has happened. There was the incident with Lakshmi's roses. Mickey's weeding.'

Ah.

It is true that when Janet spied Lakshmi decapitating the

Lady Jane Greys with all the vigour and vim of an executioner at the Tower, she had rushed towards her, commanding her to STOP! In retrospect, her voice *might* have come out at a sharper register than intended. Of course, she hadn't meant to startle Lakshmi and she most certainly did not want Patrice to think badly of her. But a tisane of rosehip could do wonders for Lakshmi's joint pain. The woman was a first-rate worker, but Janet had lost count of the times she had seen her stop to massage her wrists, rub her aching shoulders. If Lakshmi deadheaded the roses, she would never get those precious healing rosehips.

Mickey and his bally gooseberry balls were another matter entirely.

'The man's proclivity for destroying things rivals Stalin!' Janet says, keen to get Patrice on side. 'The chap was tearing up the nettles on his plot like he was cutting a path through the jungles of Borneo.' Janet had held her tongue for as long as she was able. Until she wasn't. 'There. Are. No. Weeds. In. Nature!' she had boomed at Mickey. It was perhaps fair to say that some aggro had ensued.

Janet needs to make Patrice understand. As luck would have it, an accommodating bee swaggers past in drunken delight en route from dandelion to tulip. 'See! Pollinators don't discriminate! Humans fixate on distinguishing "plants" from "weeds", decreeing who can stay and who must go. It makes no sense! Nettles are excellent for so many things!' She lists them on her gloved fingers: 'Blood pressure, muscle aches, not to mention prostate, as I made a point of telling Mickey.' Janet stares at Patrice through her goggles. 'At his age and with that expanding waistline, he could certainly benefit from some nettles.'

'I take your point,' Patrice says, nodding slowly. 'It's just . . . we have to let people make their own decisions when it comes to their plots.'

There is a pause and Janet is afraid Patrice is about to turn and go. But suddenly Patrice reaches out to examine Janet's French artichoke. Its silver hue is luminous against her dark skin. 'Not everyone sees plants the way you do, Janet,' Patrice says quietly before finally taking her leave.

Janet stands and watches Patrice walk down the grassy path across the allotments until she eventually loses sight of her behind a row of pent sheds.

Finally finished with her euphorbias, Janet gives them a quick check for whitefly, then removes her goggles and gloves, settles in her upright garden chair and gets out her tartan Thermos. Tea streams into the cup. *Not everyone sees plants the way you do, Janet.* Is that a good thing? She hopes so. Ever since taking over her plot at Seaview, Janet has tried to share her knowledge with the other allotmenteers, to disperse like pollen the endless possibilities and wonders of plants. For the love of God and Gertrude Jekyll, has she tried! Yet despite her best intentions, her efforts always seem to misfire. Janet shakes her head and dunks a Bath Oliver into her tea. Sunlight warms the hollows of her cheeks and she breathes in the friendly scent of her sage. Trying not to dwell on the many ways in which she might have upset her fellow gardeners – and, worst of all, Patrice – Janet focuses her attention on her prospective position at the National Trust, on all the new people she will meet. The future spools out, suddenly full of possibility. And to think the advert might have passed her by that day, like an airborne dandelion seed floating across her field of vision. It physically pains Janet to think she might so easily have missed her chance.

Laughter trills across the plots. Janet puts a hand to her brow and squints. Towards the front gates of the allotments, near Patrice's plot and the shed where one can rent lawnmowers, strimmers and wheelbarrows, a sizeable group are seated in a semicircle listening to a talk. No doubt some nonsense organized by Felicity (bloody Kendal!) and her crowd, certainly nothing Janet would have any interest in, had anyone thought to invite her. *Hanging Baskets That Thrill, Spill and Fill!*, *Peonies That Pop!* or, scraping the barrel, *Organizing Osteospermum for Outrageous Opulence!* A messy bricolage of overused adjectives. Not to mention a preponderance of exclamation marks everywhere like a poke in the eye. What the heck does any of that have to do with proper gardening? Why not throw caution to the wind with *Pulsating Posies of Promiscuous Petunias!* and have done with it? And anyway, whatever twaddle is going on, Janet is Far Too Busy.

More laughter erupts across the allotments and Janet peers harder. Good grief, are refreshments being served? *Cake?* Her stomach grumbles. Janet is rather partial to a nice slice of walnut cake. She brushes the pale, dry crumbs of Bath Oliver from her aproned lap. Well, blah de blah de bloody Bakewell, because her new job comes with *several* additional benefits; not only is the uniform provided free of charge, but staff are allowed to purchase refreshments from the National Trust tea shop at a significant discount! So that is bound to mean an ever-ready selection of high-quality buns at her disposal. Huzzah! At the National Trust Janet can begin anew, make a fresh start in a place where her knowledge of plants will be appreciated. There, things will be different.

And now that her online form has been submitted, Janet must get ready for the next stage of the application process – the interview! Although described as 'informal', Janet knows that one can never be too prepared. Which is why she has already started composing a detailed presentation in her head. Because one can always work a little harder, make things a little better. Janet has tried to do that. Worked hard, stayed late, gone the extra mile. The strategy proved successful for her in the early years – top marks in her exams at school, first one in her family to go to university, then straight into a good position at GCHQ. All those years in the office dotting every 'i', crossing every 't', never leaving anything to chance. Everything progressed along nicely.

Until it all fell apart.

But that won't happen this time. This time everything will work out. It has to.

Janet sits bolt upright. She knows exactly what she will wear when called to interview: her jacket-and-skirt two-piece which happens to be *the same precise shade of green as the National Trust uniform*, subliminally messaging that she *already* works there. Rudimentary psychology! She raises her Tupperware teacup in a little toast.

Janet Pimm still has what it takes.

～

It has been over a week now since her interview and Janet is wheeling a barrow of compost to her plot, brow furrowed.

'All right, Janet?' Patrice calls. But Janet doesn't hear her. She is staring deeply into the jolting mound of manure.

It should have arrived by now, Janet thinks to herself. Lowering the wheelbarrow for a moment, she stands lost in thought, returning once more to the day of the interview. She remembers slipping on her hunter-green outfit, her scrupulously polished Oxfords, dusting off her faded leather briefcase and packing it with biro, spiral-bound notebook, even a novel for the train – though of course Janet spent every minute of the journey going over her interview notes. True, she had been rather hoping the formalities would take place in the grounds of a minor stately home at least – Scotney, perhaps, an excellent example of the picturesque style – or a garden like Emmetts, which boasted some rather nice exotic shrubs. Even Kipling's old stomping ground at Bateman's would have had something to offer. The National Trust regional offices and prefab conference centre at Icklesham were therefore rather a dampener.

She told the interviewer she'd especially like to lead tours and that she would be delighted to write her own. Her tours would not be burdened with useless trivia: the names of Elizabethan heirs, the date the Trust took stewardship of the property, how many billiard tables and wig rooms . . . blah de blah de blah. No. JP's Tours would focus on evergreens and medicinal plants. She had proactively suggested roving between various National Trust properties, creating bespoke seasonal garden tours (which would require a modest travel allowance). She could, she had relayed, speak *in detail* about the box hedge at Hidcote, not to mention the cropped yews in the Pillar Garden, the conifers, the Mediterranean spurge. At Sissinghurst she could talk *at length* about the evergreen star jasmine with its glossy ovate leaves. There was so much she could impart! So much she would share. The interviewer had stared at her, visibly stunned.

How smart Janet had felt in her green jacket-and-skirt two-piece, how refreshing to be paid attention to. What a day! It really couldn't have gone any better. So where is her letter? Janet grips the wheelbarrow harder and plods heavily on towards her plot. Allowing a couple of days for the paperwork to go to Human Resources, then one day in the post – two at a pinch if sent second class (really, though? The National Trust?) – it should have arrived three days ago. Janet has been finding reasons to nip into her chilly hallway – to grab a cardie from the tallboy, make sure the light is off in the downstairs loo – and steal a glance at the coir doormat under the letterbox. She has stood sentinel in the bay window of her front room, a yellow duster clutched in her hand, waiting for the postman. But though her windowsill gleams, no envelope with an oak-leaf logo has made its way to her.

Yesterday, settling down to her lunch, she had distinctly heard the click of the letterbox and bolted out into the hallway, still clutching her sandwich. And there it was! A triangle of white poking through the flap, like the crisp sail of a boat, ready to whisk her off on her new adventure. But it wasn't from the National Trust. It was a flyer heralding the forthcoming production of *The Mousetrap* by the East Sussex Players, featuring a picture of the local butcher wearing a false moustache and a homburg hat, and peering through a monocle at a bloody dagger. On the back, scrawled in messy biro: *THIS LOOKS FUN! BEV.*

Janet crushed the flyer so viciously she dropped her sandwich. The bread slices flew apart, showering grated Cheddar up the hallway, splattering sliced tomato on the cold tile.

Today she actually went out to the gate as the postman passed and called after him.

Was he sure? Absolutely sure? Nothing for Number 11 *at all*?

The postman hunched his shoulders, shook his head.

Perhaps the hold-up is due to an administrative delay? Just one of those piddly bureaucratic things? They do happen . . . Very well, fair enough. Tomorrow, then? Yes, Janet nods assertively, tomorrow definitely. She gives the wheelbarrow a vigorous push and turns up the grassy path that leads to her plot. Tomorrow. Once she gets the official letter, all will be well. They will probably want her to start immediately. She will request Thursdays to Sundays so that she can still work at the allotment all day Monday to Wednesday. She could never give up her plot, obviously.

Will her uniform be posted ahead to wear on arrival, or will it be there for her to collect on her first day? Perhaps a green bib and braces with knee-pad pockets is already hanging on a peg waiting for her at Sissinghurst! The wheelbarrow positively rattles along the path now. Janet imagines her group waiting at the Designated Meeting Point, ready to follow her, attend to her every word. She will generously allow a couple of moments' wait for latecomers, but once they set off she will keep her group at a good pace to show they are part of something important, something to be valued. There is nothing Janet knows about plants that she won't share with her flock. She will give them everything she has.

No longer will her most sustained social intercourse of the week be talking back to *Gardeners' Question Time* – Leroy from Pontypridd wanting to know the best way to eradicate wild garlic: 'Eat it, for heck's sake!'

A new chapter is about to begin. Finally.

To meet like-minded people and make new friends?

Oh, please yes.

2

In the fortnight since Janet's interview her coriander has taken off apace and her crop of lemon balm perfumes the air, but still no letter from the National Trust. Janet stays positive. Keeps busy. Why, this afternoon alone she has bedded in some borage, whipped up a batch of nettle-and-comfrey fertilizer and broken ground on a new herb bed. The blade of her spade thrusts into the earth, turns out heavy clumps of clay. Thrust and turn, thrust and turn. She feels the tug in her biceps, the pull in her thighs. As she digs Janet imagines leading her eager tour group along the herbaceous borders of Biddulph Grange, pictures herself swapping horticultural anecdotes with her new colleagues. Thrust and turn, thrust and turn. Any day now she will hear; the letter will come.

'We've been admiring your bumper crop of radishes!' The Power Ballad couple lob chit-chat over Janet's head to the Steer Manures on her other side.

'Happy to share the harvest!' the Steer Manures lob back.

The thing about getting old, Janet thinks as she shovels, is that age erases you. Especially if you're a woman.

FANCY THIS? her neighbour Bev had scrawled on the

latest flyer, which she posted through Janet's door this morning. '*Not one bit!*' Janet muttered as she tossed it in the bin. *Paradise Lost* this time; a glossy image of Eve (raunchy), Satan in the form of a serpent (paunchy) and an apple (Bramley! A cooker, for heck's sake!). Bev seems to be labouring under the misguided impression Janet is some doddery dear in need of an outing, a lonely oldie so desperate for a bit of company she'd gratefully watch the local am-dram troupe churn out another farce as stale as jam roly-poly from the Silver Jubilee. What does Bev know about old age? She probably hasn't even broken fifty. Try being seventy-two! Janet's fingers whiten as she tightens her grip on her spade. Community centres, bingo drives, church dos – who do they think old people are? Constantly funnelled off to places that need a good sweep, where the milk is on the turn. Apart from her knees, Janet is in excellent shape, and not just for her age, thank you very much! She doesn't need Bev's charity chumminess. She has a first-class mind. She had an exciting career – went behind the Iron Curtain back in the day! But no one sees any of that. In fact, days go by without anyone seeming to see Janet at all. Janet clamps down on her back molars so hard her fillings zing. Under her unruly shock of silver hair, the angles of her face sharpen.

That was one of the things Janet had so appreciated about the National Trust advert. They were *actively seeking* elders; they clearly valued the experience and expertise that came with those extra years. In fact, Janet thinks – standing the spade in the earth a moment to rest her aching back – in the world of plants, age is revered. Just look at how people flock to the old-growth redwood forests, go bonkers about ancient oaks, not to mention all the fuss made about the five-thousand-year-old Fortingall Yew! It's the same with gardeners – experience is an asset. Hadn't she read something in the paper just the other day about a 104-year-old chap who was not only still gardening but had taken to social media to share his top tips with a new generation?

Janet gives a nod of satisfaction, mops her brow and takes a moment to admire her evergreens. How much joy they bring her. Symbiotic, really, one's relationships with plants – give and take. Not unlike parenting, she reflects, especially in those early days, when the new seedling depends on you, demands all your care and attention. That dear wobbly head needing support, that small, fragile body reliant on you for sustenance and protection. Spellbound, you chart all the firsts: first shoot, first leaf, first bud. You tether its gangly growing body to a slim stake and watch it take off like a child on its first bicycle ride with stabilizers. Whoosh! Janet reaches down to stroke a young frond of spearmint that dandles against her calf. She runs her fingers lightly over the soft fuzz of its new leaf, breathes in its familiar smell, minty-toothpaste fresh. Closing her eyes, Janet is lost in memories for a moment, until finally, with a heavy sigh, she straightens up. Even when they become less dependent, plants stay where you put them. Her evergreens will never leave her.

All they want is a bit of love. Is that too much to ask? Janet radiates love to all plants, from the agapanthus to the zinnia, but it can't be denied – her heart beats strongest for evergreens. She can enjoy the beauty of autumnal colours as well as the next person, but for Janet there is something intensely sad about that flush of russet, that last gasp of orange, that dash of magenta already fading as it falls. The very word 'deciduous', of course, has its roots in the Latin *decidus*, referring to 'that which falls down'. Janet does not want things to fall down. Janet wants everything standing tall and staying put. Evergreens are perfect; they do not seasonally shed and are never without leaves in some form or another. They are always there, full of colour. Evergreen is for life, for ever. Most certainly not just for Christmas.

Right, now, what next? Another task is required swiftly lest Janet start fretting about the missing National Trust letter for the umpteenth time. A spot more planting? Yes, planting would be a welcome break from digging. Janet reties the strings of her gardening apron and neatens the motley assembly of items in her front pocket: secateurs, dibber, roll of twine, trowel. Reaching deeper inside, she cups a palmful of seed, warm from the heat of her body. She likes the weight and shape of the seeds in her apron, the possibility of new life always carried with her. Threading a string of seeds through her thumb and finger, she sows it in a tray of dark soil, rich as chocolate. Using Adam's old baby spoon she measures out the seaweed fertilizer before adding it to the can, then waters the seeds in and carefully tucks them under one of her home-made cloches.

By the next time Janet looks up, early-evening light casts shadows across the sprawl of Seaview Allotments. Pent sheds and greenhouses perch on the edges of plots like houses on a Monopoly board. In the distance Beachy Head lurks like a secret being mulled over.

Janet watches other allotmenteers moving back and

forth across their parcels of land, chatting away to each other. Every Tom, Dick and Harriet calls themselves a gardener nowadays, but do they really know what it is to nurture, to tend? No, they ruddy well do not. If a plant shows any signs of fading, they yank it out and shove a new one in its place, something younger, fresher. People don't understand that gardening is about commitment. Fidelity. Instead of nurturing life, they spend their time fastidiously marking out their borders, delineating their territories. Still colonials at heart, Janet thinks with a snort.

Janet cuts her eye to Plot 40 opposite; its ruler-straight edges are a case in point. Mickey is never happier than when going at his grass verge hell for leather with a half-moon blade, marking out his domain. Hand-sieving his soil, for goodness' sake – what a performance! And his planting? No imagination whatsoever. Fannying around with those gooseberry bushes spring, summer, autumn and winter. He's as predictable as Vivaldi.

Not that Janet has anything against Vivaldi. At the thought of music, Janet slices her glance from Mickey's manicured border line across to Plot 35, where rows of silver CDs twirl from bamboo poles, strung up to deter the birds. Celine Dion, Bonnie Tyler and Jennifer Rush undulate and shimmy in the breeze. Janet's lips turn downward. The Power Ballad proprietors of Plot 35 are clearly happy to display their taste to all and sundry. That's not music, folks; it's just people washing-lining their emotions! But Janet has her own guilty pleasure: Rachmaninov's Piano Concerto No. 2. Oh, the passion and longing in every note! Janet takes her spade from where it stands upright in the earth and hugs it to her chest. She closes her eyes. Her favourite part is the second movement. First, the piano, *da da da dum dum dum da da*, then the flute joins in, the pure beauty carried in the exhale, perfectly controlled by that delicate embouchure, unsullied, like a first kiss. Janet's lips pucker.

'Coo-ee!' A shrill voice ruptures Janet's symphony.

Janet starts, quickly thrusts the spade into the soil, and looks up to see Felicity bloody Kendal closely resembling a blousy mophead hydrangea in some flounce of a dress, an artisan willow-woven trug of perfectly arranged shop-bought flowers swinging from her forearm. Felicity peers at Janet's plot, scrunches up her face.

'Oh dear, your green weedy things are rather running rampant this spring! I suppose it's a lot for you to manage *on your own*,' Felicity sing-songs, showing all her pearly teeth.

Felicity bloody Kendal and her Joules-decked chums have plots on a slice of the allotments Janet privately refers to as 'Belgravia', easily discernible by its pistachio-coloured Royal Horticultural Society benches and ridiculously impractical floral print Cath Kidston tools. Felicity and her Belgravia crowd tend to appear when the communal pizza oven is fired up or the sun is out, happy to witter away the hours whilst they get the chaps to mow their grass borders.

That's called gossiping, people, not gardening.

Janet comes to her plot in all weathers. She's a proper allotmenteer, like Patrice, not like those part-timers. You won't catch Janet standing around nattering about straw-berry pavlovas or whatever they babble on about. Janet is Far Too Busy.

'I just *adore* my plot in spring!' Felicity says. 'It's an absolute *riot* of colour!'

FbK's gardening expertise is as hamstrung as her deployment of idioms. <u>*Try harder*</u>! Janet wants to write in red biro, underscored twice, and stick it to Felicity's pistachio-framed shed window.

'A splash of pink here and there would cheer your plot up marvellously, don't you think?' FbK trills on. 'Perhaps in that rather dreary bed over there.' She jabs a manicured finger accusingly at Janet's japonica, which is now a delicate chartreuse in the early-evening light, droplets of water glimmering on its palmate leaves. 'Yes, a nice pop of colour here and there could really do wonders!' Felicity beams.

Dreary? Janet's plot pulsates with colour! Can Felicity not see the greens: hunter, Kelly *and* Paris? What about the parakeet? The lime? The pear and the emerald? Surely the woman has not missed the seafoam, pine and shamrock right under her nose? Not to mention the crocodile, basil, forest and jade . . .? Janet opens her mouth to tell Felicity about the greens, explain to her how full of possibility they are, the inhale before the exhale . . . but Felicity doesn't linger. She scatters her pastel words of wisdom like a handful of invasive spores and trips off.

That's all right, thinks Janet, her mouth collapsing back on itself then tightening into a thin white line. She can wait. She's used to waiting. Come November, when Felicity's plot is a slurry of bedraggled brown sludge, hers will still be vibrant, evergreen.

Hers will be a ruddy *riot*.

Janet doesn't need to look at her watch to know it is

almost six p.m. She feels it in the pit of her stomach, a grey coldness. Home time.

But there are still a few minutes left! Time to sow a few more seeds, surely? Till a bit more of the new herb bed?

But the certain call of church bells tolls the hour.

Time. For. You. To. Go. Home.

The coldness in her stomach spreads upwards to her chest.

The Power Ballad couple walk carefully around Janet's plot, crooning to each other softly. They stop to speak to the Steer Manure couple. They all laugh about something together.

'Have a lovely evening!' the Power Ballads call out to the Steer Manures as they walk on.

'You too!' the Steer Manures reply.

Janet wonders what might make an evening lovely. Preparing a nice supper, then company arriving . . . A bottle of wine, jewelled from the fridge. Two glasses. Roast chicken and a dish of buttered new potatoes, perhaps a sprig of her tarragon? Pudding, even – why not! Janet rubs her hands together. And after pudding . . .? At this point Janet's lovely evening imaginings become a little fogged. Conversation, of course – the words spilling, colliding, overlapping with the desire to . . . connect. And then . . . and then . . . a moment, a look, and finally mouths moving close, then closer still . . . Then sort of a cross-fade to the next morning and waking up to the sounds of someone whistling in the bathroom. Janet has always appreciated a good whistler – such a true and honest sound, though few people still practise the art of whistling any more. The smell of fresh coffee, the sky bright, a day opening to spend together . . . Ah yes, that would be lovely indeed.

Janet pictures her empty house and sighs. Then she tightens her gardening apron, puts her spade in her shed and gives herself a good talking to. She has her plot, her plants, and, any moment now, something else. Something full of sparkle, like a necklace of early-morning dew glittering on her beloved rosemary. Her new job with the National Trust. Soon everything will be different. Finally, her world will open up again.

3

At last! The light sigh of arrival as the letter lands on the coir. The oak leaf beckons like an outstretched hand.

Janet beams as she fills the kettle, hums as she slots bread into the toaster, chuckles as she reaches into the fridge for the marmalade then stops and instead gets the jar of cherry jam from the top shelf of the pantry. She wipes away a skirting of dust and prises the lid off with a satisfying pop. New job, new bloody jam!

Her mint-green cup trembles in its saucer as she takes it out of the cupboard. Hot water streams into the teapot, the silver strainer perfectly spans the china mouth of the cup and already she is leading her attentive tour group through Trengwainton, through Nymans, Dorneywood. Through *Sissinghurst*! She whistles the clarinet arpeggio from Rach 2 and her heart lifts. It's the phrase of the concerto used in the film *Brief Encounter* when Trevor Howard takes Celia Johnson's hand, and you know then without a doubt just how deeply he loves her. Janet has lost count of how many times she has watched that film. Splashed out on a box of After Eights, drawn the curtains and escaped into its love story, into its understated passion, just one more time.

*

A dash of milk, a sprinkle of sugar, toast pops up warm, golden, and Janet's toes curl in her slippers. She helps herself to a generous dollop of jam and reaches for the envelope.

We are most grateful for your interest in applying to the National Trust.

Tea steams in her cup, butter melts into the triangles of toast.

However . . .

The words smudge and morph before her eyes.

Not quite . . . blah de blah . . . *Unfortunately . . .* blah de blah de blah de blah de blah.

Janet blinks. Tea cools in the mint china cup.

Spring sunlight moves across the back of the house, floods in through the kitchen window, warms the cabinets, the countertop.

But Janet is cold. Frozen.

The clock in the hallway chimes the hour.

Not quite . . . Unfortunately . . .

By the time the clock chimes the quarter, Janet has found more words, further down the page, and these other words change the temperature of her body. At *We would like to take this opportunity to encourage you to join the National Trust . . .* the chill in her stomach starts to burn hot. At *Excited to let you know about our 25% discounted annual membership for seniors . . .* her chest boils. And by *Special offers in the gift shop!* her cheeks are aflame and the paper in her hand crackles and snaps.

'Join?' Her voice, parched with bitterness, whiplashes round the kitchen. 'JOIN?' Janet's words slam into the cupboard doors, crash against the milk bottle.

'Trudge round some second-rate stately home with a lot

of other old – sorry – *senior* people, staring at the worn patches in the carpet, the grime on the paintings, voices full of scorn, faces tight with envy?' Somehow, Janet is on her feet now, the letter crushed in her hand. 'Queue for ages in the tearoom for milky tea and . . . and . . . and . . . a buggering *brownie*!' Her clenched fist pounds on the table, beating out a rhythm to her words. ' "Brownie?" Why not go the whole hog and call a cream puff a "creamie"? A pistachio slice a "greenie"?' Her voice is tight in her throat, her eyes sting with tears. 'Keep your effing brownies. Keep your ruddy discount! Think *I* want to be part of the rugby scrum scrabbling for your overpriced gifts? Think *I* want to buy a jar of "Borage Honey Infused with Cinnamon" for TEN POUNDS? Based on the fact it comes with its own "twizzle stick"? Think *I* care about your "special interest book" *One Hundred and One Things to Do with Lavender*? WHAT KIND OF TWIT WANTS TO DO ONE HUNDRED AND ONE THINGS WITH LAVENDER?'

The words bellow out of Janet with such force that they wallop her back down on to her chair, where she sits, stunned, staring at the perfect triangles of cold toast, the congealing jam. In creeps that familiar yearning, the one that has haunted her over the years, the desire to turn back time, to go back to the moment *before*. Before her life became so blighted. The moment when everything was still possible.

How tall she had sat at her computer, tapping away, filling in the application form. How smug she was, laying the outfit on the bed, luxuriating in the smart slap of her shoes as she walked to the station to get to the interview, hurrying even though she was early. How pregnant with expectation.

Hasn't she learned *anything* from the past?

Janet sits rooted in her kitchen, her tea skinning over, her cheeks wet. She should have known. What a stupid, ridiculous woman she is for thinking things could be different. What a laughable old fool.

She has already written three of the tours. Printed them out, stacked them neatly on the kitchen dresser. Ready, waiting. Pushing herself to her feet, Janet stumbles over to the dresser, picks up the first page and rips right through its middle. Again and again she tears, shredding each one of her carefully chosen words. She does the same with every single leaf until a shower of torn paper blossoms across the kitchen floor.

~

Next day at the allotment Janet wearily pulls on her long-armed falconry gloves, necessary for dealing with rue. Even a small drop of rue sap can cause a nasty burn. Ingest too much of the stuff and it can kill you. It's not the kind of thing to mess about with. Janet takes her secateurs from her apron pocket.

'All alone today?' the Power Ballads serenade, appearing from around the hedge. 'Fancy a bit of company?'

Janet lifts her head, momentarily stunned, but then turns slowly in their direction, opens her mouth to reply.

'Yes, all on my tod!' says the Steer Manure man from Plot 33, who appears on the pathway. 'Mary's off to see her sister. Mind you, it's a chance to get my sweet peas in before she takes over with her beans!'

'Can be nice to have a bit of "me time", can't it?' the Power Ballads warble.

Flipping the safety catch off her secateurs, Janet eases the blades open and slips a frond of rue between them. Carefully she presses the handles and sharp metal bites through the slim stem. The severed rue falls into her outstretched glove and the words from the National Trust application thump and punch inside her skull. The words she tried not to see that day when she was filling out the form.

1. Why are you applying for this position?
   To feel useful?
   To fill some time?

Snap, snap, snap, go Janet's secateurs, fiercer now as she tries to cut those words right out. The shame of them. Lonely people, looking for something to do, a way to fill the long, empty hours. Volunteering to give up their time for free for the promise of a bit of company. That was the worst of it. The fact that the position was voluntary. The secateurs fall from Janet's shaking hand. She reaches through the rue, picks them up and waits for her hand to still before she resumes pruning. Janet would have given the National Trust everything she had, gratis. She would have given it gladly, for the chance to put on a uniform and go somewhere. Somewhere she would be valued, paid attention to, seen.

But the National Trust didn't want what Janet had to offer, not even for free.

Janet confronts another clump of rue.

Being alone is not about taking a lunch on your tod or having a day solo to dig in your sweet peas. Really being alone means every single minute of every single hour of every livelong day. It means every birthday and every Christmas, every balmy summer day and every dark winter one. It means not bothering with pancakes on Shrove Tuesday or getting excited about a bank holiday. It means never eating a meal that you didn't make yourself. Being alone is the phone sitting in slug-like silence on the table. It is perching in one of the matching upright armchairs positioned on either side of the fireplace and staring at the empty chair across from you. Alone, time moves differently. It never 'whizzes', 'flies', or 'rushes' by. It shuffles in slipper-clad feet. Alone and lonely are twinned together, Janet thinks as she slices through the rue. One sits hollow inside the other.

It hadn't always been like this. She used to have friends. Such beloved friends.

JP's here! they'd call as she pushed open the pub door on a Friday night, cheeks flushed from her cycle from college, eyes sparking with the combustion of ideas in her head. *Now the fun has started!* they'd shout, jostling to make room for her at the wooden pub table, handing her a Gin and It clinking with ice, faces turning towards her, eager to hear, ready to delight, to pay attention.

Nancy, Alice, Rajni.

Janet tips the handful of cut rue into a bucket, starts on

the next bush. You have to prune rue hard in spring in order to stop it flowering.

Janet knows what it is to be alone in every single room of her house. To eat her silent lunch looking across at the 'full' dinner service in her cabinet, all those blank-faced plates staring back at her, all those gormless empty bowls. Janet is a connoisseur of loneliness. Each morning she samples the sharp, clear cold of waking up alone, savours the dark, shadowy notes of another lone evening that tips into endless solitary night. And it's there, too, of course, that aloneness. Snuggled up in bed right beside her.

Snip, snip, snip, go the blades. White beads of sap bubble from the sutured ends of rue. Janet knows that ingesting rue sap can cause spasms, kidney damage, liver damage. Death. It can cause uterine contractions and miscarriage.

At least on her allotment singleness makes sense. Nobody expects you to have two rakes, two hoes, two watering cans. One sturdy aluminium spade is usually more than enough. Here on her allotment her singularity doesn't call her out quite so loudly. True, when she first took over her plot she had thought – hoped – that she might enjoy social intercourse with her fellow gardeners. Find herself in the company of *like-minded people* ... *make new friends*. That she might spend her time comparing notes – debating the benefits of mitochondrial fungi, say – and perhaps, if things really took off, moving on to enriching discussions about propagation and grafting, hand pollination, even ... And then – who knew what might happen? A roast chicken, a bottle of wine, two glasses ...

A moment, a look, and finally mouths moving close, then closer still . . .

But for some reason or other things hadn't taken off. Well, at least not for Janet.

Other gardeners on the allotment seem to have no problem cross-fertilizing like billy-o – like the Power Ballads and the Steer Manures forever lobbing endless chit-chat over Janet's head as if she were invisible. The Belgravia crowd in their tight-knit cabal. When was the last time anyone had sought Janet out? Asked for her recipe for manure tea as they had a jolly catch-up over the communal compost? (Five parts water to one part manure, well strained through a large burlap sack, though an old pillowcase would do the job at a pinch.)

She had thought the National Trust might give her a fresh start. One last try.

Janet looks down at the severed pieces of rue in her falconry-gloved hands, the sap seeping from its broken ends.

Alice, Rajni, Nancy.

She returns to her pruning but the blades of the secateurs hover suspended as memories twine around her like bindweed and slowly tighten. If she gives over to them, they will strangle her. Yet she can't help wondering about those women, those long-lost friends. Lost to the years. Lost to her, anyway. Where are they now? One by one all the faces that had once turned towards her, so eager to hear, so ready to delight, had gradually turned away. She had looked them up one silent grey evening in the chill of her always spare room, her eyes hungrily following the breadcrumbs that led to weddings, children, glittering careers, fulfilling retirements.

She can still see the photo of Nancy on the Australian beach, surrounded by her partner, their son and his family. Imagine Nancy a *grandmother*.

Janet's own fault, of course, in the end. All of it.

Her spearmint plant, gangly as a teen, has come adrift of its moorings. Janet gives herself a rough shake, puts down the secateurs and pulls off her falconry gloves to re-stake it, retie the fiddly string.

'There you are, my little chap,' she says, and returns to her rue, sweeps up a pile of cut stems with her hands.

'Aaaggghh!' A sharp burning rips across Janet's palms. She looks down to see the soft flesh blistered an angry raw red. She forgot to replace her gloves before handling the rue. Forgot to protect herself. *Serves you right!* Janet thinks, looking at the damage she has caused, the pain throbbing in her palms, bitterly regretting her mistake. *You've no one to blame but yourself*.

The sun moves across the allotments, lengthening the shadows of plants in nearby plots. They tower over Janet as if in judgement as she kneels in the dirt, head bent, staring down at her wounded hands, her lap full of rue.

~

Janet does not know how long she has been sitting there when she is startled by something.

A voice, shouting. Feet pounding down the grass path. Slowly Janet straightens up, her limbs stiff, her hands smarting, and looks about her.

Patrice, her face taut with panic, dashes by, shouting, 'Emergency meeting! Come quick! We need everyone!'

'What is it?' Janet calls.

'The Council say we have knotweed on the site. They're closing Seaview. We're buggered, Janet. We're bloody buggered!'

4

The ground lurches under Janet's feet. Her body feels liquid, as if she is being sucked out with the tide. She can barely stand up, let alone make it across the allotments to the meeting. Everything churns. Somehow, eventually she manages to stumble to her shed, dip a rue-blistered hand into her watering can and pull out the bottle of Boodles gin she keeps for emergencies. *Juniperus communis*, blessed amongst evergreens. Unscrewing the cap, she takes a swig, swills the gin around her mouth, swallows, and feels the burn down her throat. She takes another mouthful, wipes her lips with the back of her hand, gasps a shuddering breath and starts shakily down towards the meeting, the panicked flutter of her heart like a caged bird.

~

'They can't just throw us off our plots!'

'It's taken me five years of hard graft to get my plot how I want it! It's my world!'

'I just got my flipping bearded iris to take off!'

'What about Ken? His family have had that plot since the war!'

'Yes, yes, all right then, the Yins.' Felicity rolls her eyes as if Patrice is being unnecessarily pedantic. 'Do you think' – she lowers her voice – 'that maybe they brought the knotweed *with them*?'

'From Hackney?' Patrice says.

'No, of course not from Hackney,' FbK snaps. 'I mean from where they come from,' then adds, with all the delicacy of a 160cc engine rototiller, '*originally*.'

There is a grim silence.

'Well, after all, it's *Japanese* knotweed, isn't it?' Felicity makes a little shrug, points at Janet. 'That's what *she* said.'

Janet shakes her head. No, that wasn't what she meant. Not at all. She licks dry lips, wishes she had brought the Boodles down with her. She stutters, 'No, I simply meant that . . . the plant . . . it needs . . .' Janet can't think straight. She can't abide all this arguing, this ugliness. The only thing that matters is that the allotment is under threat. 'I just meant . . .'

'Felicity.' Patrice's voice carries across the confusion loud and clear. 'I am going to say this once and then we are going to move on. The Yins are Chinese, not Japanese. And,' she speaks slowly, her gaze cold, intent, 'THEY ARE FROM HACKNEY.'

A beat. Patrice gives Felicity a look like a hard frost, then refocuses on the group.

'Right. As I said, the Council say they've found knotweed on the site.' Patrice raises her hand to silence Mickey, who is about to shoot off again. 'Not on anyone's plot, but in the wildflower corridor on the east side.'

'Who found it?' Lakshmi asks.

Patrice shakes her head. 'I don't have all the facts yet.

The Council only notified me today; they're sending a team down to cordon off the area and do some tests. The wildflower corridor is completely out of bounds to everyone until this situation is resolved.'

'Who contacted you?' someone shouts.

Patrice refers back to the notes in her hand. 'A . . . Pete Marsh called me. New chap. He said . . .' Patrice dips her head a moment, looks at her feet as if trying to draw strength from her sturdy leather garden boots. 'He said that if there is a full-blown knotweed invasion, the land might be repossessed by the Council within the month.'

In her apron pocket Janet's fingers pearl seeds between them like a rosary as she prays, *No, please no, please no*.

Gardeners stare at each other aghast.

'They can't do that!'

'What the . . .!'

'I'm defending my title at the Egton Bridge Gooseberry Show this summer!' shouts Mickey. 'No sodding way anyone's taking my plot!'

'What about all the food we grow for our refugee drop-in, Patrice?' a woman in a red-checked shirt asks.

'Seaview is vital to us all,' Patrice says. 'I've demanded a meeting with Marsh immediately. In the meantime, let's find ways to connect with locals, get across how important the allotments are to the community and ecosystem as a whole – all the benefits we bring. Winning hearts and minds might help our case, or at least buy us some time.'

Lakshmi says, 'You're right. We need to get the word out! Get people involved, make sure they know about our

40

great conservation schemes, the biodiversity, our charitable work with the cafe, all the pollinators we attract . . .'

'Bees!' Felicity shoots to her feet. 'We should get bees! That would really get the public on side. There's an allotment in Lewes that makes their own honey and has a super range of beeswax skin products. We could do that!'

Janet shakes her head. They are way beyond bees.

'I could do a workshop on how to build a hive . . .' Checked Shirt says dubiously.

Patrice holds up her hands. 'Thanks for the ideas, but . . .'

'Bees are HUGE,' Felicity carries on, practically jumping up and down. 'We could do our own range of organic honey, honeycomb and – Oh! Oh! We could design our own labels! With little bees on! Honestly, people are bee mad – what was that novel that was everywhere last year? It was one of Richard and Judy's picks . . .'

'*The Beekeeper of Aleppo*,' says Sanjay, who runs the bookshop.

'Maybe . . . What's it about?' FbK says.

'Well,' Sanjay settles in. 'It concerns the Syrian war; the central character is a refugee who is seeking asylum in England . . .'

'Goodness, no.' Felicity shudders. 'It wasn't about that sort of thing *at all*. The one I'm thinking of was just marvellous – super fun.'

'*The Secret Life of Bees*?' offers Sanjay.

'We did that in our book club,' the Power Ballads chime in. 'None of us could agree about the ending.'

'I *loved* the ending,' says Felicity. 'So moving.'

'We liked the bit when—'

'Folks . . .' Patrice calls.

'There is also *The Bees*,' Sanjay continues. 'In fact, I should get that back in stock. Then there was *Bee Season* . . .'

'Wasn't that more about spelling bees?' asks FbK. 'Because we don't have those here in England, you see.'

'*The Hive*,' continues Sanjay happily.

Janet gently holds a single seed between finger and thumb, rolls it back and forth. She looks out across the green swathe of Seaview and all she can think about is the precious life at stake. Why are people talking about books? About honey? Don't they understand? Can't they see?

'This is serious,' Patrice's voice booms.

'*Oooh!* We should get a celebrity involved!' shrieks Felicity.

'Gail *Honey*man!' Sanjay chortles.

'Gloria *Hunni*ford!' squeals Felicity.

'*Folks, please!*' Patrice commands. 'We could lose Seaview. All the books and bees in the world aren't going to save us if they repossess the land!'

That does it. Grim reality sinks in.

Lakshmi slumps down on an upturned bucket.

'It's just hit me,' she says, putting a hand to her chest. 'Right here – what it would feel like not to have this place to come to any more.' Tears cloud her eyes. 'Seaview is a haven for me, away from my work, my family. Before I got my plot, I'd never grown anything. But then I put in a couple of rows of carrots, some beans. I watered them, gave them some compost, sort of hoped for the best. Then one day – I'll never forget it' – she smiles through her tears – 'I saw this row of little green leaves sprouting: my carrots, something I had planted. I laughed out loud I was so chuffed. It wasn't much, and when I eventually pulled them up some of them were pretty funny-looking, but it didn't matter because I grew them.'

Ken nods across at Lakshmi.

'My Brenda used to say that gardening made her feel like she'd accomplished something worthwhile in her day, that time spent gardening was never wasted. And she gardened all her life.' He sinks his hands deep in the pockets of his khaki shorts and sighs. 'Even towards the end when she was worn out from the chemo, she'd still get me to bring her over here. She said growing something made her feel she was' – his Adam's apple bobs – 'investing in the future.' He pulls a crumpled white hanky from his pocket and falters a bit as he says, 'The peppers she planted are just starting to come up.'

Lakshmi goes over and puts an arm around Ken's shoulder. Above them, swollen clouds gather; the first spots of rain start to fall, dampening spirits further.

'My plot is my little piece of home,' a woman in bright-orange dungarees called Rosa says. 'I have my cocoyam, eddoe and Jamaican tomatoes as well as my Brussels and my cucumbers. I was so homesick when I first came to England but now my whole garden smells like home – like both my homes!'

'Is that where you come from too, Patrice?' asks Felicity. 'Originally?'

'I come from Brixton,' says Patrice dryly.

Everyone seems to have a story about what their plot means to them. Even the Steer Manures join in. 'We actually have quite a big garden at home,' they admit, somewhat

43

sheepishly, 'but we love coming here for the whole community-buzz thing.'

Not quite the *whole* community, Janet thinks.

Unlike the other gardeners who one by one voice the importance of the allotment in their lives, Janet can't express what her plants mean to her. If she opens her mouth, she won't be able to stop. She doesn't feel safe after being accused of propagating the knotweed. She backs away from the crowd slightly but can't quite bring herself to go.

'What about the cafe, Patrice?' Checked Shirt says again. 'Practically everything from both our plots goes straight to the Refugee Community Kitchen. What are we going to tell them when there's no potato or leek for the soup? No veg for the curry?'

A man in a maroon cardigan says, 'I just lugged six bags of peat-free compost here from the garden centre – now I don't even know whether to put it down or not.'

'I was about to plant my second earlies,' someone else calls. 'Should I get them in the ground or . . .?'

Gardeners turn to Patrice, some hopeful, some desperate for advice, or reassurance, others demanding she take charge, that she fix it.

'What are you going to do about it, Patrice?' Mickey barks, arms crossed, glaring at her. 'You're the one who signed up to be Chair.'

Patrice pushes up her shirtsleeves, meets his stare. 'I didn't *sign up*. I was *elected* Chair. And I am going to do everything I damn well can. I promise you.' She focuses back out to the gardeners and Janet feels the intensity of her gaze. 'As you all well know, this place means the world to me. I remember when I first came down here from

44

London in the nineties. Apart from a few plots on the west side, all of this' – she waves her arm – 'was covered with shopping trollies and rubbish. A right dumping ground. But I could see the shape of what it used to be, and what it could be again. We got the Council on board then, didn't we? Took us five years but we gradually reclaimed more than a hundred plots. We fought for it once, so let's fight for it again. First, I suggest we—'

Patrice breaks off, distracted by a disturbance at the main gate. A couple of men with biohazard tape and 'No Trespassing' signs in their arms hover expectantly. Janet can't breathe. They're putting up a cordon already? How long before they block off the whole site?

From the look on Patrice's face, that muscle twitching in her jaw, she is clearly thinking along similar lines.

'Right, folks,' she says, 'I'd better go over and see what's what. I wasn't expecting things to escalate this quickly, to be honest.'

Sanjay looks across towards his greenhouse, where he has just puttied in the final pane of glass. 'So . . . will we have to take everything down?'

'Look, let's not give up without a fight,' Patrice says. 'Let's focus on what can be done. Once I've met with this Marsh at the Council – hopefully this week – we might know more. And maybe things won't be so bad after all.'

'Just you send that Marsh my way,' snarls Mickey, cracking his knuckles.

'I'm going to call NSALG to get some legal advice,' Patrice continues.

'What's NSALG?' asks Lakshmi.

'The National Society of Allotment and Leisure Gardeners,' says Patrice. 'We want to make sure we understand exactly what our rights are. In the meantime, let's not cause any trouble.' She looks at Mickey. 'Keep the Council on our side, for now at least, and please, everyone, whatever you do, *keep away* from the knotweed site. Focus on getting the word out to the local community to get their support. Who's good with all that social media stuff?'

'I'm on it,' says Lakshmi, whipping out her phone.

Patrice forces a brave smile. 'Let's all try and keep the faith – in your plants, your plots, and in each other, and I promise you all that I will move heaven and earth to save Seaview. Spread your compost, plant your second earlies! Keep the faith, my friends.'

The meeting breaks up, but people linger, surge around Patrice, barraging her with questions, or gather in groups sharing hopes, fears and the best social media strategies.

Janet, alone, retreats in the direction of her plot.

'Janet, wait!' Patrice's voice behind her.

Janet stops, turns back.

'I don't participate in social media.' Janet's shoulders sag. What ruddy help could she be to Patrice or anyone?

Patrice brushes the remark away.

'That's just one idea; there are plenty of other things we can do.' She smiles at Janet; droplets of rain bead her lashes. 'You and I are from the old-school protest generation. We could join forces – show them how it's done . . .'

Janet meets her gaze.

'Patrice!' Lakshmi shouts across the allotments. Flanked

by two officious-looking men, Lakshmi gestures vigorously for Patrice.

Patrice turns back to Janet for a moment, about to say something else.

Lakshmi calls again, 'Patrice, it's the Council – please . . .' and Patrice quickly strides away.

5

Rain javelins from a bruised sky. Janet's boots squelch as she tromps the grey streets back to her house. She is late home tonight – she was the last one to leave the allotments, breaking her self-imposed six p.m. curfew. A couple of gardeners had passed by her plot whilst she was working, peering at her herbs suspiciously, whispering to each other. But despite the ill will and the wild weather, she just couldn't leave her plants. Not that she was good for anything – her fingers trembled too much even to tie the support twine for her perennials. Buffeted by the wind, pelted by rain, she clung on to her plot as if it were a life raft in the middle of a stormy ocean. And what was it, if not that? Most days her plot was the only thing that kept her afloat. Gave a sense of purpose to her life. But now the Council was going to wrench her life raft away. How long could she last without it, flailing in the inky depths, crying out for rescue?

Janet is halfway home before she realizes that she has left her oilskin hanging in her shed. Rain pelts her apron, sodden against her body like a shroud. A man barrels along the pavement in her direction, talking loudly into his phone. Janet veers closer to the kerb to get out of the man's way. He carries on straight towards her, as if she doesn't exist. Janet steps off the pavement on to the road to avoid a collision and feels a sharp pull in her left knee. A truck hurtles by, splattering filthy water over her.

She stands in the road unsteady, dripping.

'Look at me!' Janet shouts after the man. 'There's a whole life right here!' Raindrops streak her cheeks. 'I. Am. Here.' Her curled fist beats the hollow of her breastbone. 'Can't you see me?' But her words are snatched away by the rain and wind. Because the rains did come, after all, but they are not blessed. Rather than purifying her, rinsing her clean, they have blotted her out.

~

Arriving home, Janet discovers that her neighbour Bev has shoved more of her patronizing Help the Aged bumph through the letterbox. She mashes it in her hands without even looking.

Cardboard boxes of Janet's crockery and glasses, her linens and cushions, her pans and vases, litter the house. Blindly she pushes past them into her front room, tosses the crumpled paper to the floor and, still in her sodden apron and muddy boots, slumps into an armchair. Outside, rain slashes through the sepia light of the streetlamp, dark clouds hang heavy in the sky. Janet rarely uses her front room. There is little to draw her in: a couple of armchairs either side of the grate, an old bureau, a faded rug. She doesn't turn on the radiators in here.

A lone black-and-white photograph stands on the bureau. When was the last time she even looked at it? Janet reaches out, wipes a layer of dust from the frame with her wet shirt sleeve and stares down at her family: father, mother and brother, with little Janet on the end. The picture had been taken in the photographer's studio – a rare event for people who preferred not to draw attention to themselves. Nevertheless, they all dressed up for it: Dad in a suit, Mum next to him, her hair sprayed rigid. Richard wears a striped shirt and Janet a scratchy dress with a Peter Pan collar. She remembers how the photographer took ages composing them into an unfamiliar tableau, suggesting Dad put his arm around Mum, forcing Richard and her to hold hands. *Look natural!* he directed. *As if you're all just relaxing at home!* But the Pimms never relaxed, at home or anywhere else for that matter.

The photo has the word *PROOF* stamped across it in thick black letters. The photographer sent a handful of the proofs to her parents, told them to choose their favourites, which he would then print and could, if desired, frame. For some reason they had never ordered any. Perhaps they forgot, or perhaps they weren't happy with the picture of themselves. Maybe it cost too much. Or maybe her parents looked at the photos, at their plain Pimm faces, and decided that, for them, the proof was good enough. After all, the Pimms were a family who knew their place and stayed firmly in it with the blinds down. Their motto? *Don't get above yourself!* Whatever the case, the only picture that now remains of them all together is this one, the proof.

How ironic, thinks Janet, that even the *PROOF* partially conceals them. The thick lines of the 'P' obscure half Dad's cheek and eyebrow; Mum's face is only semi-visible behind the 'R' that cuts through it. Brother Richard does slightly better, his face framed by the second 'O'. Janet fares worst, her face sliced through not once but twice by the thick black lines of the 'F', blindfolding her eyes, gagging her mouth so that the only parts of her that are left visible are her hair, her nose, her chin. She could be anyone sitting there. Anyone at all.

Janet balances the frame between her fingertips like evidence from a crime scene. From the severe expressions on their faces it certainly looks like a crime has been committed. A broken laugh erupts, flees her body and knocks wildly against the hard surfaces of the room, trying desperately to escape. Chlorophyll stains her knuckles, dark earth engrained in the whorls of her fingertips. She shares more DNA with her plants than with the people in this photograph. And without her plot, who is she? What shape is left to her days? How very small her world has become. She studies the rue blisters that criss-cross her palms. Her lifeline scored in paths of regret.

When Adam was a newborn she had felt a rush of adrenaline powering through her arteries so strong she knew that she would fight to the death to protect him. Now she has no fight left and no one left to fight for. Janet sinks deeper into the chair in the silent, shadowy room, dimly aware of the damp and cold seeping into her bones, into her chest. She closes her eyes. Water drips from the hem of her gardening apron, falls on to the faded carpet like tears. Why not just disappear altogether? It might be a relief.

~

Rap, rap, rap!

Janet jerks awake.

RAP, RAP, RAP!

There it is again – louder now, and unpleasantly close. Janet shoves her fingers in her ears.

If she ignores it, it will go away.

Sure enough, after a moment, the sound ceases. Janet slumps back down in her armchair, closes her eyes and wills herself away, back into the darkness.

A sharp new register starts up, more of a staccato tapping now. Janet's eyes startle open. What the . . .? Pressed against the rain-splattered window, something glows. It is alien, otherworldly, phosphorescent. What is it? Is it . . . a *person*?

Staring straight at her, a round face surrounded by a damp nimbus of hair. Its mouth moves, saying something.

What the heck?

Janet tilts her body slowly sideways on the chair till finally the apparition disappears.

She breathes a sigh of relief but the spectre pops up in a new pane, filling it with virulent green. The mouth moves again then hands appear and start to flap, depicting . . . what? The opening and shutting of a tiny door? If she could go back and do things differently, Janet would put up net curtains like the rest of her neighbours; she would use enough net to kit out the whole Hastings fishing fleet. The miming stops, the face vanishes.

A moment later the squelch of footsteps sounds in her hallway and suddenly a green, stocky, box-hedge-shaped figure fills the doorframe of Janet's front room.

It speaks.

'Hi there, it's me, it's . . .'

Bev.

Bev of the endless am-dram flyers is planted in the middle of Janet's sitting room, large as life, curly hair speckled with raindrops, water riveluting down her radioactive-green jacket.

'Christ, it's chucking it down out there! I was just passing and noticed your front door was open . . .'

Damn! Janet must not have closed it properly when she came in. Her blistered hands. Or her state of mind.

'. . . I knocked, then I gave your letterbox a wee bit of a flip-flap, and then I saw your curtains were open . . .'

Is there anything about Janet's life that has escaped the unremitting surveillance of this blasted woman?

'. . . and I just wanted to make sure everything was OK.'

A pause.

Janet stares at Bev, frowns.

Bev stares back, beams.

'So, is it?'

'Is it what?'

'OK? It's just that when I dropped off a flyer for *The Mousetrap* the other day – it's great, by the way! Dr Denis from Gentle Dental is in it! I'd have put him down as more of a shepherd than a Joseph, if you know what I mean – not a leading man – but the role brought out a whole new side of him. Anyway, when I dropped off the flyer I noticed you weren't in, and I thought, where's Janet from number eleven? She's usually home by now.'

Janet, unsure what to say to this, says nothing.

'And then today, same thing,' Bev goes on, 'so I left a notelet through your door just to check everything was all right. Did you get it?'

Janet shakes her head. 'What?'

'My notelet.'

Janet slowly tracks from Bev's face, down the astonishing green carapace of her jacket, across the carpet to the crushed ball of paper.

Bev follows her gaze, then gives a neat little nod. 'Aye, you did. Well, I just wanted to—'

But whatever Bev wants remains unsaid because at that moment Janet is overtaken by a violent attack of shivering.

'You poor thing!' Bev cries. 'You're drookit! You need to get out of those wet clothes right away and have a hot cup of sweet tea.'

Janet is about to protest but the shivering sends her teeth crashing against each other. She is cold, cold to her core.

Janet pushes herself unsteadily upright. She can barely feel her feet. Something crashes to the floor. The black-and-white picture of her family. The photograph skitters out of the frame.

'Let me!' Bev bends and scoops it all up. 'Nothing broken. Easily mended.'

Janet, already heading towards the sitting-room door, hardly hears her. The pain in her hands is almighty, and she can't stop shaking. As soon as she's got rid of Bev, she'll go upstairs, put something dry on, and yes, a cup of tea.

But as Bev follows Janet into the hallway, instead of turning towards the front door she heads off towards the kitchen.

'I'll put the kettle on whilst you're getting changed.'

'You don't—' Janet cries in alarm.

But Bev disappears, calling out, 'All the way at the back past the downstairs loo, right? Same layout as my house.'

Upstairs, Janet can hear Bev moving about below. It is most odd. By the time Janet returns to the kitchen the kettle on the hob is chirruping loudly.

'That's better!' Bev says when Janet appears. 'I love that you kept the gas, Janet. Ours is electric but I think cooking with gas is so much nicer, don't you? Nothing friendlier than the sound of a kettle coming to the boil, is there? It sort of makes all right with the world.'

Released from her green jacket – now hanging on the kitchen door, dripping on to a piece of old newspaper – Bev sports tracksuit bottoms and an Aertex shirt. Maybe she is a school netball coach. Despite the chill of Janet's kitchen, Bev's dimpled cheeks are flushed pink and every now and then she yanks at her collar to loosen it.

'You can tell it's you,' Bev says, gesturing towards the black-and-white photograph, now sitting on the counter-top, securely back in its frame.

Janet stares across at the picture.

'Same strong jawline. High cheekbones. Great bone structure,' Bev goes on, pointing to the little Janet in the photo. 'Not like me,' Bev laughs. 'Ageing's not for the faint of heart, is it? My chin is starting to look like a squeeze-box. And don't even talk to me about the backs of my legs!'

Janet has no intention of talking about Bev's legs, or any other part of her body, for that matter.

'Varicose veins like the Gravelly Hill Interchange!' Bev says with another laugh. 'Now, that's smart, keeping your teapot here.' Bev reaches the Brown Betty down from its place over the hob. 'So handy to the kettle. All my cupboards are on the other side, sort of opposite to the way yours is laid out, but your set-up makes much more sense. Let's see now, where do you keep your tea . . .?'

Before she can stop her, Bev flings open the pantry door, revealing Janet's humble larder. Tinned sardines, a box of stock cubes, the remains of the cherry jam, half an onion and a potato. In someone else's presence Janet is suddenly aware of how paltry it all looks.

'So nice and tidy!' says Bev, plucking the caddy from the shelf. 'You should see my cupboards! A right bloody mess!'

Unfazed by Janet's lack of crockery, Bev pulls a mug from one of the cardboard boxes that clutter the kitchen floor. 'All right to use this? You are good – I keep saying to myself that I should have a clear-out one of these days, do a car boot sale or at least take some stuff to Barbados.'

'Barbados?' Janet's forehead furrows.

'Have you been?' Bev brings the sugar, milk and the tea-pot in for a landing on the kitchen table. 'The people there are lovely.'

Janet has not been, though is, of course, aware of the Caribbean island, famous for its stunning orchids and bromeliads. What she does not comprehend is why Bev is planning on sending her stuff there, however delightful the people might be.

'They do so much for those kids, God love them.' Bev snuggles the tea cosy on to the pot as if she is tucking a child into bed.

Janet's brow clears. 'Do you mean Barnardo's?'

Bev clamps her hand to her mouth. 'Why, what did I say? Barbados?' She puffs a sharp exhalation. 'JFC, what am I *like*? On top of everything else, I've started mixing my words up. Brain fog, they call it. It's a right pea-souper in here!' She hits her forehead with the heel of her palm. 'I swear it's getting worse! Here you go.' Bev pushes the steaming blue-striped Royal Doulton mug towards Janet. 'I think tea can taste even nicer when someone else makes it for you, don't you?'

Janet doesn't know; she has been making her own tea for ever. But the tea does look good. Nice and strong. When was the last time she drank out of the Doulton? She reaches towards the mug.

'Oh pet, what have you done?' Before she can stop her, Bev has swooped down and scooped up Janet's hands. In Bev's neat pink hands, hers look even worse, rough bark. Janet tries to pull them away, but Bev draws them up to her face as if holding a bird with a broken wing. Her mouth puckers in a wince. 'These look like burn blisters.'

'It's nothing.' Janet dashes her monstrous hands away, burying them in her lap. 'Just a little phytophototoxic injury, that's all. Entirely my own fault.'

'Have you cleaned them properly? What about a dab of antiseptic Savlon? I might have some in my bag.' Bev moves towards the kitchen door, where her belongings are hanging.

Janet mutters something about yarrow-and-comfrey salve.

'I don't know that brand,' Bev says, turning back, 'but whatever you think best. You should cover them, though, so the blisters don't burst. Wouldn't you know, this would be the one time I don't have a roll of Tubigrip on me! That would really help with the soft-tissue scarring. I'll drop some by for you, if you like?'

Bev leaves an opening for Janet to respond, but Janet does not.

'Is the tea all right?' Bev eventually offers.

'I haven't tried it yet.'

Bev hovers at the kitchen table for a moment as if she is waiting for something. Janet is not sure what.

'Nothing like a nice hot cup of tea, is there? Especially on a filthy night like this.'

Janet makes a non-committal sound.

'Just hits the spot, doesn't it?' Bev continues to linger.

Janet takes a wary sip. The tea is perfect. She feels the heat and sweetness restoring her. She takes another mouthful.

'Well,' Bev says, 'I suppose I'll get out of your way . . .'

Janet nods in agreement but still Bev doesn't move. Another moment passes.

'Right, then,' Bev says eventually, and with a sigh she pads over to the door, unhooks her jacket and pulls it on. She stands there, glowing under Janet's kitchen lights in her reflective – bicycle? – jacket, then bends down, folds up the damp rectangle of newspaper from the floor and squashes it into her pocket.

'I'll show myself out,' Bev says, looking a little disappointed for a reason Janet can't quite fathom. 'Goodnight, then.'

'Goodnight.' As Bev heads out Janet breathes a small sigh of relief, takes another swallow of tea. Feels better.

'I'll pop back when I can,' Bev calls from the front door.

'Pop back?' Tea sloshes on to the table.

'With that Tubigrip!'

❧

On her way to bed Janet returns the photograph to the bureau in the front room. Dad, Mum, Richard. Her parents are long dead, swiftly following each other like dominoes. Cancer took Richard two years ago. All gone. With the tip of her index finger she traces her family, the parts still visible – her father's patrician nose, the neat helmet of Mum's hair, the abrupt angle of her shoulders as if she were permanently keeping others at a distance. Tentatively Janet's finger moves to the image of herself, follows the breadth of her forehead, the plait of her hair, the triangle of her chin. Bev's words echo: *You can tell it's you.* Janet frowns. Can you?

Slowly Janet's hand moves to her actual face, cups her chin, feels the clench of her jaw, its shape, its flesh and bone. Before, when she looked at the picture, she had seen the photo as evidence of her family's disappearance but now, suddenly, it seems quite the opposite. It is a document of presence.

Hers.

And there in her cold front room, the rain lashing in the darkness outside, it strikes her.

Janet is the last Pimm standing.

She is still here. And so is her allotment. And right there and then she decides: neither of them is going down without a fight.

6

The cheerful 'halloos' that once bounced back and forth over plot boundaries have vanished like spring petals dispatched by a cold wind. Some allotmenteers are guarded and suspicious. Others, like Lakshmi, Rosa and Sanjay, are channelling positive energy into a social media campaign raising public awareness about the many community benefits of Seaview as well as spreading the news that the allotments are in peril. Some have started panicked searches for knotweed rhizomes on their plots. Felicity bloody Kendal and Mickey have set up a vigilante 'Invasives Patrol'. Janet has seen them skulking around, taking pictures of her plot when they thought she wasn't looking. Ken is suddenly anxious about a plant he does not recognize, which is proving resistant to removal. He rubs his hands nervously back and forth on his khaki shorts.

'I'm sure it came from someone else's plot,' Felicity consoles. She looks across at Janet's plot, her eyes flashing, then whips out her phone and photographs the plant with her 'Picture This' identifier app.

'Aha!' She peers at the screen and points gleefully as if she has spied a criminal in a photofit. Reads, '"Mare's tail – invasive deep-rooted perennial, dates back to the Devonian period." '

'Maybe I won't bother it, then,' says Ken, 'if it's not dangerous. Means I'm not the only dinosaur on this plot!' he tries to joke, but Felicity shakes her head firmly.

'Dig it right out – you'll need to get the root network, which the app says can be eight to ten feet deep – and then put down weed killer,' she spits. 'We can't tolerate any more *invasives* round here.'

'I'd like to see her dig an eight-to-ten-foot hole,' Ken grumbles as the Invasives Patrol continue on their officious manoeuvres.

Janet can't settle. After Bev's visit last night, she lay awake for hours, the word 'proof' hammering against her skull. When she finally dropped off, she was caught up in a preposterous dream; Bev chasing her across the allotments in her bilious-green coat with a magnifying glass in her hand like an inspector from a hackneyed am-dram murder mystery. *Vere is ze proof?* Bev shouted in a risible French accent. *Ve need ze proof before ve can believe vat zey are saying.* Janet berated herself for the corny slapstick dream. Yet somehow she can't throw it off.

She tries to focus her mind on tending her germander but is all fingers and thumbs.

Proof, proof, proof.

The Council say they have found knotweed at Seaview and everyone has accepted it without question. Men with tape and signs have cordoned off the wildflower meadow. And now the whole allotment site is suddenly under threat of closure. It's all happening so fast, yet as far as

Janet can see, they are lacking in one key element: proof. Has anyone from Seaview actually seen the alleged knotweed? And come to think of it, what was someone from the Council doing poking around in the wildflower corridor in the first place? Decidedly peculiar. Janet knows from her days back in GCHQ that there are always myriad ways of interpreting the same piece of information. Her family photo, for example, could be seen as part of a pattern of disappearance or, alternatively, as a certificate of presence. The sudden appearance of knotweed at Seaview could be interpreted as an unfortunate twist of fate, but couldn't it equally be evidence of foul play? Could it have been planted *on purpose*? But if so, by whom and why?

By someone who wants the land.

There's one way to find out. Janet needs to lay eyes on the alleged knotweed. If it is really there, she needs to see it, touch it. She needs proof.

That afternoon Janet makes a couple of forays in the direction of the wildflower corridor but, try as she might, she can't get near it without anyone seeing her. If it's not some twit from the Council scribbling officiously on a clipboard, it's the bloody Invasives Patrol – wouldn't effing bloody Kendal and Gooseberry Balls love to catch her at the scene of the crime.

She needs another plan.

~

The allotments are a different country at night, whispering secrets in another tongue. The land unstitches its borders, shakes off the recent human imprint and remembers its wild starting place. Badgers lay waste to pristine vegetable patches and maraud through raised beds. Foxes shatter quiet-edged plots with their febrile cries and night-scented stock perfumes the air unabashed. A bank of evening primrose glows alluringly.

There's another glow, too, that of a torch zigzagging this way and that across the dark ribbons of pathway, accompanied by the sound of footsteps brushing through the damp grass. Janet is here in the small hours, armed with her torch and dressed in her oilskin. Another fox's cry shudders in the distance, lonesome, mournful, full of longing. Janet shivers, pulls her coat around her. What's that? A different sound, like a snuffling followed by frantic digging. Animals? Something else? Or *someone*! Janet freezes, her heart thumping. If her suspicions are right, who's to say nefarious intruders aren't lurking about? What would she give to have the long-handled hoe from her shed with her right now! Hold on . . . The sound seems to have stopped. Most likely an animal after all. She takes a step forward.

'Hell!'

Janet trips and falls into a raised bed of potatoes. She's barely upright again when she collides with something metallic – or is it plastic? – that knocks against the side of her cheek then spirals off. Has she walked into some fiendish trap? If there are dirty dealings afoot, there is no knowing how far these brutes will go . . .

'Aggggh!' The thing frisbees into her face again. Her arms bat out in front of her; something catches the sleeve of her oilskin. 'What on earth . . .?' Pulse racing, Janet

63

wrenches herself free of whatever is jagging her coat, dropping her torch in the process.

'Damn and blast!' She bends, wincing at the pull in her meniscus, and grasps the solid body of the torch, shines its beam about her. Silver discs spin and circulate like tiny planets. 'Beggaring blasted Power Ballads!' Janet snatches one of the twirling CDs, pulling at it so sharply that it snaps free from its string tether. She shoves it deep into the pocket of her coat with a grunt of distaste.

Another sound. Janet waits, body tensed and ready to fight, flee or freeze, but hears nothing else. At last she continues on to her destination.

The brambles are thick along the edge of the wildflower corridor. Janet catches her trousers on their thorns more than once as she picks her way through the prickly shrubs. Finally, she nears the sickly glow of the black-and-yellow biohazard tape that cordons off the alleged knotweed site.

Keep Out: Biohazard! No Trespassing! shout the signs shoved at each corner of the restricted area. Janet ignores them and steps over the ugly wasp-striped tape.

In the torchlight, Janet sees a patch of bamboo-like plants. Crouching, she inches carefully closer and peers at them, studying their leaves intently.

Her heart sinks. It *is* knotweed – the asparagus-like shoots, the distinctive heart-shaped leaves. The twits from the Council were right. Damn, damn, damn.

She stares at the plant – so mundane, yet so menacing.

'What's your story, Itadori?' she whispers.

Hunkering down, ignoring the protest from her knees, she moves her fingers gently over the earth as if she is reading Braille. She crumbles a little topsoil: rich, biscuity, like

Monty Don's voice. This isn't Sussex clay. She brings a palm of soil to her face, inhales deeply, then lets out a low whistle. Janet knows the texture and consistency of hard-packed Sussex clay as well as she knows the back of her own hand. If it feels like commercial compost and it smells like commercial compost . . . Foul play! It *is* commercial compost! She knew it! Someone's been tampering with the wildflower corridor.

Carefully she eases herself flat on the wet ground, her face level with the stalks of the knotweed. Moving the beam of her torch upwards, Janet investigates the leaves, peering at the tissue between the delicate veins. It's hard to tell in the dark and with only the sepia glow of the torch, but she would bet her pension that the leaves are displaying yellowing flesh, a classic sign of transplant shock. With her index finger she gently traces the heart-shaped outline of a sickly leaf. Using her hand as a trowel, she unearths a stalk to find short, broken roots, a sign that the plant has been dug up and replanted recently.

'You're not a local, are you, little one?' Janet mutters to the knotweed as she takes a small cutting. 'Who brought you here?' Awkwardly she pushes herself back on to her haunches and shakes her head slowly. 'And why?'

～

Janet is raring to inform Patrice about the stitch-up asap. She might not have social media skills, but she does have a pocket full of rogue knotweed. Patrice arrives at the allotments at seven a.m. sharp every day and today Janet will be here to meet her with the news and, more importantly, the evidence. Despite being tired and chilled to the bone from her nocturnal manoeuvres, Janet feels rather chuffed as she imagines how pleased Patrice will be with her initiative. Hadn't she said something about the two of them working as a team? In fact, weren't 'join forces' her very words? Their next step will be to gather more evidence on this dubious Marsh chap at the Council. Think how much she and Patrice can accomplish together! Janet eagerly checks her watch. 'Five a.m.?' She gives a snort of exasperation.

Janet waits it out in her potting shed. To make the time move faster she pulls Gertrude Jekyll's *The Gardener's Essential* from the shelf, and selects the excellent chapter 'Flowers, Shrubs and Trees', which she tries to read by the light of her torch. It's usually a real page-turner – Janet always loves the sibilance of the line *chestnut leaves in a mild breeze sound much more deliberate; a sort of slow slither* – but she is far too distracted to appreciate it now; her head is spinning.

Questions jostle. Who planted the knotweed? Why? If they want the land, what do they want it for? How on earth is it only five forty-five?

Janet glances over at the watering can. A nip of Boodles – purely medicinal, of course – would ward off the chill in her bones, not to mention calm the anxious thrum of her pulse. She wavers but ultimately resists temptation. It is essential she keep a clear head. Instead she stamps her feet, blows into her hands until finally apricot shafts of sunlight cascade across the shed window, announcing the arrival of dawn. Janet goes outside, leans against her shed, and watches the sun's slow rise. She keeps an eye trained on the front gate for Patrice. And there she is! At last!

As Janet strides towards her she notices Patrice's usually spruce work shirt is wrinkled and her friendly face tight with tension.

'Janet! Don't normally see you here at this time of day! Everything OK?'

'I came to see you, Patrice,' Janet says, staring straight at her.

'Me?' Patrice's face breaks into a broad smile, the lines of stress lifting for a moment. In fact, Janet can't help but notice that when Patrice smiles her cheeks look like damson plums. 'Well, this *is* nice!' Patrice says in a voice that sounds like she means it. 'It won't take me a mo to get the kettle on.' She picks up her red McVitie's Family Circle biscuit tin and gives it a hopeful rattle. 'I might even have a couple of Bourbons!'

Patrice sets her cream enamel kettle on to the Calor stove, lights the gas. The two women watch as blue flames snap chirpily into life. Janet reaches her chilled hands out towards the small pulse of heat. Although keen to share her news and decide on next steps for their collaborative partnership, Janet savours the moment, the warmth of the fire, the prospect of hot tea and Patrice's company.

Patrice selects a sea-blue enamel mug from her tray of assorted cups, gives it a quick wipe with a soft tea towel.

'When is your meeting at the Council?' Janet asks.

'Thursday.' Patrice carefully chooses another mug, which turns out to be an exact sea-blue partner of the first. 'In the meantime, I'm lining up some legal advice. I thought we'd better have all our ducks in a row if . . .' She gives the second mug a swift wipe and says quietly, 'If things come to a head.'

Patrice settles the matching mugs side by side on an upturned crate, prises the lid off the Family Circle tin and peers inside.

'Ah. The Bourbons have gone; only plain digestives left. Sorry.' She sighs. 'Poor old Ken came by after the emergency meeting for a bit of tea and sympathy – he hit the cream centres pretty hard. He was trying to put a brave face on it. Did you know his mum had a plot here back in the war? Digging for victory – Ken was just a little boy then, of course, helping her out. He lost his Brenda just before Christmas. They were devoted. I think this place is what keeps him going. He's not the only one, either.' Patrice gives the biscuit tin a sad shake and suddenly her face brightens. 'Oh, look, Janet, a jam ring!' She holds the tin out. 'Here, you have it.'

Janet needs to tell her about the knotweed but as Patrice steps closer, Janet is momentarily distracted by the fresh citrus scent of neroli, with maybe a touch of bergamot. Delicious. She imagines reaching out and taking the jam ring, dunking it in the cup of strong tea Patrice is making her, then sitting back and enjoying the feel of the morning sunlight on her body, the sweetness on her lips. But there is no time to lose. The fate of the allotments is at stake.

'I'm afraid I've discovered something quite shocking.'

Patrice's eyes widen.

'The knotweed was planted on purpose. Someone is trying to get us evicted and they're using the dirtiest tricks in the horticultural book.' Triumphantly, Janet pulls the uprooted knotweed from her pocket and holds it out for inspection. 'Look at this – signs of transplant shock on the leaves – and notice the broken root system.'

Patrice, still holding the Family Circle tin, stares at the plant and then slowly back at Janet.

'Janet, please don't tell me you trespassed on the bio-hazard site?'

'I did.' Janet gives a firm nod. 'And I know without a doubt that the knotweed was planted with malicious intent. The Council are trying to repossess Seaview. I'm not sure why – though my guess would be they plan to sell the land and make an absolute packet. They've sold up everything else – the cricket pitch, the rec . . .'

'Did anyone see you?' Patrice speaks abruptly, her eyes anxious.

'No, no one saw me. I did my investigating under cover of darkness.' It sounds rather derring-do and Janet can't help wondering if Patrice thinks so, too. But Patrice is frowning at the knotweed in Janet's hand.

'Did you take that from the cordoned-off area in the wildflower corridor?'

Janet nods vigorously. 'Yes, and a couple of other cuttings and soil samples . . .'

'Why did you do that without talking to me first?' Patrice's voice is strained; the lines of tension in her face etch deeper. This isn't at all what Janet had hoped for! 'Now the Council will say we tampered with the site,' Patrice continues, shaking her head. 'They were very explicit that we couldn't set foot there until they got the Knotweed Removal Services out. I gave them my word, Janet, my *word*. They'll say the rest of the site has been contaminated – it only takes one spore.'

'But don't you understand? I've got proof!' Janet shakes the wilted knotweed. 'This was planted on purpose. We just have to work out who did it and why. I thought we might do as you suggested, *join forces* and—'

'Janet, stop! Look, I'm all for activism, I really am, but we have to play this carefully or things could get even worse for us. I spoke to our old councillor, Hugh, and he told me we need to watch out for this new guy, Pete Marsh.' Patrice snaps the lid tightly back on the biscuit tin. 'To be fair, Hugh might have a grudge against him because apparently Marsh lives in one of those swanky houses they built over the old rec ground. Still, Hugh says he's a slippery customer, so he probably is. We need to do everything by the book. That's why I'm taking legal advice, trying to get a meeting with Marsh. If we have to, we'll appeal the eviction notice—'

'But we don't have time for that!' Janet cries, brandishing the knotweed again. 'For protocols and claims! They're sabotaging us, charging us with having biohazards on site. Of course there are: they're the ones who bally well put them there! They're hell-bent on kicking us off sooner rather than later. We have to do something before the bulldozers roll in!'

'I am the Chair of Seaview Allotments,' Patrice says, her voice tight. 'And I am responsible for handling the situation. I value your passion, Janet, I really do . . .' Patrice presses her lips together, unable to meet Janet's eye for a moment. 'But you have to let me take charge of this.'

The gate creaks loudly and the two women startle. Mickey eyes them suspiciously as he stomps towards his gooseberries.

'We have to play by the rules,' Patrice says quietly but firmly.

'In my experience, playing by their rules never works.'

As Janet turns and walks away she hears the sad whistle of Patrice's kettle.

7

That evening Janet marches up to the spare room with a tray of tea things and a couple of Bath Olivers and turns on the computer. Dunking her biscuit, she thinks of Patrice, how pleased she had seemed to see her, that offer of the last jam ring. Everything pointing to the distinct possibility of joining forces, but then all that had swiftly unravelled. How annoyed Patrice was with Janet's knotweed sleuthing. How disappointed. Blast, blast, blast. The biscuit takes another brusque dousing. Janet knows they can't afford to play by the rules. Patrice takes people at their word but Janet knows how the old boys' network operates. All's fair in war and property development. Look at what happened to the cricket pitch, the bowling green! Janet takes a fierce bite out of the biscuit and gets to work.

Her fingers hover over the keys. What was the name of the slippery new customer from the Council? Mulch? . . . No, that wasn't it, though she should make a fresh batch for her medicinals whilst she still can . . . Pete Marsh. That's the chap.

She taps in her search terms: *Pete Marsh + Council + Hastings*.

'Let's see . . .'

Several notices of council meetings, AGMs, bit of a jobsworth statement welcoming Councillor Marsh to the Borough Council, blah de blah . . . Photos of Councillor Marsh giving a speech at the Hastings Rotary club, holding his weekly surgery in the town hall. Clean-cut, ready smile, never slow to glad-hand a member of the parish. He's *almost* handsome but there's something a little . . . off. Is it the sharp suits? Or perhaps the gleaming winklepickers (instantly suspicious in Janet's book). Janet switches her search across to the General Register Office and discovers that Marsh was married for seven years, but divorced a few months ago. There don't seem to be any children . . . But this is just topsoil; Janet needs to dig deeper to find the roots. There will be something she can grab hold of and pull. She just needs to find the correct place to foot the spade. She rubs her hands together.

It takes her right back.

GCHQ, Cheltenham – how long is it now since she first walked through the doors? Fifty years? She'd made it. Freshly graduated, alert and eager, Janet Pimm had a seat at the table. True, her seat was at a desk with a wobbly leg by the window that didn't shut properly and funnelled in a constant stream of cold air. And yes, as one of the two female members of staff, at the end of the day there was a conglomeration of dirty cups and ashtrays that landed across her desk with the unspoken assumption that 'Janet Prim' would wash them.

Still, she was there. The rest were just minor irritations, easily solved: a wedge of cardboard under the desk leg, an extra cardigan in her drawer and a carefully curated avalanche of books and files across her desk that left no room for anyone's cup but her own. As for the sexist remarks, the lewd looks that turned to whispers of *frigid* when she ignored them – well, she tried to rise above it. She focused intently on the work. That was how she had fought her way out of the confines of her family, by work, by wanting something better for herself and striving for it. *Don't get above yourself!* might have been the family motto but it sure as heck wasn't Janet's. Janet *longed* to get above herself. Janet wanted to soar! She worked hard and she was good. Better than good! She watched and she learned. Not from the endless slew of under-qualified younger male civil servants promoted over her. No, the person Janet studied was Glynis Hatchwell.

Executive administrative assistant to James Napier, and the only other woman in the office, Glynis was the eyes and ears of the communications department. Napier, with his booming public-school voice and generous expense account, may have had the impression that he was in charge, but Glynis was the power behind the throne. Always perfectly turned out in tailored skirt and jacket, hair in a clamshell coiffure à la Maggie, Glynis was the consummate professional. Janet was book-smart, ambitious, a workaholic. Glynis possessed a whole different level of intelligence – she knew how to manage people. Savvy, sharp Glynis took no prisoners and Janet was determined to try to be more like her.

Janet finishes her Bath Oliver and reaches for another, bites down hard, scattering crumbs across the keyboard.

The more Janet achieved during her years at GCHQ, the swifter the resentment towards her boiled. Her rise through the ranks was glacial compared to that of male colleagues, but with each slight increment of advancement – her salary, her authority – the hostility swelled. That she refused to turn a blind eye to various infringements, misdemeanours and downright cronyisms rife throughout the organization didn't gain her any friends. And finally, that job, that career she had worked so hard for, sacrificed so much for, was ripped away from her. *Don't get above yourself!* Janet laughs bitterly. She never had the chance.

Swallowing a restorative gulp of tea, Janet tries to shake the memory away, shake away the shame and, more than that, the anger. Anger at Napier, at the blatant sexism, at the whole crooked system. And anger at herself for not fighting back at the time, not standing up for herself in the same way she had stood up against all the other injustices. But what could she have done in the circumstances? Because her demotion was eclipsed by something so much more devastating that she was left with no reserves, with no fight at all.

But Janet is damned if she won't fight now. Different combatants, but perhaps in many ways a similar battle; a fight for justice, a fight for equity.

Her hand frantically scribbles notes on a pad next to her:

What/who lured Marsh to Hastings?

Who planted the knotweed?

Why?

Janet spent too long as a civil servant not to know that there are practically no rules that can't be broken by those with enough privilege and power. She knows about their insider deals and secret handshakes, how the country is pockmarked with their Masonic codes. She knows how dangerous they are.

Glancing at her pad, she realizes half her notes are a mess of impenetrable squiggles and dashes. For a moment she stares, aghast – is she losing her marbles? But then her face lights up. 'Well, I'll be damned!' It's not a mess after all, it's shorthand! When was the last time she used her shorthand? And she can decipher it, too. Excitement surging in her chest, Janet returns to her quest with renewed vigour, clicking through links with one hand, jotting down notes with the other.

She stops on a picture of Marsh at some fundraiser in the Home Counties, standing next to a man with amphibious features, a veritable Mr Toad. Or, as it turns out, Mr Bringley, a building mogul. Janet flexes her fingers, types in: *Bringley Properties*. Her computer screen erupts into a brightly coloured cavalcade: shiny images of marble-tiled spas, luxury apartments, fancy hotels. She notices Bringley's seems to focus on regeneration hotspots – Liverpool, Birmingham, Slough.

She gulps a swig of tea. Regeneration. A word constantly bandied about by politicians and businessmen as if it is some sort of *deus ex machina* for impoverished towns and cities. In practice, the term usually means ruddy expensive properties built by the private sector, often without any consultation with the local community – and why would they? The new developments aren't for the locals. Suddenly the old library building is an expensive hotel, schools morph into luxury flats, low- and middle-income accommodation is levelled to make way for second homes. Locals are pushed further to the edge, priced out.

Janet pours another stream of Assam into her cup, only then realizing she is using the Doulton rather than her usual mint green. How odd. She sips her tea. It's actually rather nice, the Doulton, takes a generous pour and feels sturdy in her hand.

Janet switches her search to Companies House and breathes a low whistle. Just a cursory glance at Bringley's recent accounts shows the company is making a killing. The most recent Bringley's enterprise is a luxury hotel and spa in the Midlands. *All rooms overlook the picturesque canals* . . . blah de blah. What was there before Bringley's bought the land? Further research reveals it was a derelict brewery. Nothing to see there. And yet . . . She can smell it; she knows something is amiss.

It's dark outside; she should call it a day, heat some soup for supper. But she can't stop, not even to switch on the light. The research is propulsive, the pages of her note-pad fill with vigorous swoops and dashes, and her fingers rattle across the keys, clicking links, following clues. What with the chill of her spare room, she really could be right back at her draughty desk in Cheltenham. Back using her brain, her skill! Being of use.

Click, click, click. Bringley's certainly seems to have a gift for swooping up curiously inexpensive sites in desirable locations. Synapses firing, Janet switches her search again, this time to protests over land rights. She zips through endless cases concerning repossessions of public land . . . still nothing she can link to a hostile takeover by Bringley's or connect to Marsh. Click, click, click. Her eyes smart from the glare of the screen but she keeps on searching, scouring, all her faculties engaged, and then suddenly, right at the bottom of the screen, something catches her eye:

David and Goliath Land Grab!

A knock at the door downstairs. Janet barely registers it as her fingers trip over themselves following the story back to an allotment site in Leeds.

'Hello there!' a voice calls through the letterbox. 'It's just me – Bev.'

But Janet can't stop. Not now. Photos of distraught locals with placards fill the screen: *Allotments, Not Houses! Save Our Allotments! Reject Property Development*. The protest took place four years ago . . . case ended with an out-of-court settlement. Eyes swiftly darting, Janet scans the copy for any mention of Bringley's, her whole body alert, fingers alive, feet jigging. She scrolls through photographs; pictures of the distraught, defiant protesters and their allies juxtaposed with men in suits, smug, emotionless . . . She searches the faces . . . and yes, there he is! She is sure of it: Mr Toad. Bringley himself.

She has found a root! Blood thrums in her veins – oh, she remembers this, the adrenaline, the excitement! Now she just has to keep digging – easy does it, gently, gently. She'll need to call in some help. Help from someone who can access levels of financial information beyond the Companies House website. And she knows just that somebody! Unthinkingly her hand reaches to her phone, finger outstretched ready to dial, extension 8840, she knows the number by heart . . .

Only then does she catch herself. She's not at GCHQ and there isn't a phone on her desk, just an empty teapot and a scatter of crumbs. She is alone. That cold slap in the face. Janet slumps forward, head in hands, overwhelmed for a moment, her heart slowing, the excitement dissipating.

8840. Glynis's extension. Funny, she still remembers it though she hasn't laid eyes on Glynis in decades, not since the day when, clammy with humiliation, Janet had to pack up her desk at GCHQ. Anger at the unfairness of her dismissal simmers in her belly and reminds her of her promise to herself not to go down without a fight this time.

With an effort Janet pushes herself upright, wipes her eyes, straightens her shoulders. Glynis must be retired by now – hard to imagine – could she track her down? Janet returns her attention to the internet and searches for current contact information for Glynis Hatchwell. It's surprising how easily she finds it.

What to say? Where to start? Her hands hover over the keys. *Glynis, it's been absolutely ages so you probably don't remember me, but I wondered if you could ...* Could what? *Do some legal-grey-area poking around on what is probably a wild goose chase because I found some Japanese knotweed with transplant shock on my allotment?* Glynis would think she was an old crackpot. Keep it short. Brief and cryptic enough to pique Glynis's interest. Janet types the message and hits send before she can stop herself. Will it find its way to Glynis? Will she even read it?

When she finally heads back downstairs, Janet sees a notelet, a small roll of bandages and a tube of Savlon lying on the coir mat in the hallway.

~

Returning from the allotment the following day, Janet almost misses the unfamiliar flash of the answering machine.

She walks right past it, then stops, turns back. There it is, the green light blinking. Green for Go! Her finger hesitates a moment over the button. It's probably just someone from Age Mobility banging on about walk-in showers or foldable commodes, but when she finally presses play, Glynis's clipped tone fills the hallway, sounding like an old-fashioned telegram.

'Hatchwell here. Received message. Interested. Rather discuss in person. You'd have to come to me. I'm not in Cheltenham any more. Can you get to Windermere? If so, Thursday morning would suit.' Glynis provides her address and then, just before ringing off, adds, 'Of course I remember you, Pimm.'

~

Janet stands at the bus stop, peering up the street greasy with rain. She has meticulously planned her route to the Lake District. She will take the 3A bus to the train station, where she will catch the 10.34 to Charing Cross. From there it's the Northern Line to Euston, then the Avanti West Coast service all the way to Oxenholme, where she will swiftly change platforms for the Windermere train. An overnight is unavoidable, so she's booked The Laurels, an inexpensive guest house in Windermere. She'll take the short bus ride over to Glynis's village, Near Sawrey, in the morning. Then she will turn around and make the whole journey back home again. It's a long way, not to mention a heck of a long shot, but at least it's something rather than nothing. She can't just wait for the Council to come and cordon off more of Seaview – or, worse, stand by whilst they start razing the land.

Rain spatters against her oilskin. The bus should be here by now. She has given herself ample time, but even so . . . She shifts the rucksack on her back, wraps her arms about her, stamps her feet. Spring weather is reliably unreliable. Where *is* that ruddy bus? She's going to miss her train at this rate!

A blue car sits at the junction waiting to make a left turn, wipers flick-flacking against the downpour. Janet misses being behind the wheel, the autonomy, the speed. Her reaction time is as good as it ever was, better than a lot of the people she sees on the road nowadays. She is just thinking there is something familiar about the flagrant wodge of green behind the steering wheel when it starts waving at her. Bev.

Janet's head tortoises into her oilskin. She feels a stab of guilt thinking about the notelet Bev had squashed through the door with the bandage *for your poor hands*.

However, right now, Bev has something Janet dearly wants.

Wheels.

Janet straightens up. Waves back.

8

'Of course!' Bev says as Janet folds herself into the car. 'I'll have you there in three minutes flat. Just shove my clobber out of your way.'

Easier said than done, thinks Janet as she cranes round. Every inch of the car is crammed with overflowing shopping bags, quite literally bursting at the seams. A battered plaid suitcase that looks like it was packed in a tornado gapes open. As well as an assortment of clothes for all seasons, there is a large damask tablecloth flung across the passenger seat and . . . Good God, is that a *harpoon*?

Janet keeps her tidy knapsack perched on her knees.

'Off somewhere nice?' Bev says, pulling out so fast Janet grabs for the safety strap.

'Visiting a . . .' Friend? Glynis was hardly that. 'An old work colleague, up in Windermere.'

'DON'T EVEN THINK ABOUT IT!' Bev cries out.

Janet startles at Bev's violent reaction to the Lake District, but it turns out that the remark is aimed at a man in a black BMW trying to cut them off.

'Isn't it always the bloody Beamers?' Bev says, mopping a swathe of fringe away from her forehead, jamming her foot on the accelerator. 'Entitled tossers! Windermere?

What a treat.' The car lurches forward, Bev driving as if she is in pole position at Brands Hatch. 'What line of work were you in?'

'I worked at GCHQ.'

'You're a dark horse, aren't you?' Bev overtakes more cars and makes a sharp left. 'Catch any spies?'

Janet gives a non-committal nod.

'I'll bet you and your friend will have lots to catch up on.' Bev throws her an encouraging smile.

The last time she saw Glynis, Janet was packing up her desk, mortified, whilst half the office pretended not to watch and the rest of them ogled in delight. Glynis sat behind her desk, her face its usual professional mask of calm, but as Janet passed by on her way to the door, she could have sworn she heard Glynis whisper, *Don't let the bastards get you down, Pimm . . .*

Bev slows as they near Station Approach. They have made excellent time. Bev would make a good ambulance driver.

'Well, thank you for . . .' Janet begins but Bev suddenly hits the accelerator and speeds right past the station. Janet taps smartly on the window. 'We want to be going that way . . .' And then, because Bev fails to react, shouts, 'You missed the turn!'

But Bev keeps going.

'You know what?' Bev says, speaking quickly. 'I just remembered the works on the rails at Wadhurst. That'll mean a replacement bus service all the way to Tunbridge Wells. You don't want to bother with that, do you? Not on a filthy day like this. I'll just run you up to Tunbridge Wells.'

Works at Wadhurst? Blast, that could throw out her whole travel schedule. 'Really, I . . .'

'It's no trouble.' Bev gives her forehead another swipe, her curls sticking up in an abrupt margin about her face. 'I'm going that way myself.'

'You are?'

Bev keeps her attention firmly focused on the road ahead but nods vigorously. Rain pelts against the glass. Janet has a long day of buses and trains ahead and it is dry and warm in Bev's car.

'Well . . . if you're absolutely sure it's no bother.'

'Nae bother at all!' Bev says, her face breaking into a broad smile. 'Now, you just relax and make yourself comfortable.'

Janet hesitates for a moment, then wrestles her knapsack into the seat behind and sits back.

Swiftly the sea fades into a blue smudge in the distance then disappears, replaced by tangles of vineyards, rolling fields, land exploited by the Romans for its rich deposits of iron ore. They speed past the historic town of Battle, past the ancient woodlands of Brede, where oak, sweet chestnut, hornbeam, birch, alder and aspen flourish. The wood anemone will be blooming now, Janet thinks, imagining their dear star-like faces shining up at the trees above them, carpeting the forest floor like a fresh fall of snow . . .

An arctic blast of air hits her. She traces it to the air-conditioning nozzles, all energetically emitting icy streams. Bev grasps the steering wheel with one hand and fans the other violently up and down in front of her face like an angry seal. Suddenly she flushes the exact shade of a Bonny Best tomato, the colour soaring up her neck, across her face, into her hairline. If only Janet had her plant mister to hand, she could give Bev a cooling spritz.

'Thar she blows!' Bev gasps, angling the air-conditioning nozzles so they blast directly at her face, breathing deep lungfuls of the frigid air. 'Having a bit of a day of it, I'm afraid!' she says after a moment. 'I had the first one before I could even get out of the house this morning!'

The first what? Sherry? Janet worries.

'I should be used to them by now, but hot flushes are such a pain! I try and control them, especially when it happens at work – you know, mind over matter. I try and think cold – frozen Russian lakes, tubs of vanilla ice cream, Torvill and Dean – but nothing seems to stop the meltdown.'

Janet knits her brows in concentration. '*Majorana hortensis* might help . . .?' she offers.

'I'll take all the help I can get!' Bev says. 'This Marjorie a friend of yours?'

Janet takes a breath. 'Marjoram is an excellent anti-inflammatory and antioxidant – highly beneficial to hormonal health.' She had bedded in that excellent crop only the other day and it was already coming on apace; the sprinkle of nettle-and-comfrey fertilizer really was just the job. In a few weeks her marjoram would be abundant. A sudden twist in her gut – in a few weeks her plot might be gone.

'Marjoram, eh?' Bev scrunches her eyes. 'Hmm . . . wonder if there's any in the cupboard . . . mint sauce . . . piccalilli . . . no, I'm pretty sure I haven't got marjoram. I'll look out for it. I know that evening primrose is good for cramps; I recommend it for some of my mums . . .'

'*Oenothera biennis*. Relieves PMS symptoms, minimizes breast pain and can also reduce hot flushes.' Janet sits up a little straighter. Perhaps Bev might like to know about her patch of evening primrose at the allotment, how at dusk it glows golden. Janet turns towards Bev with new appreciation.

'Mind you, I'm not much of a plant person.' Bev swiftly overtakes the car in front. 'Don't get me wrong, I never say no to a nice poinsettia at Christmas, but when it comes to treating my own aches and pains, I reach straight for the Anadin Extra, every time. Or a single malt.'

'But where do you think your Anadin Extra comes from?' Janet cries out before she can stop herself. Patrice's words echo in her head: *Not everyone sees plants the way you do.*

Bev glances across at her, confused. 'Well, I usually get mine from Boots . . .'

Janet shakes her head and says in what she hopes is a more neutral tone, 'I mean what it is *derived* from. Aspirin comes from meadowsweet and white willow. So many drugs come from plants: morphine, codeine, quinine . . . single malt whisky,' she adds, shooting Bev a quick look before continuing with her list. 'The Madagascar periwinkle produces vinblastine and vincristine for cancer treatment, chemotherapy drugs are derived from yew, then there's the galantamine in daffodils that's being used to slow Alzheimer's . . .'

'Daffodils! That's a new one on me, and I'm in the business, so to speak.'

Janet raises an interested brow.

'Healthcare. I'm a nurse and a midwife.'

Janet pulls her coat closer. She feels chilled to the bone.

'When I first started on the maternity wards,' Bev carries on, 'I'd often sprinkle a bit of lavender oil on flannels, put it on one of my mums' foreheads or slip it behind their necks. It definitely helped.'

'It would,' Janet says quietly.

'Never time for any of that now, though – it's all accounting for every swab and cotton ball and drowning under mountains of paperwork.' Bev shakes her head and tightens her grip on the steering wheel.

'I grow lavender on my allotment. At Seaview.'

'A work mate of mine used to have a plot there. It's meant to be lovely.'

Janet nods. 'It is,' she says and then adds in a rush, 'but it's about to be destroyed by the Council.' Hearing the words coming out of her mouth makes her throat tighten. Bev looks at her. Janet drops her gaze to her hands, sees them curled like roots in her lap, gnarled and scarred. Heck, don't let Bev start asking her about the Tubigrip. It's still rolled up like crêpe paper on Janet's kitchen table.

But all Bev says is, 'I'm sorry to hear that. You must be gutted.'

～

' "Garden of England"!' Bev reads as they pass the sign at the Kent border. The proud cones of oast houses flash past, lime-green splashes of farms. 'What do you grow on your allotment? Veg? Or are you more flowers and soft fruit?'

Janet's eyes close for a moment as she pictures the

kidney-shaped leaves of her lady's mantle, cleverly designed to hold droplets of rainwater. 'Yarrow, borage, juniper.' The words sound like an invocation as her fingers straighten and bend, feeling her way across her plot. 'Lungwort, sage, comfrey, thyme.' It's disconcerting to be speeding away when her plants are so vulnerable.

'You've clearly put a lot of work in,' Bev says. 'Is it a dead cert that you're going to lose it? Can't you do anything? All club together? How many of you are there?'

'A hundred and twenty plots – and the people, couples, families that tend them. I don't know yet if it's a dead cert. I hope not.'

Janet sighs. She knows the knotweed was planted on purpose very recently and has a pretty clear idea why, but she needs more. She needs proof. She turns, stares out of the window for distraction. Scotney, Bodiam, Bateman's – how many more brown signs to National Trust properties do they have to pass! Mind you, the High Weald looks fetching even in the downpour: sandstone crags, wildflower meadows, dense forests. Years ago, she had some wonderful hikes out here with Nancy. They covered swathes of the North and South Downs, though their favourite was proper fell-walking up in Cumbria. Nothing like it. Janet rubs her knees, not sure what kind of hike she could manage now. Back in the day, the two of them could hike ten miles before lunchtime, often more, no bother. Like walking on air.

'Phew. That's better.' Bev turns off the air conditioning. 'Hope you didn't get too chilly? When I get a flush, I just want to throw open all the windows and doors – even on a day like this. Eddie hates it. Ever married, Janet?'

Janet's hands cup her knees. 'Yes.'

'Eddie and I have been together twenty-two years. Creeps up on you, doesn't it? How long were you and . . .?'

'Brian.'

'How long were you and Brian together, if you don't mind me asking?'

Janet looks at the back-and-forth slice of the wipers, grateful for their mathematical angles, their clean lines.

'Long enough.'

She can still remember that day, the sound of her shoes on the pavement, like a Murray mint clicked between the back molars, clipping along the street to her house. She remembers coming in the back way and, through the kitchen window, seeing Brian with his trousers askew, the apples spilled all around him. They had gone to a pick-your-own the previous weekend. Ribston Pippins, Kentish Fillbaskets, Royal Gala. Brian, his eyes glinting like bright milk bottle tops, panted like a dog as he grabbed the woman from Wales amongst the Feltham Beauties, the Howgate Wonders, the Autumn Golds, and rutted himself in and out of her. She had slithered and shrieked against Janet's mint-green Formica table, a rash of crimson blooming across her breast.

'Right,' Bev says carefully, 'so did Brian . . .?'

After she saw them, Janet turned and just carried on walking, as if it wasn't really her house or her life at all, which, from that moment on, it wasn't. She carried on walking as if she were another woman altogether, on her way to another house in a different street in another life. Off she went, clicking along the lane, past the backs of the houses where other husbands might or might not be having affairs in their kitchens, right to the end of the street, to where the houses stopped, and the road became a muddy track that led to the field with the old piebald pony who stood at the gate swishing away flies with its tail. Janet remembers standing at that gate, her back pressed against the wooden slats to keep her upright.

When she finally returned to the house and walked into the kitchen, everything was in its proper place. The woman from Wales was perched neatly at the Formica table, carefully slicing a Battenberg she had brought for Janet as a treat. Brian was warming the brown-bellied pot just as Janet had taught him to; the apples stood neatly in russet and green pyramids on the countertop. So perfect was the scene, so believable, that Janet had wanted to give everyone a quick round of applause.

'Brian's in Llandudno,' Janet says.

A beat.

Janet un-cups her knees, sits back, traces the path of a raindrop skittering down the window.

'I love Eddie to bits,' Bev says at last, 'but there are rooms in my head he will never enter.'

Janet tries to keep Brian out of every room in her head. Tries to keep them all locked up tight. Yet as the road flashes by, propelling her forward, she feels the past tapping at the windows, pulling at the brickwork like clinging ivy. She sees Nancy, her tear-stained face turning away from her. She remembers the last time she held her son close. She clutches at the safety strap, grasps on to it so tightly her fingers turn white.

9

11.05. Five minutes later than when she last looked. When does her London train leave Tunbridge Wells? Janet only knows the Hastings and London platform times. Whilst she appreciates the lift, she doesn't like losing control of her schedule.

'Almost there,' Bev assures her as the sign for Tunbridge Wells flashes past.

Janet feels a jolt of relief. She glances at her watch once more. She would usually be pottering in her house, preparing her lunch, impatient to head out to the allotment. How root-bound she has become. There was a time when a journey like this would have been nothing to her.

'Looks like all the world and his wife are heading to Tunbridge Wells,' Bev says cheerfully, hitting the brakes as she eases into a traffic queue for the exit.

11.09. Janet's jaw tightens.

11.12 and they haven't moved.

11.14. Janet sighs loudly. Bev seems perfectly relaxed. Perhaps even a little excited? She must really like driving. Or sitting in traffic. Or Tunbridge Wells.

Janet's feet tap on the floor, pumping an imaginary accelerator. *Come on!* She folds her arms, stares at an ugly concrete structure along the side of the road covered in graffiti.

'If people are going to risk life and limb, not to mention arrest, to spray paint on walls, you'd think that they'd want to write something worth saying.'

Bev glances across at Janet, eyebrow raised.

'If you have a ruddy great public canvas in front of you, why fill it with a load of bulbous drawings and scrawl? I mean, what the devil is that?' Janet presses her finger to the window, squints and reads out, ' "Zig luvs Kazza 4 eva." I rather fear Kazza is wasting her time.'

'Oh, I don't know,' Bev says. 'Zig sounds very devoted to me. So what would you write, then?'

'Something useful.'

Bev nods thoughtfully. The car inches forward.

Janet looks at her watch for the umpteenth time.

Bev suddenly turns to her. 'Why don't I just take you?'

'You *are* taking me – if this traffic would get a move on.'

'To Windermere,' Bev says, then adds casually, 'I'm going that way.'

Janet stares at Bev. Agog.

'You are *also* going to Windermere?'

'Well, no, no, not Windermere. What I mean is . . .' Bev swipes a hand across her brow. 'What I mean is I'm going in that direction. I'm heading to Kirkcaldy. Fife.'

'*Scotland*?' Good grief, and the woman only thinks to mention this now!

Bev nods vigorously. 'My sister still lives there. I've got a couple of days off work and thought I would drop in, take Rona a few family "heirlooms".' She gestures to the overflowing back seat. 'Our mum died last summer, and I thought Ro might like some bits and pieces as keepsakes.'

Janet computes the five hundred-odd miles between the English south coast and Fife and Bev's casual use of the term 'drop in'. Mind you, Janet's trip to see Glynis in the Lake District isn't exactly round the corner. Clearly they each have their reasons.

'In fact,' Bev says, already turning the indicator on, 'it'll be nice to break the journey in the Lakes. What do you say? I'll have you delivered to your old friend in no time.'

Janet frowns, fiddles with her seat belt. Her plans are being uprooted faster than nettles in Mickey's gooseberry patch. Janet has been rather looking forward to the train journey; she has a window seat booked on the Avanti West Coast service and there is supposed to be a refreshment trolley on board. It really is bucketing down, though, and what if the trains were delayed or she missed a connection?

'In the car we'll get there in a flash, much quicker,' Bev says.

Janet pauses. Is Bev right? Would the car trip allow her more time once she got there?

Bev, sensing weakness, shoots her a hopeful look.

'You can really make the most of catching up with your friend, a lovely long visit.'

'Um . . . Very well, then. Thank you, Bev.'

Bev focuses back on the road, clearly delighted with her powers of persuasion.

But it wasn't Bev's comment about spending more time with Glynis that made Janet change her mind. She and Glynis had never known each other outside the office. She can't picture them palling around now. Janet has something else in mind. When she unearthed her old rucksack yester-day she found the Bartholomew *Walk the Dales* map still tucked into the inside pocket. If she arrives early she could take herself on a hike; a small one, of course, just long enough to retrace a familiar route. Just long enough to let her remember the life she could have had. The life she should have had.

~

Janet experiences another tug of frustration when, after a mere handful of miles, Bev slows down and pulls over at a service station to get petrol – 'Whoops! Nearly empty!' Bev then wastes an inordinate amount of time fiddling around with her phone – 'Just putting the route in my GPS, pinging Eddie a wee text whilst I'm at it.'

Really, the woman is exhibiting a startling lack of readi-ness for a long road trip. Did she not think to fill up the tank before setting off? Younger generations always seem a bit more slapdash about everything. Janet likes to plan a route, to know where she's going, be prepared. Order and Routine.

Finally, they're off again. Bev picks up the pace and the car whizzes along. Fields, towns, bridges scud by, and with them a tangle of thoughts; the rejection letter from the National Trust, slippery Pete Marsh. Brian amongst the Ribston Pippins. Nancy. Adam. Janet tries to shake free of them all.

Music might help. Sometimes they play Rachmaninov on Radio Three and Janet will stop whatever she's doing and listen, stand transported, the music entering her cells.

'Spot of radio?' Janet suggests.

'Broken, I'm afraid.' Bev casts an eye at the radio. 'The aerial took a bit of a knock at the drive-through car wash.'

'Never mind,' Janet sighs.

'But the CD player works.'

Would it be too much to hope that Bev might have Rachmaninov's Piano Concerto No. 2 in the glove compartment?

Whenever she hears those first passionate chords of Rach 2, Janet is transported to a train station at dusk – the smell of steam, a refreshment room with a tea urn, a proper brew served in a china cup *and* saucer. From the first chance meeting on the platform . . . *I seem to have something in my eye . . . Shall I take a look? . . . Oh, how kind . . .* to the devastating final parting when Celia Johnson says goodbye to Trevor Howard for ever. It's there on their faces, all the pain and torment they are feeling, but they *keep it in*. You don't need Celine Dion emoting all over the place to share their agony, to know that as they say goodbye, their hearts are breaking.

There's your train.

I must go.

Yes, you must.

Goodbye.

Goodbye.

No big, showy gestures, no heaving bosoms, no quivering, glossy lips.

Just his hand on her shoulder.

And then he walks away, out of her life for good. The shriek of the train, the hiss of steam – and then he's gone. What desire! What a love story.

'Why don't you go ahead and pop in your CD,' says Bev.

'*My* CD?' What the heck is the woman on about?

Bev points towards Janet's coat.

'In your pocket?'

Confused, Janet reaches into the pocket of her oilskin and her hand closes around a flat circular disc. She pulls it out. A silver CD. *Even Bigger, Even Better: Power Ballads IV.*

'Aye, Janet,' Bev says, glancing over, 'you're full of surprises.'

How on earth . . .? Oh. Her stealth night on the allotments, caught in a sudden assault of polycarbonate.

'Go on – pop it in,' Bev smiles.

Janet hovers, the disc balanced on the tips of her fingers, quivering like the scales of justice. Which will weigh on her most heavy? The tumult of her thoughts, or a so-called *power ballad*? How bad can it be? What's the worst that can happen?

'Go on!' Bev encourages. 'It will speed us along.'

Janet slides the disc into the player. Her regret is instant and deeply felt.

'Bonnie Tyler!' Bev exclaims as a woman's voice moans through the car, reverberating off all the surfaces. 'I haven't heard her in ages!'

Janet's lips thin. People seriously call this music? Actually listen to it *on purpose*? As if in answer, Bev starts to hum along, taps a button and increases the volume.

As far as Janet can make out, the only thing Ms Tyler seems to be feeling is a persistent desire to turn around. At this particular moment, Janet can see the appeal of doing exactly that.

As they drive on, the downpour increases and the wipers go full blast, making their immediate future seem blurry and uncertain. Janet reaches for her rucksack and pulls out her Bartholomew *Walk the Dales* hiking map. She flaps it noisily a couple of times as Bonnie turns around yet again, then she flattens out the creases in the paper and studies the soothing tracks and pathways. Janet's finger lightly traces a small footpath and her shoulders relax. She has always enjoyed an orienteering map. She prides herself on being a very able reader of their codes, easily deciphering the shadings and marks that depict slope lines, earth walls, open land, crossable watercourses, vegetation. Nancy always deferred to Janet as their designated map-reader when they went backpacking. *You are my True North, JP*. Janet liked the responsibility of being the pathfinder, leading them on their way, keeping them safe.

Turn around . . . Bev veers on to the M40, towards the Cotswolds, still humming away.

The thing that's so reassuring about a map, Janet thinks as she folds the Bartholomew into a smaller rectangle – precisely encompassing the Three Peaks trail – is that there are no surprises. As long as you pay attention and read it properly, you can see what lies ahead. So different, of course, to life. Janet strokes the map between her fingers, feels the promise held in its nap.

Brian was a stationery salesman. He seduced her with quality writing paper. He was sent to the wrong floor by a new girl on reception and ended up at Janet's desk in the Cheltenham office with his ready salesman's smile and his briefcase full of samples. By the time he realized his error a pool of watermarks lapped between them, whispering a lilting language of grammage and grain, of folio and foolscap, a language that Janet understood and in which Brian was fluent. He slipped Janet thick sheets of paper to press between her fingertips, gently encouraged her to feel the weave of the embossed and the debossed. He had all the right words: *luxurious* and *deep velour* and *fully saturated*.

Turn around . . .

Janet was supplicant to the sheets that rippled across her palms. *Woven, vellum, linen*, Brian murmured, *pinstriped, smooth, uncoated*. Reams of paper in bridal shades of ivory and oyster, cool as silk and just as soft. Light streamed through Janet's window, warming the woodgrain of her desk and the leather of Brian's briefcase splayed open upon it, creating an intoxicating miasma of oak, leather and parchment. With each sheet Brian fluttered on to her outstretched hands came the dependable scent of paper, a smell that conjured for Janet a familiar world of books, libraries, maps. A world where she excelled. A world she knew, a world that was safe, conventional, traditional.

Three months later they were married at the local registry office.

She had settled, of course. Because she was a coward. And so, although it had shocked her – the fact of Brian and the woman from Wales in her kitchen that day – in the end, how could she blame him? She knew enough about real love to know that she and Brian had never had it.

*

There is a rip in one corner of the Bartholomew. Janet slowly runs her finger along it, tracing the ragged edges where the land is severed in two. She remembers the exact moment it was torn, when Nancy wrenched it out of her hand. *Be brave*, Nancy had said. *Fight for the life you want!*

She could tape up the rip, but the mark would always be visible, like a scar.

10

Bev hums away to the endless power ballads as they drive past the polite curves of the Cotswolds. By the Midlands she is singing along under her breath. From Cheshire, inhibition apparently waning, Bev's volume increases with every mile, even when she doesn't know all the words and fills in with *shoobie doobie doobie do dah*. The power ballads must be on their fourth repeat cycle, so Bev has certainly had time to brush up on the monotonous lyrics. When traffic sludges to a crawl for over an hour on the section of M6 that runs between Liverpool and Manchester, Janet has to fight the strong physical urge to grab the CD and throw it out of the window. She'll never arrive in time for a hike at this rate.

Just as Bev bursts into an unabashed chorus of 'I Will Survive' – a particular favourite – Janet gets her first glimpse of the clefts of the valleys and the soar of the fells. As abruptly as it started, the downpour stops, the clouds roll aside and in a slant of early-evening sunlight the land sparkles. Wind turbines cartwheel deliriously amid a landscape of endless green: wine bottle, aquarium, slate, waterfall, seaweed, parrot, avocado . . . More shades than Janet can even name. Despite everything, she feels a stir in her chest and with it a sliver of memory as bright and precious as a thread of saffron. A memory of being completely happy.

'Almost there,' says Bev as a sign for Kendal flashes by. 'What's your friend's address?'

'I'm not meeting Glynis until tomorrow. I'm booked into a guest house tonight.'

Bev nods, checks the time on the dashboard. 'I might call it a day, too – see if your place can squeeze me in?'

The woman isn't a planner! What if there isn't a room available for Bev? Will she be obliged to offer to share? That would be most inconvenient. Also, will they have to dine together? What on earth will they talk about? Janet looks at her watch and sighs. The train would have been much faster. Perhaps she can make time for a hike tomorrow after her meeting with Glynis. She's so close now – can she really go home without setting foot on the fell?

Despite Janet's many and varied concerns as they pull up at the guest house, there is a comfort in not having to go in alone. The Laurels in Windermere promises more than it offers. There are zero laurels for a start, and Janet thinks fleetingly of the abundant *Prunus laurocerasus* on her plot. Here, she can make out only a scrap of pock-marked box hedging and a yew with root rot, but after a day cramped in Bev's car, she is grateful to un-concertina herself and escape the damn power ballads.

They wait at reception where venomous carpet is paired with dark wood panelling that gives off a sticky sheen. A receptionist with a flamboyant ponytail deals with a middle-aged couple in front of them. The couple sport identical outfits: spotless duck-egg cagoules, squeaky-clean leather brogues and fawn trousers with sharp creases.

Janet feels scruffy in her muddy hikers, her mannish coat. Instinctively she brings her hand to her waist, reaching for the comfort of the tools in her apron pocket. But there is just the flat of her shirt. She clutches her ancient knapsack closer to her, feeling suddenly awkward, old. Glowing gently next to her in her luminous coat, Bev looks chipper, and completely at ease.

The receptionist nods at them.

'With you in a mo, ladies.'

'Any recommendations for dinner?' the man in the cagoule is saying. 'We don't want anything *too* nice.'

His wife concurs anxiously, 'No, nothing too *fancy*.'

The receptionist nods at them, her ponytail swinging wildly. 'You want pub grub,' she announces.

The couple look visibly relieved.

'We do,' says the man, his shoulders relaxing.

'Burger and chips, steak and chips, cod and chips,' Ponytail trots off, 'nothing fancy, nothing special?'

'Right,' they say. 'Exactly.'

'The Oak on the corner of the high street.'

'Perfect.' The couple smile at each other, thrilled, and disappear into the evening.

There is an awkward moment when Ponytail thinks Janet and Bev are a mother and daughter sharing a room, which makes Bev chuckle and Janet blush, but things are quickly clarified, and Bev manages to nab the last single.

Once in her room, Janet is unsure how to occupy herself till dinner. The sloping ceilings mean she bangs her head on the way into and out of her lozenge of a bathroom. Places like this make her feel gawkier than ever. The room is a contradiction. On the one hand it seems to welcome the visitor with a daintily laid tea tray and a fresh pastille of soap in the bathroom, but at the same time it seems to want to keep them in their place with a series of strategically placed shouty 'Please Do Not!' instruction cards. Someone has been industrious with the air 'freshener' and the room is drenched in an astringent spray of ammonia under the guise of 'Spring Blossom'. Janet considers leaving her own 'Please Do Not!' note. Instead, she pushes open the small leaded window, pokes her head out and breathes in greedy lungfuls of the evening air. Wisteria drapes the window frame, scents the breeze. On Janet's plot right now circadian rhythms will be kicking in; the star jasmine will be opening to the dusk whilst the wood sorrel will be shutting up shop for the night. Her fingers twitch, restless. She takes a closer look at the wisteria – despite the perfume the leaves are pale, with leggy growth; at some places stems crowd each other out. Should have been pruned back in February in order to let in more light and air. Janet retrieves her Huntsman Swiss Army knife from her rucksack and snips at a few places where the growth is too dense. She breathes a contented sigh. That's better. Her hands relax.

Outside, the sun melts its colours across the sky, like a child's crayons left on a warm radiator, purple, orange and crimson rays slanting. Beyond the tumble of the town, she can make out the navy smudge of the lake and in the distance the noble profiles of the mountains. Buoyed by her smidgeon of pruning and the nature that surrounds her, Janet rallies. She lays her plaid pyjamas out on the bed, puts her toothbrush in the bathroom, underwear and socks in a drawer and, having entirely unpacked, gets ready to go out to dinner.

Janet's concession to dressing for supper is to smooth down her shirt and use the sphere of soap to wash her face in the doll-sized basin. She catches sight of her appearance in the mirror and feels suddenly uneasy. Why didn't she pack something smarter? Glynis was always dressed to the nines. It simply hadn't occurred to her. In fact, Janet had instinctively reached for her hiking clobber when she knew she was coming to the Lakes, grabbing her rucksack and flask, automatically feeling for the orienteering map. Old habits die hard. She peers closer at her reflection. Does she always look so stern? What was it Bev said the night she came round? *Same strong jawline. Great bone structure.* All Janet sees are wrinkles, the furrow of her brow, the lines she never saw coming but which are now etched deep by the sorrow that put them there. She is speckled with sadness like rust on a forgotten spade.

Whilst she has a map, flask and knapsack, Janet has neglected to pack a hairbrush, and despite her best attempts not one of the seven components of her Huntsman Swiss Army offers anything remotely serviceable. In the end she wets her hands and flattens down her shock of silver hair as best she can, then heads to reception to meet Bev, who, she is relieved to see, is still in her sports clobber.

'What do you fancy, Janet?'

'Anything but The Oak,' says Janet.

~

Ascotts is a self-satisfied building comprised of thick slabs of honey-coloured stone. A disinterested waiter deposits Janet and Bev at a table at the back.

'Could we have a . . .' Bev starts, but the waiter is already gone.

Bev frowns, considering something for a moment. Janet is about to sit down but Bev remains standing, so Janet stuffs her hands in her pockets, waits. That awkward feeling again, out of her comfort zone, an unwanted 'weed'. When was the last time she was in a restaurant? She can't even remember. How much will it cost? What if Bev wants to order three courses? And yet . . . a tendril of excitement unfurls as she takes in the linens on the tables, the light shimmering on the glasses, the hum of conversation. Ascotts seems to cater to well-heeled couples, business-people and golfers. Many of the diners seated towards the front of the restaurant are already enjoying food and wine.

Bev seems to have finally made her mind up about what-ever it was that was bothering her because she unzips her coat, flings it on the back of her chair, sits down and picks up the menu. Janet follows suit.

'I'm starving,' Bev says. 'I could literally eat everything!'

Janet glances at the prices. Maybe they should have gone to The Oak for *something and chips* after all.

' "Cuttlefish and broad bean surprise",' Bev reads. 'Sounds more like a nasty shock. Mind you, if someone else is cooking, I'll eat most anything. Eddie and I used to go to the Old Lions Tavern in Hastings every Friday. They did a lovely mushroom risotto. Eddie always ordered veg-gie lasagne. Did you ever go?'

Janet shakes her head.

Bev shrugs. 'It's a wine bar now. A bit trendy. Eddie says he prefers the food we cook, but for me . . .' She trails off, looks about them. 'It's not just about the food, it's the candlelight, the sense of an event, getting ready – something that takes you out of your routine. A date. Eddie and I always had the best conversations when we went out. That's what I thought, anyway. See anything you fancy?'

Janet glances at the menu. The catch of the day comes with chervil hollandaise.

'I foraged some wild chervil once on a backpacking trip, served it with roast trout, and wild garlic cooked over the campfire.' Did she just blurt that out loud? She's too used to being in her own company, talking to herself. The memory breached the surface of the past so vividly, like a trout jumping for a mayfly. She can smell the fish roasting, hear the crackle of the flames.

'JFC! I can just about manage sausages and sweetcorn on the barbecue, but roasting wild fish over an open fire – that sounds Eagle Scout level!'

Janet bats Bev's words away. 'Cooking it was a doddle. Catching the bugger was the hard part.' Pinking slightly, she adds, 'But it was tasty.' Bev looks at her intently – probably can't imagine Janet up to her thighs in freezing water, reeling the blighter in as it thrashed and twisted, then slicing open its belly and gutting and scaling it. Even Janet struggles to align that image with her sense of herself now, her staid sandwich lunches in the silent dining room, her hopeless knees.

'Anyway, that was a lifetime ago,' she says, vigorously unfurling her napkin, flapping the memory away. 'I was another person entirely.'

'You're still her, though, aren't you?' Bev says after a moment.

'What do you mean?'

'The woman who caught the fish, cooked it over the fire – she's still in there.' Bev slaps her hand to her chest. 'In here.' Three fierce slaps. 'We are all the women we've ever been, aren't we? They are all still part of us.'

Janet is not sure if Bev's question is rhetorical and lets a moment pass. Bev looks at her, her eyes the grey-green of spring sage.

JP's here! That Janet – sparkling-eyed, flushed-cheeked, rushing into the pub, eager faces turning to her – was she still her? Or the Pimm Glynis remembers – what about her? But when she looks inside, searching for those other versions of herself, it's like staring down the mouth of a long-forgotten well, dank, dark and hollow.

The waiter slouches back to their table with the enthusiasm of an orderly bringing a bedpan.

'Yes?' he says, staring at the back wall.

Bev smiles up at him. 'We'd love one of those wee candles everyone's got, wouldn't we, Janet?'

Janet nods. In truth she had been more focused on a dish of olives and perhaps the Italian breadbasket, but to each her own. Her stomach emits a noisy gurgle.

'And water . . .' says Bev, glancing round at the other tables.

'Sparkling or still?' the waiter intones.

'Janet, what do you prefer?'

Tap? Can she ask for tap? Is that still done? Do they really have to pay for water?

Bev looks across at her. 'Cumbrian tap?'

Janet nods, relieved.

Bev returns her attention to the waiter, giving him another friendly smile. 'A large . . .' She frowns, shakes her head, presses her fingers to her temples. 'What's the word? Tip of my tongue . . .' She winks but there is a tiny jag at the corners of her lips, a tension in her jaw. 'A large . . . oh, what is it? The thing you put the water in?'

'Carafe?' the waiter suggests with a slight sneer.

Bev looks back at him, cuts her eyes. 'Ewer,' she says. 'A large *ewer* of water, please.'

Bev orders the fish pie and Janet the catch of the day with the chervil hollandaise. The waiter is already turning to go when Bev picks up the wine list.

'I'd love a glass of wine. How about you? Nice chilled white? It would be cracking with the fish.'

Janet hesitates. The wine is bound to be pricey in a place like this. But Bev is right, it would be a perfect accompaniment to the fish. It's turning into quite a night! The quiver of a smile crosses her lips. If only the Steer Manures and Power Ballads could see her now, dining out, ordering wine. *Have a lovely evening!*

'We only do wine by the bottle.'

Bev looks to Janet for permission. 'I see, OK then, well . . .' She closes the wine list, hands it to the waiter.

In the old days Janet could down a flight of vodka faster than a Russian diplomat, but now, apart from the odd medicinal nip of Boodles from the watering can in her potting shed, she doesn't drink. Alone. Too dangerous.

But she isn't alone, is she? She's miles away from home, on the shores of Lake Windermere, in touching distance of the Dales, dining out, in company. And Bev, who has driven her all the way here, looks like she fancies a glass.

'We'll have a bottle of the Sauvignon Blanc,' says Janet.

*

'I hope I didn't embarrass you,' Bev says when the waiter goes.

'How?'

'Not remembering the word for jug . . .' Bev claps her hand to her mouth. 'Jug! *That* was the word I was looking for – carafe. Snooty sod!' She shakes her head. 'This brain fog drives me crazy. I never know when it's going to happen, what words are suddenly going to go missing. I was making the shopping list the other day and couldn't remember the words for washing-up liquid! Can you believe it? And the thing is, Janet, I could see it – the shape of the bottle, the green liquid, the red cap – I could even smell it, but the name?' She clicks her fingers. 'Gone.' Bev smiles but there's a trace of disappointment in her eyes. 'Daft, isn't it? I can go to work and deliver a baby, do the neatest episiotomy you've ever laid eyes on, but simple words keep eluding me.'

'Sage is good for memory,' Janet says, 'as well as the marjoram. You can brew it into a tisane. Also, lady's mantle, borage. For the hot flushes, the brain fog. Oh, and *Trifolium pratense* tea might help.'

'I'm thinking that's not covered by my usual Yorkshire Gold?'

'Red clover. It's excellent for menopausal symptoms. It's also known as bee bread, sugar plum and, for some ungodly reason, suckles.'

'I went on HRT a couple of months ago, and it's already starting to help with the flushes – mind you, the circles I had to go in to get it. My GP suggested sleeping tablets when I told him I was up all night with hot sweats! I held my ground and got the hormones, but it made me think about the poor women who don't know what to ask for and are fobbed off with sleeping tablets – or, more often than not, antidepressants.'

'Pregnant horse urine,' Janet says, 'is what HRT was made of in my day. I steered clear of it, as you can imagine.'

Bev nods. 'My mum, too – she had a terrible time with the change and nothing to help it along apart from an occasional Drambuie. Funny expression, isn't it, *the change*? Change into what? When you first get your period it's a bit of a shock, but people celebrate and say, "You're a woman now!" But what does that make us when we hit menopause? Are we not women any more?' She takes a breath, then carries on brightly, 'But HRT has come a long way. Yams – that's what they make it from now – bioidentical to the body's own hormones, apparently.' She shakes her head. 'You wouldn't think it, would you? Yams.'

'Never underestimate the healing power of plants,' Janet says.

'To be honest, I get yams confused with sweet potatoes, but whatever the case, I'm bloody grateful to them!'

The waiter flashes past, depositing a bottle of wine and a basket of bread without stopping.

'And a candle—' Bev starts, but he is gone. Reaching for the bottle, Bev pours them two generous glasses. 'What shall we drink to, Janet?'

Janet holds her wine glass out, aware how slim and elegant it is in her scarred rough hands. A businessman at a nearby table looks across at the two of them and says something to his companion, who turns in their direction and barks a harsh laugh.

'To . . .' Janet starts, but her throat constricts. She can't think of a single thing. Except what is she doing here? Like the knotweed, she suddenly feels her own transplant shock. She needs to be with her plants or working to save the allotments, not out for dinner in some fancy restaurant. Her chest tightens.

'To yams!' Bev chinks her glass loudly against Janet's. 'And to lady's whatsit? What was that other plant you just mentioned?'

'Lady's mantle?' Janet mutters.

'To lady's mantle and to Marjorie marjoram, to clover and sage!' Clink, clink, clink. 'Any more, Janet?'

Comfrey, thyme, flax. Janet gasps a breath. *Evening primrose and yarrow.* Another breath and she feels her chest start to relax. She sees her plants, bedded down for the night, for now, safe.

She clinks her glass to Bev's.

As they tuck into the wine and bread rolls the restaurant fills up around them.

'This is going straight to my head,' Bev says, happily topping up their glasses. 'Good job I'm not on the wards tomorrow!'

'Do you like being a midwife?'

Bev slowly butters a crusty roll, then says, 'You know how people ask you the question about what sense you would most hate to lose?'

Janet sips her wine. It isn't quite the path she thought the conversation would lead down, but she is starting to realize that Bev is more of a lateral thinker.

'Well, for me, it's touch,' Bev says. 'For me, touch is the centre. I see it with my patients all the time. You can give them operations and drugs, but I think one of the most

111

healing things you can do is just hold their hands. It doesn't have to be much – a cool palm on their forehead, a hand on their shoulder, but I think it can make all the difference. Just a wee bit of physical contact, letting them know someone's there for them. It brings their blood pressure right down.' Bev takes a slow sip of wine. 'You don't need a nursing qualification to know that, do you? It's instinctive. We all need to be touched, don't we, Janet?'

Janet busies herself slicing a piece of focaccia into two perfect halves. She can't remember the last time someone touched her.

'I suppose so,' she mumbles.

'My mum was a big hugger,' Bev goes on. 'I think I get it from her . . .' She picks up her wine glass again but doesn't drink, just stares at it, a little lost, and then carefully puts it back on the table. 'She'd hug anyone – the old ladies at her church, the man on the street selling *The Big Issue*. Even her letters were like hugs – she was a great letter-writer. People don't send letters any more, do they? But Mum did. She would pop all these other bits in the envelope, too, along with the letter – a recipe she had torn out of the *Radio Times*, a picture she'd cut out of a magazine of a jumper or coat she thought might suit me. These chubby envelopes would fall through my letterbox. She always told me to take the time to write a letter, or even just a postcard, something to let people know you're thinking about them. I really miss her letters.'

Janet sees the flyers and notes Bev has put through her door, the notelets she has crushed, thrown out, and feels a flush of shame tinge her cheeks.

'But to answer your question,' Bev goes on, 'yes, I like

that part of my job, being there for my patients one hundred per cent. And I love holding the newborns. But nowadays we're run off our feet. It's go, go, go. Give them drugs and get them out. Free up the beds.'

There's a pause during which Janet's stomach emits another loud grumble. Bev waves her arm and smiles at the waiter, who walks right past them.

'Aw, in the name of the wee man!' Bev exclaims. 'It's like you hit middle age and someone flicks the lights off.'

Precisely.

'Just the other morning, I was coming back from a night shift and a man on a motorcycle nearly bloody flattened me! So do you know what I decided, Janet?'

Janet feels sure she is about to find out.

'I decided that I needed a new look. Remember that song, "She'll Be Coming Round the Mountain"?' Bev whets her whistle with a swig of wine and sings a few bars.

Janet nods quickly to show that she does indeed remember and that there is no need for any further singing, but Bev sings on.

'*Singing aye, aye yippee, aye, aye yippee, aye, aye yippee yippee aye!*'

'I do remember,' Janet says, louder now, nodding again for extra emphasis.

'*She'll be wearing big red bloomers when she comes—*'

'I thought it was pyjamas?' Janet interrupts. 'Pink pyjamas?'

'Pyjamas? Was it? It may well have been – wouldn't trust my memory right now, that's for sure. But bloomers or pyjamas, I bet they bloody well saw her coming, eh, Janet? That's what gave me the idea for my new look.'

Janet's eyes widen, a startling mosaic of images colliding before her: Bev patrolling the maternity ward in bright-scarlet knickers, striding into the Hastings post office in fuchsia-pink pyjamas.

'I was straight down to the outdoor store,' Bev says. 'At first, of course, the shop assistant took me over to a rack of women's jackets in pastels. "Oh no," I said, "I want something that I can be spotted in for miles." "Oh, high-vis?" she said. "We've only got that in Men's." Which says a lot right there, doesn't it? Anyway, I found this.' She flaps the sleeve of her jacket. 'Visible from outer space! So whenever I'm walking down the street or going into the bank or coming round the bloody mountain, they will definitely see me coming!'

Janet doesn't doubt it.

'Like four o'clocks,' Janet says, but is drowned out by the loud businessmen at the table near them.

'How are you finding the Merc?' booms the man to his companion.

'Sorry?' Bev says to Janet.

'Like four o'clocks,' Janet repeats, 'fluorescent flowers. They date back to the Aztecs.'

'It doesn't have as sleek a profile as the Jag,' the man motors on, 'not such a looker.'

'You do know your plants, Janet. I'd love to see one. Why are they called four o'clocks?'

'Because—' Janet starts, but is drowned out again.

'The Merc is fine for cruising, but the Jag is quieter. A real pussycat. Nice little purr when she really gets going.'

Bev turns round to look at the businessmen and then says, her own voice raised, 'Now there's a man who's keen on high visibility, eh, Janet?'

The kitchen doors open and two steaming plates come out. Bev sits up, adjusts her napkin. 'Thank Christ! I'm starving.'

But the plates waft by them to the car-talk table.

'At least the scran will shut them up for a while,' Bev says. 'What were you saying?'

'Nothing. Just how they open every day at four o'clock, that's all.'

'Isn't that clever? Just in time for tea! Mind you, it'll be dinner at midnight for us at this rate.' Bev waves vigorously at the waiter, who walks off in the other direction. She puffs a frustrated exhalation. 'I'm half tempted to roll my sleeves up and get in that kitchen myself.' She stares back over at the car-talk men. 'You know they came in after us, don't you?' Bev narrows her eyes, then picks up the wine bottle and empties it into Janet's glass.

'Finish that off.'

Raising her own glass, she downs the rest of her wine, then picks up the breadbasket and tips the contents into her handbag.

'Drink up, then grab your sou'wester whatsit.' Bev stands up, hoists her handbag over her shoulder and picks up her coat.

'What?' Janet looks at her confused, but obediently gulps the remains of her wine and reaches for her oilskin.

'If they're going to treat us like we're not here . . .' Bev says with a determined jut of her chin, 'then so be it. Come on!'

And just like that, Bev in the lead, Janet loping close behind, the two women march out of the restaurant.

*

'I hope you're not disappointed about the chervil sauce,' Bev says as they walk briskly along the pavement away from Ascotts. 'I just couldn't take another minute. Hiding us at a table by the toilets, ignoring us, putting our order at the end of the queue. And we never got a sodding candle! I used to put up with it. Not any more.'

Janet breathes in the cool night air, the fresh smell of the countryside, feels the quick beat of her pulse. No, she doesn't mind about the chervil. She is ravenous, though.

'Let's get a move on before they come after us for the wine,' Bev says. 'Shall we try The Oak? Suddenly I quite fancy a plate of nothing special. What about you?'

The Oak doesn't have a free table, but the local chippie is a beacon in the dark and supplies them with a generous serving of saveloy and chips. They eat their meal on a bench, looking out across the rippling waters of Lake Windermere. A bright wedge of moon lolls in the sky, delighted with herself.

Bev takes a bread roll out of her handbag, makes a chip butty and chuckles.

'What is it?' Janet asks.

'I was just thinking about the first time I ever stole anything. I must have been about nine or ten? A birthday party at the house next door. I think I had a wee bit of a crush on the boy whose party it was. Well, his mum had a fancy glass bowl of liquorice wheels on the coffee table, and I really, really loved liquorice . . .'

Heat radiates from Bev's body as if a blowtorch has been ignited.

'What did you do? Purloin the crystal?'

'When no one was looking, I took a big handful of wheels and then – I was wearing a dress with no pockets – I shoved the liquorice down my knickers to hide it. I had to stay pretty still so they didn't fall out. Made the rest of the party a bit tricky. When I got home, they were stuck to my bottom like barnacles. What do you think of that?'

What does she think of that? Janet dabs mustard on her saveloy, considers and then says:

'Well, it's not up there with the Brink's-Mat robbery, but it was certainly a novel way to hide the lolly.'

Bev laughs.

'Speaking of which,' says Janet, 'if I'd known we were going to skip the bill, I'd have ordered the Sancerre.'

A huge snort erupts next to her, and she turns to see Bev, head tipped back in reams of laughter.

Janet is sitting by Lake Windermere, surrounded by countryside and listening to laughter caused by something she said. If it wasn't so dark it would be obvious that she is smiling.

'I'd love to have seen that bampot when he finally got round to noticing we're gone,' gasps Bev. 'He'll have had a face like a well-skelped erse!'

11

Bev is already sitting at a table for two pouring tea when Janet enters the Laurels' breakfast room the next morning. Janet relishes the unfamiliar pleasure of sitting down to breakfast across from another person despite the feeling that there is a self-propelled lawnmower loose in her skull, a result of the copious wine consumption, no doubt.

'Morning,' says Janet, slipping into her chair.

She takes a triangle of toast from the rack, knifes a golden curl of butter on to the side of her plate. She wants to tell Bev what a good time she had last night. She reaches eagerly for her words, like the seeds she carries in her apron pocket waiting to be sown, but Bev gets there before her.

'That was one of the best nights I've had in ages,' Bev beams over her teacup. 'Unexpected but perfect.'

Janet nods enthusiastically. Couldn't have put it better herself. Unexpected but perfect, exactly so. That smile again, coaxing at the sides of her mouth.

'When I left Hastings yesterday,' Bev continues, 'I could never have imagined I'd be spending the night in a guest house in the Lake District! Oh my God – the complete bliss of having the whole bed all to myself! I spread out like a starfish and watched some crap telly. I didn't have to worry about waking Eddie up or Eddie getting cold when I had a night sweat and threw the duvet off.'

Janet nods, dollops marmalade on the edge of her plate. She always has the bed to herself.

'It was amazing waking up this morning not having to think about anyone else's wants or needs. I suppose it's what people mean when they go on about having . . .' Bev taps her spoon on the side of her teacup. 'Oh, what's that expression?' Tap, tap, tap. Tap, tap, tap.

Janet's lips flatten; her fingers tighten over the butter knife. *Don't say it don't say it don't say it.*

'Me time!' Bev clatters the spoon into the saucer, shakes her head, making her curls jostle and bounce. 'I ran myself a nice big bubble bath with no one moaning about using up all the hot water or taking too long. I just lay there and soaked in the silence – it was so nice just to be on my own.'

Janet stares down at her tea. Being on your own isn't one single night in a lakeside guest house.

'And after I got out of the bath I thought, I've got the whole day ahead of me and no one to please but myself!'

Janet nods, takes a bite of the toast. It's dry in her mouth, tasteless. She chews slowly. The National Trust rejection rattles in her head. The day after the rejection, she opened her cupboard to get out her mint-green teacup and just stared at the other mugs all lined up and looking out at her expectantly, their gaping handles longing to be held. She stood for a moment, gripping the cupboard door, then suddenly turned and grabbed a cardboard box from under the stairs. Returning to the kitchen, she shoved the teacups inside it. The cups were followed by dinner plates, bowls and side plates. A couple of plates cracked as she threw them in. It didn't matter; no one was ever going to use them. She grabbed another box – in went the glasses and most of the cutlery. She left the mint-green teacup and saucer, one bowl and one plate. A knife, fork, spoon. A single water glass. But that was just the start. On and on she went that night, racing through the lonely rooms of her house, boxing up all the spares, the extras, the other halves of the matching pairs. And when she was done, when the shelves and cupboards were empty, for a moment she felt jubilant, as if in some way she had cheated loneliness, got one over on it.

She hadn't, of course. Because it was too much to bear, the emptiness echoing around the solitary mint cup and saucer. Shelves shell-shocked by the ruthless evacuation, empty hangers shivering. In the end she realized why she needed a tier of plates, a pack of placemats, a tower of dessert bowls, and why it was better to launder two pillowcases even though only one was ever used. Because at least in their presence there was the *promise* of company. But she didn't have the energy to put everything back, didn't have the heart. She just left the cardboard boxes strewn across her house, stepping stones back to another life, a life that was long gone. Those were the boxes Bev had noticed when she came round. But Janet wasn't having a clear-out, as Bev assumed; she was trying to stop herself from being so lonely that she thought her bones might break.

Janet picks up her tea, hugs the cup in her hands, desperate for the warmth of its touch even though it makes her scars smart.

Last night, despite being patronized and ignored by the staff, there had been so much pleasure – Bev raising her glass: *To lady's mantle and to Marjorie marjoram, to clover and sage!* The quick beat of Janet's pulse as they marched out of the restaurant three sheets to the wind. Sitting side by side on the bench in the moonlight. Making Bev laugh like that. Laughing herself. Janet had savoured it all.

All the while Bev was probably counting down the minutes to her 'me time'.

Bev is smiling away, chatting on about where her route might take her, what stops she might make. Should she go up via Dumfries and Galloway or through the Scottish Borders? Blah de blah de bloody blah. Clearly she is dying to be off, away from dull-as-dishwater Janet.

Suddenly Janet is on her feet. 'I'm off.'

Bev looks up, puts her cup into her saucer, half rises.

'Oh . . . right . . . already? You haven't had your breakfast.'

'I have a very important meeting. I have to get on.'

Bev nods quickly. 'Of course. Would you like a lift?'

'I'll get the bus,' Janet snaps, and then adds, 'I am perfectly capable of using public transport, you know. I'm not some doddery old lady who needs to be chauffeured everywhere by a healthcare professional.'

'No, of course not. I—'

'Thank you very much for the lift.' Janet opens her knapsack and takes out her purse. She lays down two crisp twenty-pound notes next to Bev's teacup.

Heat rises in Bev's cheeks. 'What's that for?'

'Half the petrol. Safe travels.'

Bev pushes her chair back, stumbles to her feet. 'Janet . . .'

But Janet is gone.

12

'Punctual as ever, Pimm,' says Glynis, standing in her doorway.

Glynis's hair is no longer sculpted into its regulation clamshell coiffure but tied in a loose chignon, blonde tresses now thickly threaded with silver. Rather than her trademark battle-grey skirt suit, she wears a cashmere polo-neck jumper and a pair of navy cords, but Janet would have known her anywhere. And, of course, there are the shoes. Glynis had always allowed herself to rather 'walk on the wild side' in the footwear department. The two buckled crème caramel creations she sports today show that much at least hasn't changed.

Janet had tried to gather her thoughts on the bus ride out to Glynis's village, but her heart skittered under her oilskin and her mind remained cluttered. She loitered for ages at the end of Glynis's street, feeling foolish, feeling old.

Pull yourself together, she scolded herself. *Focus on what's important; focus on Seaview.*

'Walk with me,' Glynis says, grabbing a dove-grey rain-coat, landing a stylish navy fedora on her head.

· Seeing Glynis combined with the olde-worlde charm of their surroundings makes Janet feel as if she is travelling back in time. The traffic-free streets are laced with narrow ginnels and dotted with whitewashed stone buildings with slate roofs. The whole thing looks like an old-fashioned chocolate box – smells like one, too; scents of sugar, cream and cocoa waft from the Famous Fudge and Chocolate Shop. One could easily imagine Mrs Tiggy-winkle dashing out from behind the cheery red post office or the entire Flopsy, Mopsy and Cotton-tail trio hopping into the baker's for iced buns. It is all completely at odds with Janet's sense of the whip-sharp woman who clips alongside her, the heels of her shoes sparking off the cobbles. A woman who knows where the bodies are buried. Glynis looks like a film noir cut-out slotted into this cutesy environment.

'We moved here because of Douglas,' Glynis says, as if reading Janet's thoughts. She leads them upwards towards a grey stone church at the top of a small hill. 'When he got his prognosis, he said he wanted to live out the rest of his days here.'

'Do you like it?' Janet asks as they reach the top of the hill.

Glynis considers. 'I think one can make a good life anywhere, if one has the wherewithal. And it makes Douglas happy. I can't be happy if he's not happy.'

The one chink in her armour.

'Esthwaite Water, Claife Heights, Latterbarrow,' Glynis rattles off, calling out the names of the glittering lake, the soaring hills, as if she is reading her weekly shopping list – not that Janet can imagine Glynis making a shopping list.

Janet gazes out at the landscape and her heart lifts for a moment. She recognizes what she thinks might be the peak of Helvellyn and . . . are those the Langdales in the distance?

Glynis marches them over to a large stone bench at the far end of the graveyard and sits down. 'No one can over-hear us here.'

She hasn't changed one bit, thinks Janet, settling herself on the bench next to Glynis. Everything has been perfectly thought out. No one to witness their meeting save the gravestones.

Glynis crosses her ankles, knits her gloved fingers together and turns to Janet.

'Tell me.'

Janet's words gallop. 'I think our newest borough coun-cillor is in cahoots with a big property developer and they're coming after my allotment – not just mine, the whole allotment site, a hundred and twenty plots. It's a whopping big parcel of land, central to town with sea views. Worth a lot of money if you can get it out of com-munal hands and into private ones. They've planted an illegal invasive, Japanese knotweed, to hasten our demise by classing the site as a biohazard.' She pauses, gulps a breath.

'What is your suspicion of the alleged "cahoots" based on?' Glynis cocks her head to the side, eyebrows at a stand-off. It is the exact expression she used to wear all those years ago back in the office when someone handed in a dodgy travel expense claim. Without fail the puff would go out of whatever fool was standing before her and they would fal-ter, take the document back just to give it one more quick check.

'The knotweed was definitely planted on purpose,' Janet

124

says. 'I'll swear as to that. But exactly how Marsh, the councillor, is connected to Bringley, the property developer – that I don't know for certain, but . . .'

'But you feel it in your bones?' Glynis says, her look piercing.

Janet meets Glynis's stare, returns it.

'Enough to come all the way up here to ask for your help.'

Glynis uncrosses her ankles and her shoes sparkle softly in the morning light.

'Well,' she says after a moment, 'that's good enough for me. I'll see what I can do.'

Janet feels her body relax, a lightness. Glynis will help. She isn't on her own.

'When I got in touch, I thought you might still be at GCHQ. Even though we must be fairly close in age, I just couldn't imagine you as retired.'

'I left last year when Douglas got sick. You know they call it the Government Communication Headquarters now, don't you? Or worse: the Doughnut. But you never worked in the new place, did you?'

Janet shakes her head.

'It's got an open-air garden courtyard in the middle. I preferred the old-school brutalism of our offices. I believe they are a Sainsbury's now.'

'So you can't get into the system any more?'

'You don't think I left before making sure I had secured an excellent replacement, do you?'

Realization dawns on Janet's face. 'The new Glynis – Glynis's Glynis.'

Glynis tips her head back and laughs throatily. 'Well

said. I have my own Glynis. My own Giulia, actually, but a chip off the old block, if I do say so myself.'

Her smile disappears. 'Look, I can't promise you that I – or Giulia – can find anything. If your Councillor Marsh is taking backhanders from a property developer, you can be damn sure they'll take care to cover their tracks. But let's see what a little investigating reveals. Leave it with me. Let's avoid all digital comms. No emails. No texting. It's always so much trickier to delete digital files than shred good old foolscap. In an emergency, call the landline, but don't leave any voicemail you wouldn't want used as evidence in a court of law if this gets nasty.' A twitch of a smile at the corner of her mouth. 'I have to admit, I'm rather looking forward to it. It will be an excellent distraction from this.' She gestures disparagingly out to the perfect little village, the jaw-dropping landscape.

'Thank you,' says Janet.

A moment's silence and then Glynis says, 'The atmosphere was quite different after you left, Pimm.' Her tone is almost accusatory.

'I didn't have a choice in the matter,' Janet replies. Again that spark of fury in her chest at how easily her career had been destroyed.

'Napier told me you'd put in for a job with less pressure.' Glynis narrows her eyes, stares at Janet intently. 'Said you wanted to focus on family. I must say, I had my suspicions . . .'

'They threw me out,' Janet says, her voice flat.

There is a pause. From somewhere the sound of children screeching and shouting as they are freshly released into a school playground.

Glynis re-crosses her ankles and folds her hands in her lap. 'What really happened? Tell me your side of things.'

And Janet does. She tells Glynis how she had gone to Napier, querying the fact that the decorating company brought in to do the refurbishment of various ministerial offices, including his own, seemed to be owned by Napier's brother-in-law. Napier had pooh-poohed her away. Not long afterwards, Janet had 'failed' her annual review.

'Mistakes I hadn't made were blamed on me,' Janet says; again that thrum of anger. 'Within weeks I was transferred to Whitehall, demoted to pushing papers in the basement.'

'Leaving Napier to order leather-topped desks and tufted ottomans to his heart's content.'

There is a short silence before Glynis says, 'Well, it was a poorer place without you, Pimm.'

Janet shifts on the bench. 'Not for Napier.'

'Damn Napier!' Glynis's voice betrays no emotion but her eyes flash. 'You were the smartest in the office, you had the most integrity, you set the tone. You should have been the division head.'

Janet opens her mouth but then closes it again. She sits a little taller.

Glynis shakes her head, purses her lips. '*Plus ça change*, eh. The rules might change but the game is always the same. The old boys' network might have new tools, hide behind their digital avatars, but their grubby little hands are still sticky as hell.' She shrugs. 'Who knows, maybe this time we'll get lucky.' Abruptly she stands. 'I'd better get back. I don't like to leave Douglas on his own for too long.'

'Might his health improve?'

'It won't.' Glynis's eyes rest on something in the distance for a moment. 'I'll have him with me for another year – a bit more if I'm lucky. And I'm going to make damn sure he enjoys every day he has left. Right, then' – she looks back at Janet, her voice brisk, back in control – 'off I go. Remember' – she turns up the collar of her mac, tips the brim of her fedora – 'you never saw me.' She smiles almost imperceptibly and sets off down the hill on her sugared heels.

As Janet watches Glynis go, she is tempted to whistle a few bars of the Harry Lime theme tune from *The Third Man*. Suddenly Glynis stops, looks back over her shoulder.

'I hope your allotment crowd know how lucky they are to have Janet Pimm on their side. And remember, don't let the bastards get you down.' With a final wave Glynis is gone.

Janet sits for a moment looking out at the rolling hills, the mountain peaks. Glynis has promised to do what she can. Clearly she is hungry for a distraction. Still, she respects Janet's instinct, believes in her. Warmth floods her chest. It is the same feeling she had the other day, threading her seeds into the earth, tucking them under the cloche. Hope.

After a while Janet wanders into the church to look at the wall paintings, thinks about how easily things can be covered up, whitewashed over and, unlike these rescued murals, never see the light of day again. It is dark and cold inside the old church and Janet doesn't linger. Whatever Napier fudged all those years ago to get her demoted had certainly worked. At the time she didn't have the strength to fight. But now she will do whatever it takes.

Outside in the light, she slowly turns 360 degrees, taking in the beauty of the landscape until finally her hiking boots nose east like two excitable golden retrievers itching for a run. Janet sniffs the air, the whiff of limestone, that distinct minerality of this part of the country, the particular sense of spaciousness. She wants to feel the swish of grass against her legs, the pull of her muscles as she clambers along the fells, her lungs filling with fresh Cumberland air.

She's so close. She could pick up the local bus in Windermere and be in Sedbergh in a flash. Verdant pathways open up before her: Ilkley Moor and the Twelve Apostles, Buckden Pike, Hawes to Sedbusk, a stretch of the James Herriot Way – she and Nancy had walked them all. Bev is probably over the Scottish border by now, relishing her 'me time'. She's no doubt singing power ballads at the top of her lungs – good riddance to that blasted CD. Janet shakes the thought of Bev away. Aysgarth Woods and Waterfalls, Horse Head Moor. So many favourite hikes . . .

But Janet already knows where she is heading. Whernside. The highest of the Yorkshire Three Peaks, its whale-like shape cresting the valley. She'll start in Dent, see if she can get far enough to get a good view of the cairn. Maybe she could even stay over in the old youth hostel if it's still there. Or a B & B. No, mustn't get carried away; she needs to get back to Seaview, protect her plot.

It was on Whernside that she and Nancy had hunted for the rare northern hawk's-beard, partial to limestone pasture with a northerly aspect. How they had searched! And they had been close, Janet was sure. Could she retrace their steps? The plant won't be in flower just yet, but she could probably identify it by its basal leaves and the rugose lamina of its conspicuously anastomosing veins. One more fell hike for old times' sake. When might she get the chance again?

The fact that Whernside is within such easy striking distance is a happy coincidence. Not the deciding factor in Janet's trip up here at all.

13

The bus back to Windermere passes a park planted with striking horse chestnuts, their friendly hand-shaped leaves an eye-catching green. Soon they will be in flower, always such a magnificent sight.

I hope your allotment crowd know how lucky they are, Glynis had said. But Janet is certain they don't feel one bit lucky to be saddled with her. Especially not Patrice. Was it today Patrice was meeting with Pete Marsh? What would she say if she knew what Janet was up to? Would she think Janet was just making things worse? All Janet wants is to make things better. From nowhere she suddenly remembers one day last autumn when Patrice came by her plot with an offering of some handsome cauliflower plants for her vegetable patch. Without thinking, Janet had blurted, 'I don't like cauliflower.'

Patrice said, 'I bet you'd like it if you tasted my Brixton charred cauliflower with mint-and-tamarind dipping sauce.'

Janet didn't know what to say, so she just shrugged.

Needless to say, Patrice hasn't offered her any more plants or cuttings since then.

Maybe she should offer Patrice some sweet marjoram cuttings. Return the favour. A bit late, but still. Does Patrice already have marjoram on her plot? Janet doesn't recall seeing it there. In any case, what she really needs to do is come up with something to save Seaview. If she can do that, then maybe Patrice would like a cutting.

Janet sighs and presses her forehead against the cool of the window.

~

Back in Windermere, Janet stands at the stop for the Dent bus, due any moment. As she waits she pulls the Bartholomew out of her rucksack to study her route. She is just folding the map up again when something bright green catches her eye across the square.

'Bev?'

Bev sits on a bench shivering and eating a 99 Flake ice-cream cone. She looks up when she hears Janet's voice. She gives her a smile and a small wave but as Janet approaches she can see Bev's eyes are red-rimmed. A confetti of scrunched-up paper napkins covers her lap.

'Are you all right?' Janet asks. 'Did something happen to your car?'

Bev dabs her eyes. 'No, the car is fine.' She takes a sad lick of her ice cream.

Janet hovers. 'I thought you'd be well over the border by now.'

Bev gives a loud sniff. 'I decided to treat myself to an ice cream before I set off. Cheer myself up.'

From the looks of it, the idea does not seem to have been successful, but Janet decides it is probably wisest not to point this out.

'I used to love a Ninety-nine,' Bev says. 'How perfect the swirl of ice cream was, how you got a whole chocolate flake too. It was like eating a fairy tale.' Bev looks at the cone in her hand. 'I haven't had one for years. It's smaller than I remember, and I couldn't believe the price. That's the thing with fairy tales, I suppose. Too good to be true.' She takes another bite, slowly licks her lips. 'It still tastes lovely.' A fat tear rolls down her cheek.

Across the square the bus to Dent rumbles into view.

'I expect you'll want to be on your way,' Janet says, shoving the Bartholomew back in her knapsack and rootling for her bus pass, 'if you're going to make it all the way to your sister's?'

Bev looks up at Janet through her tears, confused. 'My sister?'

'Rona?'

'Rona.'

'In Kirkcaldy?'

'Kirkcaldy.'

They suddenly seem to be involved in some bizarre form of call and response.

Bev takes another small lick of ice cream. 'Rona in Kirk-caldy.' A further tear takes its marching orders, closely followed by another and then another.

Janet can see her bus idling at the stop now.

'Right, well, I'd better . . .' Awkwardly she takes a step backwards, then one more.

Tears course freely down Bev's cheeks and it appears she has come to the end of her supply of paper napkins. Janet hesitates, then rummages in the pocket of her coat and pulls out a large, crumpled but clean white-and-blue-checked cotton handkerchief. She thrusts it towards Bev, though the gesture only serves to bring about a fresh onslaught of tears. Bev grabs hold of the hanky and mashes it to her face, but in the process her ice cream tumbles to the ground. The two women stare at it, splattered on the pavement.

'The thing is,' Bev gasps, 'I'm not going to Scotland.'

'Why on earth not?'

'Because . . . my sister, Rona, lives in . . .' Bev hiccups another sob 'Croydon.'

'Croydon!' Janet's brow creases. Trying to make sense of Bev is like trying to stake overgrown cucumbers in a brusque wind. 'But . . . if you aren't driving to Scotland, then where the heck are you going?'

The green jacket shudders.

'Barnardo's,' Bev sobs. 'I was on my way to Barnardo's!'

'*Barnardo's?*' Janet is the one doing call and response now.

Bev gives her face a vigorous mop with the hanky. 'When I came to yours that night – saw all the boxes everywhere – I thought, that's what I need: a good clearout. I thought it might make me feel better, lighter, to get rid of some of the stuff that's been . . . weighing me down. Some of my old things and a few of Mum's bits I've been . . . holding on to . . .' She takes a juddering breath. 'So I bagged it all up, threw it in the car, and was popping to the charity shop, but then . . . then . . .'

'Then *what*?' Janet asks, incredulous.

Bev slowly raises her blotchy tear-stained face. 'Then I saw you.'

Across the square the Dent bus turns the corner and disappears.

Janet sighs, drops her bus pass back into her pocket and sits down heavily next to Bev.

'Perhaps you'd better tell me all about it,' she says.

Bev nods gratefully.

'I saw you standing at the bus stop in the rain, and it just seemed neighbourly to give you a lift to the train station. And then you said you were going to the Lakes, and that sounded so lovely. I didn't mean to horn in on your trip. I didn't have a plan. I just couldn't stop driving . . .' Bev twists Janet's hanky in her hands. 'I wanted . . . something.'

Despite Bonnie Tyler constantly telling her to *turn around*, what Bev really wanted that day was to keep on going.

'It only took a couple of minutes to get to the train station in Hastings, so then I thought maybe I could just drive a wee bit further – run you up to Tunbridge Wells. And then we ran into that traffic tailback and I realized that I didn't want to go back. I just wanted to keep on driving, and the thing is, you . . . you . . .'

'I what?'

'You let me,' Bev says simply, and smiles at Janet, wet-cheeked.

Janet stares back, open-mouthed.

'You gave me the excuse,' Bev says after a moment, 'to keep on going. And it felt so *good* just to be out on the road, leaving everything behind, not being accountable, not going to work or getting the shopping. I was just driving, moving forward, letting the day unfold in its own way. And then, last night, eating that greasy saveloy on the bench, looking out at the lake – I was so happy. But this morning you left so suddenly, and I knew I had to go home

135

and I just wasn't ready.' Bev gives her eyes another swipe with the hanky. 'Also, you were a wee bit short with me.'

Janet shifts. 'I got the impression that you wanted to be alone.'

Bev stares at her, then her face softens. 'Och, Janet, no, not a bit of it. Look, I can't remember exactly what I said but I just meant that it was so different, so nice, to have a whole night in a room by myself. When I woke up drenched from a night sweat I didn't have to worry about disturbing Eddie – I just got out of bed, flung open the windows and stood there starkers, looking at the moon – bloody good job I was on the top floor!'

'Agreed.'

'And it's not just about not waking Eddie up,' Bev goes on, her hands clenched. 'It's about not having to tiptoe about or pretend everything is OK or pop fresh sheets on the bed. It's about being free to pace back and forth like a . . . like a lion in a cage, to open my mouth and roar at the top of my lungs if I feel like it, because sometimes, Janet . . .' Bev stares at her, eyes wide. 'Sometimes lately that is the only thing that I want to do. Just throw my head back and roar.'

Bev's phone pings. Janet watches the light flash from inside her green pocket. Bev takes it out, looks at the screen and then switches it off.

They sit in silence for a moment. A raven in its black-lacquered dress suit swoops down, inspects Bev's cone, gives it a suspicious peck.

Janet has an idea. It might be a terrible one, but Bev's sporty clothes suggest someone who enjoys physical activity. Her canvas pumps are a bit of a worry, but if they stick to flatter terrain . . . And Bev has a car.

'Look, I was planning a bit of a leg stretch; a friend and I used to hike the fells nearby and I rather fancied retracing one of our routes. Also, there's a plant I wouldn't mind having a bit of a scout for, northern hawk's-beard – pretty rare and it's unlikely we'd find it, but we could try. I don't know if that appeals but—'

Bev is on her feet, her tear-stained face shining.

'Yes, it does appeal. It appeals very much! Yes!'

Janet pushes herself upright. 'Right, let's make a move. We should press on whilst the weather holds.'

'I'll call in at a shop on the way,' Bev cries, 'and get us a picnic!'

A picnic isn't at all what Janet has in mind, but Bev is already off and right then Janet hasn't the heart to argue.

14

Janet had assumed that Bev dressed in sporty clothes because she was indeed sporty – a cyclist or a jogger or one of those speed-walkers. It's true that Janet's knees prevent her from keeping the pace she once did; as she pants up the rocky ascent she needs to stop for a breather more than once. However, each time she turns around Bev is further and further behind, ambling up the hillside helterskelter, stopping here, there and everywhere as if she is on an Easter egg hunt as opposed to a hardy fell hike. Bev slows things even further by leaving the path at various junctures, dashing off this way and that, shouting that she thinks she has spotted the northern hawk's-beard, even though Janet has already told her quite clearly that the plant prefers to grow at a bit of altitude, so it's not really worth scouting till they get higher up. Not likely to happen if Bev doesn't pick up the pace. But no sooner is Bev back on the path than she stops to chat to a fellow hiker on the route. Infuriatingly, every time Janet takes a breather to allow Bev to catch up, Bev takes a breather too. Janet is starting to see the appeal of 'me time' after all.

They are behind Janet's schedule, having already lost a full half-hour in the bakery in Dent with Bev oohing and ahhing over crusty loaves of bread and thick slices of home-made cake. Much as Janet tried to chivvy her, Bev kept finding yet another picnic essential – 'Look at the size of these cheese straws! Did you see the fruit buns? Who can resist a home-made sausage roll?' Janet had stared glumly at Bev's overflowing shopping basket. Janet's idea of a fell hiker's picnic was an apple, a flask of water, and perhaps – if one was really pushing the boat out – a tablet of Kendal Mint Cake.

But just look at where they are! Janet rolls back her shoulders, breathes the Cumberland air and takes in her surroundings. What magnificent countryside. The lime-stone enables rich plant life; such an abundance of wild thyme! Janet takes another deep inhalation, notices that the thyme smells muskier than the patch on her allotment. Another deep breath – isn't that . . . Yes! Sweet cicely! There must be a crop of the wildflowers near by. The scent reminds her of the aniseed balls she loved as a girl. An ounce each Saturday from the glass jar in the sweetshop; the rest of her meagre pocket money she saved for note-books and fresh pencils, but she just couldn't resist the temptation of a small paper twist of those sweets. She still remembers happy hours sitting on the back step – the Pimms had no garden – studying her lessons and slowly savouring the spicy, aromatic taste of the aniseed ball, sucking till the red streaked her tongue and the sweet was just a tiny white dot. She can almost taste it now.

What else? Janet looks about her. Dense spikes of bis-tort abound and she can spot plenty of the perfectly named bird's-foot trefoil – an invasive, yes, but such a vibrant pulsating yellow! How the pollinators adore it. And what views! She puts her hand to her brow, takes in Great Coum, Dentdale, Howgill Fells. It is all just as she remembers, just as it was the last time she was here, all those years ago with Nancy. They had been walking in the other direction, starting at Chapel-le-Dale and hiking from Ingleborough to Pen-y-ghent, finishing their arduous Three Peaks hike at Whernside.

They had set off in such high spirits, the miles stretching deliciously ahead. They weren't in a hurry; they would be 'going off piste', Nancy had declared, whenever the fancy took them, camping at night and searching for the northern hawk's-beard en route.

By the time they finally summited Whernside, the final peak, they were filled with such a sense of achievement. The two of them stood not far from where Janet stands right now, tanned arms draped round each other's shoulders, gazing out. Back then, with Nancy right beside her, muscles singing, charged with life, Janet felt herself at one with the soaring hills, the expansive verdant green. Now, standing alone, she takes in the prehistoric limestone scars and aligns them with her own scars, the places where over the ensuing years she has felt stripped away, exposed. She feels the cracks and fissures caused by an accumulation of sadness, a slow erosion of regret. And yet . . . just like the arteries of ancient dry stone that thread the land, she is still standing. Battered by time, crumbling in places, yes, but still here.

The timelessness of the landscape means that the view before her looks just as it has for millennia. And just as it did when she stood here with Nancy that day. She feels a giddy moment of time travel, her very same body standing in this very same spot, looking at the very same view.

And yet everything has changed.

'Halloo!' Bev's voice bounces up the hillside.

Janet shields her eyes with both hands and tracks her gaze down the path until it comes to land on a shining green speck with a smaller orange speck of a picnic bag. As Janet waits for Bev to catch up, she recalibrates their hike. What with her knees and Bev's perambulations, they'll never make it anywhere near the top of Whernside. Could they at least get as far as the place where the majestic cairn comes into view? The sky has clouded over and she can smell rain, but it feels a way off.

'This is wonderful!' Bev pants as she finally reaches Janet's side, pink-cheeked and bright-eyed. 'Amazing views! How did we get so high so fast? We must have walked about five miles already.'

'We've probably climbed about a thousand feet,' Janet says.

'No wonder my legs are killing me. Are you thinking what I'm thinking, Janet?'

That they need to pick up the pace?

'That this is the perfect spot for our picnic!' Bev glances towards Janet hopefully.

'The views are even better further up,' Janet encourages, indicating the way.

For the next quarter of a mile or so they follow a stone wall, side by side, Bev semi-trotting to keep up with Janet's long strides, Janet forcing herself to hold back.

'Did you come here a lot?' Bev pants.

'Yes, it was a favourite of ours – my friend Nancy's and mine. Last time I was here we did the Three Peaks walk. Twenty-four miles.'

'We're not doing that today, are we?' Bev looks anxious.

'No. Five-mile circular if we're lucky. We'll barely make a dent in one peak.'

'Thank Christ for that!' Bev says, and then after a moment asks, 'So, you and Nancy are big hikers?'

'Used to be. After university Nancy got her first job in Edinburgh, and I got mine in Cheltenham. The Dales were a good meeting point.'

Two pairs of hiking boots walking in easy rhythm. Tufted grass underfoot. Summer and the flash of a tanned calf. Hills rising in the distance. The clunk-clunk sway of a knapsack expertly packed – basic camping essentials at the bottom, sandwiches wrapped in greaseproof paper on top. The sun high in the sky and all that is asked of them is to keep traversing these ancient pathways at their leisure, stopping now and then to marvel at waterfalls and limestone flags. Picnicking by a riverbank, high on nothing more than sugar from the flask of tea and the generous possibility of youth. Afterwards, boots tied around necks, they balance their way out on the stones that perfectly span the stream. Then a splash as one of the boots tumbles into the water. Janet hunkers down, reaches forward, fingers stretching to retrieve it. Nancy holds on to the frame of her knapsack to anchor her, keep her from falling in. 'Don't let go!' Janet calls, leaning out further, closer to the water. 'Never, JP, never, never, never.'

'Do you and Nancy still meet up?'

'No.'

'Well, it's a long way, I suppose, between Edinburgh and Hastings.'

'Nancy's in Melbourne.'

'Ah. Even trickier, then.'

'Haven't seen her in years.'

Decades.

'That's a shame. Do you think—'

'Shall we pick up the pace?' Janet says.

'We could,' Bev wheezes, 'or, and here's another thought . . . we could stop for a minute and have our picnic?'

～

'You brought a *tablecloth*?' Janet says as Bev unfolds a large piece of damask which she drapes over the ancient stone wall. She watches as Bev proceeds to lay their picnic out on the cloth.

'Aye. I thought, well, it's in the car anyway. We can have our picnic in style, what do you say? Treat ourselves to the fancy meal we never got at the restaurant last night.'

Despite her misgivings about the picnic, not to mention the tablecloth, as Janet leans against the stone wall eating a hunk of bread with cheese, biting into a juicy tomato, she feels she can't complain.

'Are you still rolling your eyes at my tablecloth?' Bev grins over at her. 'Because I think I might have a candelabra in here.' She peers into her bag, gives it a shake.

'No, I was just thinking how uncommonly good this is, which is idiotic because I have cheese and tomato for lunch every day. This tastes so much better, though.'

'Well, you'll have worked up an appetite with the hundreds of miles we've walked. I certainly have.' Bev tucks into her lunch.

It's true, of course – eating outside feels totally different, one of the things Janet loved about camping. But it's not just the view, the fresh air, the exercise. Instead of sitting in her dining room, she's leaning against a moss-freckled stone wall in the middle of rippling moorland, sharing a picnic. Silence, she reflects, has such a different quality when it is shared.

'Ah, that hit the spot,' Bev sighs as she pops the last bite of fruit bun into her mouth. She stretches, then gets up and shakes the crumbs from the tablecloth. The cloth flutters in the breeze. 'I got this on our honeymoon in Florence,' Bev says, looking at it. 'It was pricey. The saleswoman was lovely, you know, so Italian. She came right over and took it out of the tissue paper.' Bev holds the cloth before her. 'It sort of . . . shimmered. There's a satin thread woven in that really shines under the light. The saleswoman kept telling me to touch it, feel how soft it was, fluttering it out, saying, *bellissimo, bellissimo*.'

Bev slowly folds the cloth in half and half again, and then in a triangle shape as if for a military funeral. Her fingers trace a worn patch where the thinnest of threads hold the fabric together.

'Christmas, anniversary, birthday – it's been there, decorating our table for years. I washed it on gentle, kept it in the drawer with a lavender bag. Then the other day I was about to put it out and I looked at it and realized the hem had unravelled and it was well past its best . . . never mind the wine stain I could never get out.' Bev stands there for a moment before gently slipping the cloth back in the bag. She turns to Janet. Smiles brightly. 'Right, then, time to find your hawk's-beard!'

Janet glances up at the sky, grey as pencil lead. As well as losing the time they are soon going to start losing the weather.

'Actually, I think we'd better turn back.'

Bev's face falls. 'When's the next time you are going to be all the way up here? Let's just keep going for another twenty minutes, what do you say? I bet I can find your plant. I feel lucky.'

Janet frowns, takes out her Bartholomew.

'Where are we now?' Bev asks, joining her and peering at the map.

Janet points to where she thinks they are.

Bev takes the map from Janet, puts her finger where Janet's was and then straddles her thumb to Dent. 'Christ,' she cries, holding up her finger and thumb. 'We've barely done an inch!' She shakes her head. 'My legs beg to differ!' She returns to the map, studying it for a moment, and then says, 'I use GPS all the time but it's nice to hold a map in your hands, to see everything all laid out. Kettlewell, Starbotton, Appletreewick,' she reads. 'Oh, look, here's one for you! Janet's Foss – is that a hill or . . .?'

'It's a waterfall,' Janet says quickly, heat flaring in her cheeks. Taking the map from Bev, she snaps it back into her knapsack.

'Fifteen minutes,' Bev bargains. 'Ten. I'll find your hawk's-beard, then we'll head home.'

Against her better judgement, Janet nods.

They walk on beyond the trusty stone wall and out on to open hillside. They pass the turn-off for Boot of the Wold, which leads to the Whernside Tarns, bodies of water that seem to balance precariously on the slopes. For a while they are silent, both searching for the northern hawk's-beard. Just the thwomp of their footsteps and the distant baaing of the sheep that dot the hills.

'What is it you love about gardening, Janet?' Bev asks eventually, looking up from the clump of sweet cicely she is examining.

Janet puts her hands on her hips, stares out at the land-scape. One winter, not long after she first got her plot at Seaview, she had looked at the leafless trees, the bare branches, and seen the buds of spring. She had stood on the frozen earth and felt fruit ripening in the summer warmth. She had breathed in the chill of winter and smelled the autumn harvest. It was all there, a promise held in the dark earth, in the sculptural branches – a prom-ise of the future, a promise of life.

'It's a sort of time travel,' Janet says.

'Time travel!' Bev says. 'I like that! Say more.'

'Gardening links you to past, present and future. When you garden, you're collaborating with invisible hands from the past, labouring for the future. It's about faith, I suppose.'

'Faith?'

'You wait and you wonder and you hope and then, one

day, if you are lucky: a shoot. Green and alive and right there where there was nothing.' Janet is talking more to herself than Bev now, her fingers gently opening and closing. 'And you do everything you can for it because you feel somehow that your fortunes are bound to each other. It keeps you in the present, but it promises all the possibility of the future . . .' Janet thrusts her hands in the pockets of her oilskin, shrugs. 'I don't know if that makes sense?'

Bev stands up, comes over. 'Completely. We're birds of a feather, you and me.'

Really? Janet is hard-pressed to think of any similarities between them; even their faint shadows that stretch along the grass mark them as entirely different, one lanky, angular, long, the other short, round, curvy. 'How so?'

'We both help deliver life into the world,' Bev says simply.

They agree to search for just a few more minutes and stay within hooting distance of each other. Janet strides along the edge of a stream on her left, turning back now and again to see the glowing green shape of Bev zigzagging this way and that. After a while the light starts to dim noticeably as a mist rolls in. The path climbs gently along the ridge but sadly the summit of Whernside is no longer visible. They need to head back, no matter what Bev says. Janet knows how quickly the weather can change out here; the mist can come in fast and once you lose visibility you're buggered. She turns and makes her way back down the slope. Disappointing in a way – no summit, and no northern hawk's-beard . . . and . . . hmmm, no sign of Bev. Janet curls a hand to the side of her mouth. 'Woo, woo,' she calls.

Bev's answering call comes back, but where is she? Janet

147

retraces her steps, keeping close to the curve of the stream now on her right side. Still no sign. Janet hoots again and once more hears Bev's return cry, but it seems further away, coming from a more westerly direction . . . Janet leaves the pathway, following the sound of Bev's voice. She probably got distracted chatting to some hikers. Even so, Janet quickens her pace, stumbling slightly on the soggy ground. Finally, she spies the glowing lantern of Bev's coat on the other side of the stream. Bev has wandered quite some way off the path and is waving her arms backwards and forwards vigorously as if she is trying to land a plane. In that jacket she probably could.

'I've found it!' Bev cries. 'It's over here!'

A burst of pleasure spans Janet's chest. Just when she was about to call it a day! She knew it was here somewhere, she just knew it! Janet strides faster now, eager to see the plant. She imagines Nancy beside her. *I told you, I knew it was here!*

'Come on!' Bev calls.

Come on, JP! Nancy's voice in her head. *Race you!*

Quickly Janet looks for the narrowest point of the stream. Ah, here will do – wider than she would like, but one good leap should be enough. Janet jumps across the stream but lands on a slick rock, her foot twists violently beneath her and a gut-wrenching pain slices through her ankle. She falls backwards.

The sound of her cry echoes around the fell.

15

The exquisite pain in Janet's ankle knocks the breath out of her. Other sensations leech in: the sharp chill of the stream, hard rocks beneath her head. The back of her skull throbs. Tentatively she feels along her jaw, behind her neck, touches wetness. Water? Blood? She brings her hand to her face, peers at the blur of her fingertips. Where did the light go? Hulking shadows rear up across the steep scree of the hillside.

What happened? Her heart pounds high in her breast, the only sound in the brooding silence about her. Where is she? All alone? She needs to move, keep the blood circulating, get off the fell before this mist gets any thicker, but as she tries to sit up, put weight on her foot, pain slices through her ankle. Thrusting her hand into her mouth, she bites down on her knuckle, squeezes her eyes shut.

'Janet!'

Not alone. Relief floods her chest and she shudders a sob. Not alone, that's right – there are two of them.

The sound of their footsteps, side by side, the grass swishing on bare legs, rucksacks on their backs, the sun on their shoulders – the Three Peaks! Almost there, aren't they? What a feeling of exhilaration. Laughter, yes, and a

picnic . . . and never wanting the day to end. And some-
thing else – searching . . . for what? Something she wants
dearly, has so longed for . . . and now it is almost in her
grasp, she could just stretch out her hand and take it, pull
it back to her finally . . .

Janet reaches out into the mist.

'Nancy?'

'Janet? Can you hear me?'

Tears wet her lashes; a tightness in her throat. Her fingers stretch outwards. 'I'm here.'

'Hold on, I'm coming.' Footsteps in the grass, then strong arms under hers, lifting her gently upwards.

'You came back,' Janet croaks.

'Lean against me. I've got you. That's it, grab hold.'

The strong arms pull Janet from the edge of the stream and help her into a sitting posture.

'Let me take a look at you . . .'

Her foot is lifted, boot unlaced, sock off. Cold air on skin, but warm fingers pressing along arch, heel, ankle. Heck, it hurts.

'I know, I know,' the voice soothes.

The hands go away for a moment, a rustling and then a ripping sound. Her foot is lifted again and then something is bound tightly around it. Too tight, too tight! . . . but . . . it's helping. Yes, the tightness helps. Janet inhales, exhales.

'Now, I know you might not approve' – Bev crouches on her haunches alongside Janet – 'but I'm afraid that I haven't got any of your marjoram to hand. I do, however, have two very nice Anadin Extra in my pocket and you are going to take them. Right now.'

Janet rubs her eyes, takes in the round face, the startle of fringe, the kind, concerned eyes. Bev. Of course.

Janet doesn't argue. She scoops the two white pills and swallows them dry.

'You gave me a fright there!' Bev says, holding out the water bottle.

Janet nods. Yes, she frightened herself, too. Lost the plot there for a moment. Slowly Janet looks around her. A damp fog is descending, thickening by the minute. The storm is coming in. She should have known. They shouldn't be out here.

Bev starts rootling in her jacket pockets, then in her trousers and finally in the picnic bag. She goes through her search again then stops suddenly. 'Oh no! I left my phone in the car . . . bollocks! Hey, where do you think you're going? Keep off that ankle!'

'There's no time,' Janet gasps, trying to stand. Raindrops fall.

Bev looks up at the damp and darkening sky then down at Janet's ankle. 'Maybe we should find shelter.'

'We need to get off the fell now whilst there's still some visibility.'

Janet lurches to her feet, stumbles.

'Lean on me.' Bev expertly hoists herself under Janet's side, helps her upright.

With each step Janet clenches her jaw. Leaning on Bev, she focuses on getting back on the main path. As soon as they find their way to the picnic spot, they can follow the stone wall back down towards the village. Simple. Downhill will be a bugger on her ankle, but they'll be safe. They aren't going to make it home tonight. Perhaps they could find a B & B in Dent and set off early in the morning? Or maybe, depending on how things go, they could make it at least part of the way back? Stop in the Midlands – the Cotswolds, even. Right now, though, they just need to get on the path . . . but where *is* the path? Surely they should have reached it by now? Don't panic, *keep the faith*. Any moment, they will find it. Just keep following the gradient of the hill, that's it. Easy to get discombobulated when visibility drops and you're fatigued, not to mention when you're in ruddy agony, but she can still follow the signs.

'All right there, Janet? Have those painkillers kicked in yet? Do you need to stop for a minute?'

Janet would love nothing more than to stop, just lie down on the cold, wet ground. She still feels a bit dizzy. For a moment back there she had thought . . . Nancy . . . She gives herself a little shake. 'We need to keep going. I'm fine.' Then, remembering she is putting most of her weight on Bev, she asks, 'You?'

'Don't you worry about me,' Bev replies. 'Midwives are stronger than Bruichladdich whisky!'

They stagger on. As they approach an outcrop of rocks, Janet's spirits lift a little – she thinks it's the same one they passed on the way up . . . but is it? This one seems larger, more jagged. It's so hard to tell in the gloom; the fog distorts shape, distance. Nothing looks familiar. She stops, tries to get a sense of where they are. Slowly she turns around, trying to orientate herself to the peak. But where is it? Behind her? The gradient should make it clear but the ground here seems oddly flat. They must be on a ridge.

Why hadn't she packed her compass? In the old days she would never have gone on a hike without it. Basic training: water, torch, compass, matches.

Just a day hike. The most foolhardy words a hiker could utter. That was precisely when things went wrong. A hiker should always be prepared. Janet hadn't been prepared at all. She had ignored all that, driven by a fierce longing . . . for what? To find the northern hawk's-beard? Or something else? What was she really searching for out here on the fells?

They continue on, but with each step Janet second-guesses herself. They could be going in completely the wrong direction. She can't sense the peak of Whernside in front or behind them. All she can feel is pain, cold and a rising sense of panic.

She stops them again. 'I don't think we are going in the right direction.' She needs to gather her thoughts, make a plan. They take a precarious seat on some rocks, not entirely comfortable, but it's a blessed relief to take the weight off her ankle. Pulling out the Bartholomew, she holds it up to her face, peers at it, turns it this way and that. Where are they? Raindrops skitter across the map. Janet crushes it on to her lap. What use is a map when you can't even get their bearings? What a fool she has been.

What a fool she is.

'Here.' Bev holds cupped hands towards her. 'I forgot to give you this in all the palaver. This will cheer you up!' Bev opens her fingers. 'Look, Janet, the hawk's-beard! We found it!'

For a moment Janet forgets everything and looks down at the little plant lying in Bev's hands. She has wanted to find it for so long, and now, after all those years, here it is. Yes, yes, of course Bev shouldn't have picked it . . . blah de blah . . . but all that is too late now. Gently she lifts the stem, lays it across her own palm like a bookmark in a bible, and her face softens. She feels along the delicate scalloped edges of its tiny leaves, strokes the tip of her finger across the yellow fronds.

Through the gloom Bev smiles at her, eyes bright. 'That's something, isn't it? Even if we are a bit turned about.'

Janet brings her face closer to the plant, then shudders a sigh that sucks all the happiness out of her.

Loathing seeps through Janet's body like poison; her veins pulse with toxicity. Who did she think she was, striding out here on to the fell, behaving like a bally group captain? *Follow me! This way!* Letting Bev pack a cumbersome picnic and a ruddy Italian tablecloth but forgetting the essentials: no matches, no compass. The truth is, she isn't fit for this, and neither is Bev.

What is she even doing here? Trying to recreate the past? Retrace her steps and get it right this time. But she is wrong, wrong, always wrong: babbling on to the National Trust interviewer about JP's Tours, shouting at Lakshmi about deadheading her roses, disappointing Patrice. Janet's fault. All of it. The look on her fellow allotmenteers' faces when she talked about knotweed – suspicious, untrusting. The men in the restaurant had seen her for what she was – an ugly old misfit.

The plant in her hand is not a hawk's-beard, it's a dandelion, and underneath its wilted body her open palm is scarred by an angry score of rue burns. Rue for regret. Perfect for a woman who just keeps on making mistakes.

And now she's done it again. She has heard of walkers stranded out here, just a mile or two from safety but injured from a fall or plagued by bad weather. Disorientated, they wander off, fall, succumb to hypothermia, leaving rescue teams to discover them after it was too late.

What if she can't get them back?

Fear and guilt fill her throat like quick-dry cement.

'Shall we wrap the hawk's-beard in something?' Bev suggests. 'I've got the bread bag here somewhere. Or we could use your hanky?'

Janet balls the plant up, tosses it away. 'It's just a dandelion.'

'Are you sure? I really thought . . .'

Janet sees disappointment flash across Bev's face. Sees, too, a smear of mud on Bev's cheek, damp hair plastered to her head. Would it have hurt her to pretend to Bev that it was the blasted hawk's-beard? After all, it is extremely similar to the dandelion, especially to an untrained eye. Couldn't she have afforded Bev that scrap of goodwill? No. Instead she hears herself saying:

'You also thought that it would be a good idea to waste time shopping for a picnic. Now look at us! I told you we didn't have time for all that.'

'You did. Sorry, Janet. But look, I'm sure we're not far from—'

'Sure?' Janet spits back, feeling the words twisting up and out of her before she can stop them. 'Like how sure you were about the hawk's-beard?'

'I just wanted to find your plant . . .'

'Want? WANT? WANT?' Is she shouting? Janet stops, her jaw hangs open. Forcing her mouth closed, she chokes her words back, all that she wants. She told Bev gardening was a sort of time travel, faith in the future. Yet all she wants is to go back into the past – go back and change it.

'Did you think I needed your help? Is that why you picked me up at the bus stop yesterday? Because you felt sorry for me? Thought I needed an escort – a damn nurse?'

Bev stands her ground, stares back at Janet. 'Rage all you want, hen, you don't frighten me. I've heard more shouting and swearing than a sailor in a hurricane. When you've pulled a twelve-pound baby from a woman's vagina, you've heard it all. If you want to take it out on me, give it your best shot.'

But Janet doesn't want to take it out on Bev. Not at all.

Bev's face softens. 'Look, I know your ankle hurts, I know you're worried about how to get us out of here. But we're in this together.'

Get us out of here. Bev is right. That is what she must focus on. Janet takes a jagged breath, then another. Focus. Think back to training. Get the lie of the land. Slowly the crumbs of a plan start to emerge.

'Wait here,' she instructs Bev. 'I am going to walk in radials, until I can get my bearings.'

Bev shakes her head. 'No way are you going anywhere.' Her voice is firm. 'If there's more walking to be done, I'm the woman for the task, not you.'

And despite everything, Janet knows Bev is right.

'Agreed?' Bev says, giving a neat little nod. 'Good, so tell me what a radial is.'

Janet steadies herself, takes another deep breath. 'When people are lost, they tend to walk in circles without real-izing it, especially when visibility is poor like this. They get more and more disorientated. Doing radials from a fixed position as soon as you realize you're lost can help orientate you back to your path again without leading you further astray.'

'OK.'

'So you need to walk in as straight a line as you can. Count each of your steps as you go. As soon as you get to a hundred, stop, turn one hundred and eighty degrees and come back here to me.'

'What am I looking for?'

'Anything: ridges, rocks, a stream, whatever landmark you can see – ideally the path. Try to notice if the gradient is going up or down – I think we're on a ridge here, but obviously we need to be going downhill.'

'Right you are. And what if I don't find anything like that?'

'Just come back and try again. Keep shifting the angle by forty-five degrees and carry on walking until . . .'

'Until I find the path – or a clue as to where we are. Got it. I'm off, then. You keep that leg elevated.'

'Remember, you need to retrace your steps exactly, so pay attention to everything you see on the way out. Don't walk further than a hundred paces, then turn around.'

'Right.' Bev starts to walk away.

'Bev!'

Bev stops.

'Count out loud, count so that I can hear you!' Janet orders.

'Right.' Bev sets off again.

'Don't forget! Loud!'

Bev stops again, swings back to face Janet, arms folded.

'Janet, I've delivered more babies than you've had hot dinners. I'm good in a crisis – have some faith in me! Now, why don't you focus on what *you* need to do – which is to get that fecking ankle elevated and let me get on with the radials!'

Bev turns and stalks away, booming loudly, 'ONE, TWO, THREE . . .'

Janet watches Bev till the fog devours her. All that is left is a trace of her voice – 'twenty-five, twenty-six . . .' – until that too is silenced, and Janet is alone.

16

'Eighty-nine, ninety, ninety-one, ninety-two,' Janet counts out loud. The counting comforts, helps take her mind off the pain in her ankle, keeps her with Bev. Her eyes try to stay focused on the spot where Bev disappeared into the mist, but it's tricky. She wishes for the umpteenth time that she could have been the one to go.

'Ninety-eight, ninety-nine, a hundred.' Bev should be turning, heading back now. She strains to hear her voice, catch her footfall. 'One, two, three . . .' She wills Bev back with her counting.

An owl – a tawny, she thinks – calls out from somewhere directly above. Janet gasps, tries to catch a glimpse of him. He sounds nearby. She can't make him out but . . . there he is again! Must have been startled from his nest to be calling at this time of day. Perhaps a warning? Nothing for a moment, then . . . the return call.

His mate.

Janet's hand presses against her chest, feels that pull of longing, like a plucked string, sounding its lonely note. Her heart. Her seventy-two-year-old heart that weighs . . . how much? Seven ounces, maybe eight? No more than a young rosemary plant. But it feels so much heavier. 'Twenty,

twenty-one, twenty-two,' she counts, and then finally gives in to the pull of the past.

The moment she first saw Nancy, arriving late for an English lecture, Janet was captivated. Nancy had jet-black hair, cat-green eyes and a curling smile that always seemed to promise mischief. She was utterly different from anyone Janet had ever met – a wild, free spirit who read war poets not love poets and did so out loud, ideally at night on a cliffside or in a graveyard. Nancy's hands were always ink-stained from the stories she scribbled when she should have been studying. She never joined in the impending graduation conversations about getting married, or stressed over the presumed conundrum of balancing a career with a family. Nancy was happiest outside; only vast landscapes of land and sea could contain her boundless energy and spirit.

And – for a reason that Janet could never fathom – Nancy liked Janet. *We fit, JP, like the contours of a map where the land meets the sea.*

But what had Nancy seen in her? Catapulted from the cul-de-sac of her shuttered suburban upbringing into the noise and thrill of university life, Janet was wide-eyed and hungry. But even now as she looks back across all the years – sees her younger self, studious in her button-down shirt and lace-ups – she still wonders at how on earth she drew Nancy's attention. Admittedly, their first meeting was notable. Late for a lecture and pedalling furiously, hair unravelled from its elastic and streaming about her face, Janet didn't see Nancy until she was almost on top of her. With a shriek of brakes and scorch of rubber, Janet's red Raleigh screeched to a halt, her front wheel grazing the toe of Nancy's suede boot. Red-cheeked, heart racing, Janet apologized profusely, but Nancy just smiled, casually leafed through the copy of *Antigone* that had fallen from Janet's pannier, then suggested they go for coffee. Replaying the incident later as she patched her bicycle tyre, Janet realized that although she had not seen Nancy, Nancy had seen her. In fact, it was almost as if she was standing there just waiting for her, waiting for Janet to crash right into her.

We fit, JP.

At home with her parents, life had been about knowing your place and staying in it, but with Nancy there were no borders, no boundaries; with Nancy there was freedom and endless possibility. Sometimes a group of them would go away together in the holidays. Once, they spent a week in Provence – Rajni, Alice, Nancy and Janet in a rambling whitewashed gîte with a burnt-red terracotta-tiled roof, stone floors and white shafts of linen billowing in the windows like sails. The gîte was tucked away down a road lined with scented pine trees and surrounded by lavender and rosemary bushes. Endless days spilled into each other; morning walks through nodding fields of sunflowers, pineapple bright, then long tipsy lunches at bistros feasting on *moules frites* and crusty baguettes, carafes of blushed rosé set out on chequered tablecloths, then late afternoons spent dozing with novels teepeed over sleeping faces, the silence punctuated by the sudden splash of a body shattering the impossibly aquamarine surface of the water, Nancy arcing a dive that scattered diamond droplets of water on to Janet's bare thighs, hot from the sun and slowly turning golden.

Most treasured were the times when they would strike out, just the two of them: a weekend hiking in the Cotswolds, the South Downs Way, a week following Hadrian's Wall. Tromping across fields, over hills all day long, then making camp in the evenings, Janet catching fish, grilling it on the campfire, washing it down with beakers of red wine. Their conversations were voices sliding over and under each other, full of life, of energy, plans for the future. Sometimes they would just lie sprawled on the ground, tired limbs overlapping like their chatter, which flowed, then slipped into languid pools of silence as they stared up at the stars.

Janet is cold sitting on the rock. Where the heck is Bev? She should be able to see her by now. Janet strains into the gloom and finally hears the faint sound of Bev's voice.

'Ninety, ninety-one, ninety-two . . .' And then, at last, a bloom of blessed green appears through the mist.

Janet, flooded with relief, looks at her expectantly. 'Anything?'

Bev mops her brow. 'I don't think so. The ground felt flat, couldn't see more than a few yards ahead, but definitely no path. How's that ankle?'

Caught up in the past, Janet had almost forgotten. 'I'm fine.'

'So, forty-five degrees clockwise and off I go again,' Bev says, carefully angling her feet.

'Bev . . .' Janet says quietly.

But Bev is already quick-marching away, disappearing into the mist once more. Janet can picture Bev on the hospital wards: focused, attentive, capable. She can clearly see her in the labour room, there in the sweat and the blood, guiding her patients through the pain, putting a cool hand on their forehead. Janet listens until Bev's voice fades into the gloom again, and she wraps her arms around herself.

Nancy had always been the careless one. Heedless of sticking to the map, she preferred the less trod route. But Janet could always steer them to safety. Sometimes Nancy chided her for being too conventional, following the rules, sticking to the path. After they graduated and started their careers, Nancy teased her for trying to fit in at GCHQ. *Leave the old boys to it. Let's travel the world, JP! Let's have adventures! Get a Mustang convertible and drive across America – move to Australia!* Life was completely different for Nancy; she came from money. Janet had to work hard for everything – to get a place at university, to get her job, to work her way up. Much as she would have liked to, she couldn't risk everything on a lark. Thankfully, for all her talk, Nancy didn't move abroad. The idea of Nancy not being in her life was unthinkable. With Nancy, she knew who she was, felt completely seen. In some ways it was as simple as that.

The rain drizzles on and a cold wind picks up. Maybe it will help shift the mist. Janet shivers and hugs herself tighter. She misses the comfort of her apron, its assembly of tools. Will Bev be able to read the signs to find the path? Will she retrace her steps exactly? Janet's teeth start to chatter. She clamps them tight.

The last time Janet was out here it was high summer and she was in her twenties. Hard to imagine those endless sunny days now, as she sits shivering on the rock, her clothes damp about her. Back then, some afternoons were so hot they would siesta for an hour or two and continue their hike in the relative cool of the evening. Janet takes herself back to an afternoon early in the trip when all three peaks still lay tantalizingly ahead. So long ago, and yet she remembers the smell of the grass, the sound of their steps . . .

It is already warm when Nancy and Janet start their climb and by noon the sun scorches the fields and hillsides. The ascent is steep and the rhythmic sound of their breathing punctures the still air. Occasionally Janet points out something of interest: a place where the stream has exposed a flat bed of limestone, the delicate mauve corollas of a rare bird's-eye primrose, the drum of a woodpecker in the ancient trees. Conversation trails off as they climb higher, saving their energy. They fall in step with each other, striding over the rocky terrain. Sun beats on their bare shoulders; sweat pools under their arms.

Janet stops. 'Listen!'

The roar of water, not far off. The sound urges them on and as they crest the hill they see it, a silver-grey torrent cascading down the limestone rocks into a pool of water, startlingly blue. Nancy races towards it, tearing off her rucksack, pulling at her clothes, kicking off her boots and jumping in with a noisy splash. She stays submerged for a moment then appears, gasping, laughing. Droplets of water spray across her face and neck.

She calls out something, but her words are swallowed by the sound of the waterfall.

Janet stands and watches Nancy for a moment, then lets her own rucksack tumble to the ground, rolls her shoulders, blissfully released from the heavy load of tent, sleeping bags, cooking pot. Then she bends, unlaces her boots, pulls off her socks and sits at the water's edge. She dips her feet into the exhilarating coldness and watches rivulets gully down her calves and ankles, sparkling in the sunlight.

'Come in, JP, it's electric,' Nancy calls.

'Bloody freezing, more like!'

'Just plunge in. The first couple of seconds are a bit of a shock but then it's gorgeous!' Nancy pulls at her feet.

Janet shakes her head. She watches Nancy float on her back, then lies on the grass, listens to the roar of the water, looks up into a cobalt sky, feels her body relax on to the baked earth.

'Come on, JP! Don't be a coward!'

Sweat trickles down the back of Janet's shirt, tickles her top lip. Finally, she can bear it no longer – the heat, the taunting. She looks around and, seeing no one, pulls off her shirt and shorts, and wades in.

The cold takes her breath away.

'*It's effing freezing!*' she gasps. 'You pig!'

Nancy laughs, splashes water at her and swims away, reappearing directly behind the wall of cascading water.

'Be careful!' Janet calls.

'Come on! There's a cave back here,' Nancy shouts.

Janet swims towards her, takes a breath, dives under the fall. The sound of the water is deafening. For a moment everything disappears but the surge of water and the pulse of her blood in her veins. She feels shudderingly alive.

Nancy is shouting something.

'What?' Janet shouts back. She climbs up on to the limestone rock behind the fall.

'It's yours,' Nancy roars, the curtain of water streaming down before them. 'Janet's Foss. This is your power, your force. You are bold and brave and powerful. And I love you!'

'Janet's Force,' they shout. 'Janet's Force!' they scream at the top of their lungs.

A man in a gilet stops at the edge of the pool to look at the waterfall. 'Pipe down!' he barks, before walking on, plunging his sticks into the ground in self-satisfied thrusts.

'Pipe down!' Nancy yells, louder now.

'Pipe down!' Janet thunders, and they stand laughing into each other's faces until they are no longer laughing, just staring. 'I love you,' Nancy says again. Behind the screen of water they are hidden in their own secret world, and as Nancy kisses her Janet is aware of two things: how unexpected it is, and how completely natural. When they finally stop kissing and emerge back out on to the other side of the fall, she feels reborn.

They lie on the grass, listening to the deluge, feeling the sun warm their wet legs until the dusk falls. Then they make camp and share salty baked potatoes, red wine and a sky hung heavy with stars.

'Janet's force,' Nancy whispers. And then, reaching out, she pulls Janet's body into hers.

Janet shivers. Did she not know what she had in that moment? She must have, because even now she can remember her whole body vibrating with happiness. The day everything changed and everything stayed the same between them was perfect, as were all the days after, the nights under the stars, in each other's arms. They were alive and in love and life stretched out like the endless landscape surrounding them. As they hiked, Nancy planned out their future, the trips they would take, the places they might live. At first Janet let herself believe in it all, but as they headed down towards Dent and back towards their everyday lives, Janet felt herself retreating. Fearless, unconventional, privileged Nancy wasn't afraid. But Janet had been raised in a family who kept inside the lines, who didn't draw attention to themselves. Janet had fought so hard to escape the confines of her upbringing, to forge a career for herself. At work she was already bullied because of her gender. If they knew about Nancy? They would tear her apart like a pack of jackals.

At the end of the day, she was a coward. When Nancy sensed the change and confronted her, Janet had turned away, pretended she was busy working out their route. Nancy ripped the map from her hands, tearing it. From that moment on there was a rupture between them.

Losing Nancy was like having a limb hacked off.

On their first day at GCHQ, Janet always told the new recruits: *Everybody has a weakness and sooner or later it will cause you to make a crucial error.* Hers was the cowardice that made her choose Brian. But by the time she realized it, it was too late. She sought respectability at the registry office, secured safety in the weightiness of Brian's 400gsm wedding invitations. But they had never made each other happy. It was almost a relief when he left her. And in the end, her precious career was destroyed anyway.

But, of course, that wasn't the worst thing that happened.

'Ninety-one, ninety-two, ninety-three . . .' and Bev breaks through the mist. 'Ninety-seven, ninety-eight, ninety-nine, a hundred!' Bev finishes the final steps as four giant leaps. 'Bull's eye! I'm getting this down to a fine art!'

Despite her cheery disposition, Bev looks tired and her shoes squelch mud. Dirt licks her trousers, her jacket, the side of her neck.

'Took a bit of a tumble myself,' Bev says, brushing off the front of her coat. 'It's getting pretty slippy underfoot. But I've made a discovery – it's uphill that way and the ground was rockier, so I'm going to try this way next.' She points in the opposite direction.

'No. Stick to the system.' Janet tries to push herself to her feet.

'I'm going to try my plan, if that's OK. I have a good feeling about this direction.'

'No,' Janet snaps, 'you need to do this methodically, not willy-nilly. You need to listen to me.'

Bev takes a breath. 'Look, Janet, I know you're the hiker, and I don't know these trails the way you do. But let me tell you what I do know: you're hurt, so I'm the one doing this. And I have an instinct about this direction.' She points ahead and then adds, 'You need to trust me.'

'It's not about trust! I'm sure you think I'm just a foolish old—'

'Christ's sake!' Bev's voice cuts across Janet's. 'Stop telling me what I think.'

'What I mean is . . . you don't really know me—'

'Not for want of trying,' Bev shoots back.

'I don't—' Janet starts, but Bev turns on her.

'Yes, I noticed you in the street. I admit, I started to look out for you – but not because I pitied you or thought you needed looking after.'

Janet doesn't know what to say. But it doesn't matter because Bev is suddenly full of words.

'You're an oddball.'

Janet flinches.

'The first time I saw you, do you know what I thought?'

Janet steels herself.

'I thought, that woman looks like she ploughs her own furrow. You stood out from everyone else – no one else in our street strides around with their pockets clanking with tools. I couldn't take my eyes off you! I wanted to get to know you. I didn't really know how to go about it . . .' Bev shifts. 'It's harder to make new friends outside work when you get older. Most of our neighbours are families with kids so they're wrapped up in all that. But I thought, stop making excuses, Bev, give it a go.'

Janet thinks of the flyers, the notelets.

Bev squares her shoulders. 'But you made it clear that

you didn't want to know me, and that's fine. But then, because I'd sort of got a sense of your comings and goings, I did get a bit worried when you broke your pattern. I thought maybe you were ill – or you'd had bad news or something. And then I saw your door left open that night . . . I didn't feel sorry for you; I was just concerned. Then I saw your poor hands . . .'

The bandages pushed through the letterbox.

'. . . and I'm sorry if I barged in, but that's who I am, that's me. It's also my job and I'm not going to apologize for that. So yes, I wanted to do what I could to help that night. But mostly I just saw you living your life on your own terms and I thought, Christ, that woman looks like a force to be reckoned with!'

Janet opens her mouth to speak but Bev doesn't yield.

'I never planned a road trip. I wasn't trying to stalk you or kidnap you. Don't worry. And when we get back to Hastings I won't bother you, I promise. But right now, we're in this pickle together and I'm doing my best to help get us out of it. I'm sorry about the picnic and how it slowed us down and I'm sorry I was wrong about the hawk's-beard. And I'm really sorry that because of me you've hurt yourself – that's the last thing I wanted. And you're right, I don't know a thing about orienteering, but I do know this . . .'

Janet tries to say something but Bev holds up a finger and says, all in one breath, 'One: you need to stay off that ankle as much as possible and two' – she holds up a second finger – 'if we don't find the path soon then we at least need to find some shelter because I don't need to be a bloody Girl Guide to know that otherwise we will be up you know where without a paddle.' Bev inhales loudly, blows out an exhalation, then says, 'So, three: I'm going this way.'

And before Janet can stop her, Bev marches off, her feet squelching until all sight and sound of her are swallowed in the mist.

Though Bev has disappeared, her words swirl in her wake. *Ploughs her own furrow . . . a force to be reckoned with.* Janet presses her hands to the hollows of her cheeks, shakes her head. *You stood out . . . I wanted to get to know you.* Who the heck had Bev seen when she had looked at her? What version of Janet? Bev's words from the restaurant return to her. *We are all the women we've ever been, aren't we?* She thinks again of Bev's flyers and notes, sees them suddenly for what they were: invitations. Bev had not only seen her, striding down the street to the allotments, but she had liked what she had seen! She wasn't invisible to Bev. Instead, Janet is the one who's blind, who didn't see what was right in front of her.

And now she stares into the mist, desperate for a glimpse of that green coat.

'A hundred and fifty, a hundred and fifty-one, a hundred and fifty-two,' Janet counts. Bev should be back by now. 'Hello?' Janet calls into the gloom, waits, listens for Bev's return call. But no sound comes. 'A hundred and seventy-one, a hundred and seventy-two, a hundred and seventy-three . . .' Where is she?

'Two hundred and fifty-six, two hundred and fifty-seven, two hundred and fifty-eight . . .' Janet forces herself to her feet. Which direction did Bev go in? That way – was that right? Her memory is starting to blur in the mist.

'Hello?' She calls again and then again. 'Bev . . .?' No sound, no sign. Janet stares ahead, willing Bev to appear. But there is nothing save the swirling fog.

Janet shouts again, shouts until her throat is hoarse.

But no answering call comes.

17

Janet composes the recipe for a tonic, the most curative, uplifting menopause elixir known to womankind.

She'll start with marjoram, of course. As well as being queen of hormonal balance, it will give the tonic pleasing olfactory notes of pine and citrus. Then rosemary, a generous pinch. Not a menopause-specific plant per se, but an active ingredient in all the best tonics. Or if not, it should be. What else . . . what else? Janet inventories her plot, mentally taking cuttings. Red clover – what *can't* that plant do! Cast off so often as a 'weed', it's an excellent remedy for menopausal symptoms, especially hot flushes. Janet has a feathery bed of it slap-bang in the middle of her plot.

The tonic is Janet's bargain with the universe, with Mother Nature herself. She will make Bev the best menopause tonic the world has ever seen if only she will come back.

Janet calls out for the hundredth time, shouting Bev's name into the fog, holding her breath, waiting, waiting, waiting. No sign for well over forty minutes now. Janet forces herself to stay put. She can't risk Bev coming back to an abandoned base camp or getting more lost herself. Then they'd both be wandering about in the mist. It would be like a double drowning where one person goes in to save another and they both perish.

Janet shivers and roughly rubs her arms, legs and chest to keep the circulation going. She reaches across to the picnic bag, grabs the handle with her fingertips and drags it towards her. Pulling out Bev's tablecloth, she tucks it between her shirt and coat. The feel of it is strangely comforting and reminds her of her gardening apron. Bev had torn a strip from her beloved tablecloth, holder of happy memories, without a second thought to make a bandage for Janet's foot. Its destination may well have been the charity shop, but still, to tear it like that, for Janet ... Reaching into the bag once more, she balls up the paper wrappings from the food and pushes them up her sleeves for insulation, hears herself crackle. Scarecrow. Wrapping her arms about her knapsack, she hugs it to her and hears the slosh of her Thermos. Hot tea. Suddenly it's all she can think of: pouring a steaming cup, warming her hands. No. Not until Bev is back. Then they will have tea together. She looks at her watch. Almost seven o'clock already. They're losing time. What little daylight they have will be gone within the hour. Then what? Janet's stomach contracts. She desperately scans for any meagre signs of shelter – trees, hedges, even a dip in the slope. Where is Bev? She sets her jaw. *Keep it together!*

In her mind she returns to her plot, to Bev's elixir. Sage helps with memory but has also been used since ancient times for boosting female energy – not to mention warding off evil. She harvests generous handfuls, buries her face in its soft fronds, comforting herself with the memory of its earthy scent. She draws on its powers. Next to the sage grows her bank of evening primrose. The flowers will be opening soon, glowing in the dusk, their decadent bowl-shaped petals on full, glorious display for an audience of night-prowling creatures. She wishes she had a meadow of evening primrose right here to light a pathway for Bev to find her way back.

'Bev? BEEEVV?'

Keep the focus, *keep the faith*. She returns to her plot, takes a cutting of yarrow. Human appreciation of the healing qualities of the plant dates back centuries. Achilles used it to staunch the wounds of his men on the battlefield. She'll take a couple more sprigs, for what is this if not a battlefield as Janet tries to hold out against cold, pain and fear as well as her familiar enemy: regret. Another slow minute passes. Then another.

Come back come back come back.

What else does Bev need? *Think, woman, think*, she commands as she rubs her hands together, tucks them into her armpits. *Cimicifuga racemosa* of course, you numbskull! A member of the innocuous-sounding buttercup family, but such a bold warrior. The little plumes of star-shaped white flowers can soar upwards of eight feet. Astonishing. There's nothing like it for hot flushes and night sweats. She doesn't have any on her plot, though. An oversight. Might Patrice have some? She's the only gardener at Seaview with botanical knowledge and skill to rival Janet's own. Felicity bloody Kendal wouldn't know black cohosh if it bit her on the backside. If only she were at Seaview now. Thank God Patrice can't see what a mess she's made of everything. Her self-aggrandizing plan for single-handedly saving the allotments is a farce. Maybe worse. April is the cruellest month. Hypothermia is a real possibility. She could get Bev killed out here. Idiot! Janet pushes her fists into her eye sockets. God, she's going mad, Lear in the storm, crazed and railing against the world. *Blow, winds, and crack your cheeks!* Was Lear blind, or was it someone else? Gloucester!

'*Pluck out his poor old eyes!*' Janet shouts into the wind.

'Steady on, lass!'

'Bev!' Janet's hands fall from her face.

From the mist a streak of colour moves towards her. And what a colour it is! Chlorophyll! Luminous, vivid and alive. Janet mutters a silent thanks to the universe. Bev's tonic, when she makes it, is going to be ambrosial.

'Phewee!' Bev plonks herself on a rock next to Janet. Mud-stained, windswept and out of breath, somehow she still has a smile on her face.

'I know that took longer than it should have, but no need for either of us to pluck out our eyes just yet. Mind you, I'm a bit worried your blood pressure may be low.' Bev scrunches up her eyes and peers at Janet. 'Hard to tell in this light, but you look a bit peely-wally.' She reaches for the pulse point on Janet's wrist and tips her head to one side, counting. 'Hmm, yes, your pulse is a bit sluggish. How about we roll you on your side for a moment—'

Janet snatches her wrist away. 'We will NOT roll me on my side. My pulse is perfectly fine! For heck's sake, woman, where were you? You were gone for ages!'

'Sorry. I was so hoping I was on the right track, I sort of stopped the counting and just kept going. I was afraid we were running out of time, so I took the risk. I didn't find the path but I have found somewhere less exposed to the elements. Desperate as I am to get you back to Dent, I think we're going to have to change tack and take shelter before it gets dark.'

~

Bev has done well to find this spot; she could so easily have missed it. They both almost come a cropper getting down the overhang to it, but when they do Janet can see a natural earthy burrow in the hillside, barely big enough for the two of them. A couple of overgrown hawthorn bushes, no doubt planted as a boundary line at some point, create a little windbreak.

'Well,' Bev says, 'it's not quite up to the Laurels' standards – no mini soaps, or fluffy towels – but will it do?'

If the wind picks up, probably not. But for now . . .

'It's excellent,' Janet says and is touched to see how pleased Bev looks.

But there's work to be done.

'Right, first rule of survival?' Janet asks.

'Sustenance!' Bev says. 'I'm starving.' She rootles through the worse-for-wear picnic bag. 'I thought there was a bit of cheese left . . . I must have eaten it. OMG, Janet, look what I've found!'

Triumphantly, she produces a box of fudge. *A Gift from Dentdale* loops across the lid in old-fashioned cursive. 'I bought it for Eddie. When I spoke to him this morning, I said I was taking one more day for myself. I didn't mention another night, too. He's going to be thinking I've run off. Poor Ed. He'll be worried sick when he can't get me on the phone tonight.' Bev shakes her head sadly.

'Food is actually quite low down the list of survival priorities.'

'It is?' Bev says, incredulous. 'Because it's pretty high up on mine.' She looks mournfully at the fudge box, which depicts a sunny picture of Dent on the front. The village looks welcoming. And a world away. Bev reluctantly puts the fudge back in the picnic bag. 'OK, so what is at the top of the list? Staying warm, staying hydrated.'

Janet nods. 'Both vital, but when you're lost in the wild, your best hope and first task is signalling in case someone can help you. So let's tackle that one first.'

Bev moans, 'I still can't believe I left my phone in the car! I'm tethered to the bloody thing all day. I shoved it in the glovebox because I wanted a day off the radar. Certainly got that.'

'I'm not sure you'd get any reception out here anyway,' Janet consoles. 'Anyway, there are other ways of attracting attention.'

'Aye! Like an SOS! We could make a giant "X" on the ground with big stones. But I don't see any. Or we could use my coat' – Bev starts struggling out of it – 'hoist it up a tree – high-vis!'

'Keep your coat on,' Janet barks, 'you'll need it tonight. We need all our layers for protection. Hypothermia is our number-one danger. But I like the way you're thinking.'

'I know! My tablecloth!'

Fully spread, the cloth is sizeable. It could certainly be put to use.

'If you're sure?'

'Yes! Let's cut it in half,' Bev says. 'Use one half for a signal and the other half to wrap around you! Keep your kidneys warm.'

'We will use the other half to curtain the mouth of our shelter to keep the heat in as best we can,' Janet says firmly. 'Every degree will help.' Getting out her Huntsman penknife, Janet flicks the blade open, cuts a nick midway across the tablecloth and tries to tear the sheet in half, but it's hard going. 'This thing is like chain mail. How the devil did you tear the strip for my ankle without a knife?'

'Never underestimate a midwife. Arms of steel.'

Bev rips the tablecloth into two halves.

'Well done. Now tear a couple of thick strips along the two corners that you can use as ties. That's right. We passed a birch a few yards back up the hill. Try to rig it like a flag. Hopefully you can find a good strong branch to secure it to. Fasten it as firmly as you can. I have a nasty feeling it's going to storm.'

'I'll look for a couple of crooks in the branches and apply the classic figure-of-eight bandage wrap to each end. I defy any storm to get one up on my binding technique.'

Whilst Bev tends to their flag, Janet works on fashioning the other half of the tablecloth into a bivouac. Collecting the biggest rocks and stones she can manage, she works along the overhang of earth at the entrance to the burrow, anchoring one edge of the cloth so the rest falls in an awning. She is tired and it's slow going. A breeze tugs at the fabric and it flaps about, and more than once she puts too much weight on her ankle and her eyes water, but she is filled with determination. Now that Bev is back she has a new fire in her belly. After some wrangling and a few well-chosen expletives, the fabric looks pretty secure, but just to make sure, Janet stabs her Huntsman through like a tent peg. Unless they get gale-force winds, their biv- ouac isn't going anywhere. Suddenly light-headed, she rests against the side of the hill. Bev is right, her blood pressure is probably low. Damn and blast old age. Janet forces herself to take a couple of deep breaths.

'Hey, Janet,' Bev calls, 'how do you like our flag?' Janet looks up the hill to the square of cloth tied to a silver birch. It snaps in the wind.

'Funny to think of all the meals I've served on it over the years,' Bev says as she watches it flap. 'All the Christmas dinners.'

'I was certainly in the wrong to complain about you bringing it. Turns out it should be a staple in every survival pack!'

Bev tilts her head to one side and says quietly, 'It was lovely in its day.'

Despite everything – the cold, the weather, and the gen- eral direness of their situation – Janet looks at the hopeful pale shimmer of their flag against the darkling sky.

'Still looks good to me,' says Janet.

Bev turns to her, eyes bright. 'You know what, Janet? You're right. It looks bloody *bellissimo*!'

'Right,' Janet instructs, 'our priorities are: stay dry, keep off the cold ground and stay warm. We need a dry layer of undergrowth. Can you gather materials to make a good thick layer that we can sit on? Get as much foliage as you can – dead leaves, grasses – anything dry. Try to avoid pulling anything up by the roots; rip out leaves instead. Bracken is the most common plant on the planet. I'd go and find a patch of that.'

'When I get back,' Bev says hopefully, 'do you think we can make a fire?'

'Not unless you have matches?'

Bev shakes her head, then disappears. Whilst she is gone, Janet cuts along the seams of the picnic bag to make a small water-repellent groundsheet.

'Something in here smells amazing,' Bev says, returning with an armful of leaves and bracken.

'Fern.' Janet nods.

'Mmmm, I can't get enough of it, it's so sweet and woody! Not edible, is it, by any chance?'

'I wouldn't recommend.'

Bev works industriously, gathering armloads of raw materials, which Janet fashions into a mattress of foliage across the floor of their shelter.

'Ouch!' Bev drops her next bundle on the ground and rubs her arm.

'Bramble?'

'Um, stinging nettle, I think.'

'Ah yes, there are a few stingers.' Janet reaches over and plucks a nettle leaf.

'Careful!'

'Now, they *are* edible! Pinch 'em in the centre' – Janet demonstrates – 'that avoids the hairs on the edges – then you won't get stung.' She dextrously rolls the leaf into a cigar shape, pops it in her mouth and chews.

Bev watches wide-eyed. 'Doesn't that sting your tongue?'

Janet shakes her head. 'Chomp it with your teeth; it

neutralizes the acid. Try it. This is the best time of year to eat nettles.'

Bev shrugs. 'I'm hungry enough.'

Janet rolls another leaf between her fingers and hands it to Bev. 'Bung it straight in, that's it.'

Bev bites the leaf, unsure, but then smiles, surprised. 'It's quite nice, almost spicy. Gives you a wee rush, doesn't it?'

'Full of vitamin C. They increase your energy levels, strengthen your bones and connective tissues, and they're good for PMS and menopause. Oh, and they give you lustrous hair, amongst other things – clean liver and kidneys, too. I've a vigorous patch on my plot, much to the consternation of my neighbours.'

'They should prescribe them on the NHS! Right, now, do we need any more leaves and stuff?'

'We've got enough here for a good insulation layer. Come in. I don't think there's a lot more we can do apart from wait for the visibility to come back.'

They pat down the bracken bed, removing any nettles or twigs they can spot in the last of the fading light. Bev scoops up some of the bracken and bundles it under Janet's ankle.

'I'd say take your boot off, Janet, but I think in this weather you're better off keeping it on – let's just loosen the laces a bit.'

She unties the laces then settles herself in the dark burrow next to Janet. The mattress crackles and subsides.

'It's quite springy!' says Bev. 'Better than the mattress we've got in the spare bedroom. How cold do you think it will get tonight?'

'I'm hopeful that it will stay above freezing, but it might get down as low as two or three degrees Celsius, so we'll need to really watch each other for signs of hypothermia. Keep rubbing your hands and feet.'

'Will do, and I'll tell you if your lips turn blue!'

'For an extra layer we'll add some insulation to our clothing.'

Janet starts shoving handfuls of leaves between her shirt and her jacket.

'Christ, you really do love plants – isn't that going to be scratchy?'

'Thermoregulation. An extra layer of material between your shirt and your jacket will help keep your body's heat in. Go on . . .'

'I feel like the Michelin Man, but itchier!'

'And we have to do something about those.' Janet points accusingly at Bev's shoes.

'They're just a bit damp,' Bev says, apologetically.

'Take them off. Socks, too,' Janet orders. 'Put the socks down your trousers, one on each thigh – they'll dry out a lot faster that way. Leave them there for an hour then put them back on. We've got to be careful with our extremities.'

'Always am, Janet,' Bev quips. 'Always am. Now what?'

'Now we settle in. And hope for the best.' Janet sits back on to the bracken bed and breathes a shuddering sigh of relief to be off her ankle. She plucks a frond of fern from the mattress, traces its delicate leaves, twirls its slim stem between her fingers. A plant that pre-dates the dinosaur – the fact never ceases to amaze her. The extraordinary resilience.

Bev is watching her.

'Were plants always your thing?'

Janet could let loose a waterfall of words, could write a

book on plants. Plants are the recipients of all her love and repay her daily with their beauty, resilience and medicinal miracles. There's too much between Janet and plants to summarize with a pat answer. She ponders a moment then chooses one pillar fact.

'I love plants because whatever challenges come to them – fire, flood, drought, pests – they stand their ground, and survive.'

Bev sits back, a curl of leaf caught in her hair, taking in Janet's words. 'I've never thought about it like that,' she says slowly, 'that having roots means you have to stand your ground no matter what.'

The women are quiet for a while, listening to the crackle of the bracken, the light patter of the rain. Janet imagines their flag waving valiantly in the wind, signalling their presence . . . to whom? Perhaps just the tawny owl whose call occasionally punctures the darkness. In her mind's eye she sees the owl flying alongside its mate, the two of them out hunting, swooping through the shadows under the stormy clouds.

'How do you know all this stuff about radials and fern thermal underwear?' Bev asks. 'Did you do survival training at GCHQ?'

'I needed a whole different kind of survival training for GCHQ. No, I just used to backpack a lot when I was young. You learn to keep the basics covered – compass, penknife, torch, matches, water-purifying kit and VIP clothing.'

'VIP?'

'Ventilation, insulation and protection – layers for changing weather conditions.'

'You and Nancy.'

'Me and Nancy.' Janet pauses for a moment and then adds, 'Mind you, if she'd had it her way, Nancy would have just gone off with a jaunty scarf round her neck, a corkscrew in her pocket and a winning smile. I was the sensible one. Or dull, depending on your perspective.'

'You're far from dull,' Bev laughs. 'I've been in your company for less than two days and already I'm lost in the wilderness, eating raw nettles for dinner with half a hedge shoved down my bra.'

'Fair enough.'

'Your Nancy sounds fun,' Bev says. 'What's she like?'

Janet stiffens. She had been so enjoying their chat, couldn't remember the last time she had talked so much, but suddenly she doesn't know what to say. There is an awkward pause and then Bev says, 'If your Nancy was a plant, what plant would she be?'

Janet feels her body relax. 'Bougainvillea. Sun-loving, captivating and impossible to train!'

'I like the sound of her even more,' Bev says warmly. 'Now, what would Eddie be . . . Hmm, I wish I knew my plants better.'

'What's he like?'

'Affable, a bit of a homebody and completely dependable.'

'Then a house plant, perhaps?'

'Definitely a house plant!'

Janet narrows her brow. 'Let me see, affable and dependable . . . Perhaps Eddie is a bit of an *Aspidistra elatior*?'

'Well, he has his moments,' Bev chuckles. 'What's that like, then?'

'The aspidistra is extremely reliable, a steadfast grower, can put up with irregular watering and drought, sail through a load of calamities that might scupper another plant.'

'Sounds just like my Eddie! What about you, Janet?'

What kind of plant would she be? She struggles to think of a plant alter ego – it feels too much like self-flattery to compare herself to majestic evergreens or potent and powerful herbs.

Another silence settles between them. They shift positions, try to keep warm.

After a while Bev puts her socks back on and is delighted with the results.

'That actually worked! What other tricks do you know?'

Janet feels a surge of pride. She had no idea she remembered all this stuff, or that she would ever put it to use after all this time. But somehow it is still there.

'I'm pretty good at foraging. At this time of year, if we had to stay out here and really live off the land, we could look for ground elder, fool's parsley, wild garlic, chervil, columbine. The sap will be rising in the silver birch – that's a bit like drinking sugar water – and there's plenty of sweet cicely around, which tastes like aniseed. Did you say you were partial to liquorice?'

Bev laughs. 'You're making it sound like a feast. What about insects? Please don't make me eat spiders.'

'I think we'll stick to plants. Though apparently some ants taste like lemon drops.'

'I wish you hadn't said that.'

'Why?'

'Janet! I'm *starving* and you're going on about sugar

and aniseed and lemon drops! Sorry, but it's no good. I give in.' Bev grabs the *Gift from Dentdale* fudge, rips off the cellophane and tears the box open, releasing a sweet sugary scent. Bev moans her pleasure. 'Sorry if this means I don't make it out of here, Janet, but at least I'll go with a smile on my face!' Paper crackles as she unwraps a piece of fudge, pops it in her mouth. 'Absolute bloody heaven!'

Janet watches her for a moment then shrugs. 'Well, if we're going to have fudge, we might as well have a cup of tea.'

'Tea?' mumbles Bev, as Janet pulls the Thermos from her rucksack. 'You've got *tea*? Christ, Janet, you're like bloody Derren Brown! Hold on, is it . . . *proper* tea?'

'Yorkshire Gold, I believe.'

'You're having me on!'

'I made it this morning at The Laurels for the train back to Hastings. When I realized we were lost, I decided to save it for when we really needed it. Which seems, from the look on your face, to be now. Let's have half now and save the other half for later. Always coldest the hour before dawn, and all that. We'll have the other half then – give ourselves something to look forward to.' Janet unscrews the top and pours a stream of tea into the Thermos cup, then hands it to Bev, who takes a sip and sighs in reverent pleasure.

'I can't believe you didn't drink it when you were waiting for me – you must have been freezing sitting out on that rock!'

Janet shakes her head. 'Absolutely not! All rations must be shared equally.'

Bev carefully sups just her share, and says, 'I've waited

ages for you to offer me a cup of tea. But it was definitely worth the wait.'

'Waited? When?'

'That day in your house?' Bev says, 'I made you a cuppa, and was gasping for one myself, but . . . well, none was on offer.'

Janet remembers Bev hovering at the kitchen table and is about to make an excuse, but then dips her head and admits, 'I'm not used to company.'

'Well, never you mind, because this is literally the best cup of tea I have ever had in my life. Couldn't like it more if I were having it at the Ritz. Living the dream, eh, Janet?' Bev passes the cup back to Janet along with a piece of fudge. 'Here.'

Janet takes the square Bev hands her, lets its creaminess dissolve on her tongue, takes a sip of the tea, feels the precious comfort of its warmth. Small gifts in the dark and beside her the stolid presence of Bev, chatting away, making her laugh. Keeping her company. They settle into a routine of silences and little ripples of conversation. Every half an hour they shift positions, staying close, keeping as warm as they can.

~

'Janet, are you awake?'

'Mmm.'

'Don't drop off.'

'I won't.'

'I was thinking about time.'

Janet leans forward, peeks under their curtain and peers

up towards the sky but can see only blackness. The rain is in earnest now. Janet tucks herself deeper into their nest and tries not to think about the cold. It must be about seven degrees. Bearable if it doesn't drop any lower, but still dangerous without proper equipment. She tries to ignore the constant shaft of pain thrumming in her ankle, the dull ache at the back of her head.

'I reckon it's about two a.m., maybe a bit later, but I can't see my watch.'

'No, I mean time itself,' Bev says.

'Ah.'

'When you're young, time is different, isn't it?' Bev goes on. 'Things just happen – exciting, unexpected things – and you just sort of embrace it all. Christ, I remember one weekend, when me and my friends were eighteen, we were just out on a Saturday night, then suddenly we're on the sleeper train from Edinburgh all the way down to London, totally spur of the moment. The next morning, we're posing by the lions in Trafalgar Square, running around Chinatown and it was like . . . like the whole city was ours, the whole world. Mum nearly killed me, but it was worth it. But now . . .' Bracken and leaves rustle as Bev shifts. 'Now it's like I always have a "to do" list on the go, forever planning – must do this, must do that. Why do we stop having adventures?'

'You're rather getting your fill of adventure tonight.'

'Too right!' Bev laughs, but then her tone becomes more serious. 'I was thinking about what you said, about the plants. About how they don't run away, but instead they face what's coming.'

Janet nods.

'When I called Eddie this morning, he asked if I was running away. He wasn't being unkind, just trying to understand where my head was. But the thing is, I don't feel like I'm trying to run *away from* my life – more like I'm trying to run *towards* it. Does that make sense?' Bev blows on her fingertips, then thrusts her hands in her pockets.

Janet considers. Hasn't she also been searching for something? If not an adventure exactly, maybe a quest. Or a pilgrimage. Everything about being out here reminds her of Nancy, of the life she could have had. When she made the decision to meet Glynis, she knew deep down that she wasn't undertaking this trip for the sake of the allotments alone. A part of her, a long-hidden part of her, wanted to come back. To retrace her steps.

And then what?

'What do you think you are running towards?' Janet asks.

Bev turns to look at her. 'I don't quite know how to explain it . . . It's like this: the other day Eddie said I didn't quite seem like my old self. And something just came over me. I wanted to scream at him. "*Old self?* What about me – the woman right here in front of you! Does anyone care about her?" Last week I stood at the chilled cabinet in Morrisons holding two frozen chicken fillets in my hands for what must have been twenty minutes. Couldn't for the life of me remember what I'd come in for. Then at work a couple of days later I was writing up my ward notes and realized I'd spelled "antenatal" completely back to front. I mean, I couldn't do that on purpose if you paid me, but there it was in black and white.'

There's a different note to Bev's voice now, another layer under its usual cheery warmth. Something fierce, wild.

'Sometimes I feel like a boat that's been cast adrift – not some snazzy cruise ship, just one of those wee ones you can rent for an hour. A rowing boat. I feel . . . what's the bloody word? Unmoored. I feel unmoored.'

Janet thinks of her plot, her life raft in the storm. Unmoored, yes. She knows what that feels like. And Bev, who seems so full of life, so positive, purposeful, is floundering too. Janet wishes she knew how to help, feels ill equipped. Someone like Patrice would be good in a moment like this. But Patrice isn't here. Janet must do her best.

'I read a magazine article that described a hot flush as an aura,' Bev says. '*Aura?* Aura, my arse! It's real, it's physical, it's bloody chaotic! It's like melting from the inside out. It's like becoming a volcano. And I'll tell you what it's not – it's not feeling "irritable" and having "mood swings" – not for me it's not. I've got one consuming mood, Janet, and that mood is rage. I'm so . . .'

A vein pulses in Bev's neck as she tries to give shape to what she is feeling, tries to find the words.

'Angry?' Janet offers.

'I'm apo-fucking-plectic. I'm spoon-snapping mad. Do you have any idea how high the suicide rates are amongst menopausal women? No! Nobody does, because talking about menopause is so stigmatized that most women going through it don't even know they're suffering from it. There are millions of us, Janet, millions, and we're not being taken seriously – we're ignored, or we're being made fun of. Why do we put up with being shamed? We deserve better.'

Bev's eyes flash.

'I'll tell you something, when I wake up in the night drenched with sweat, I feel wild. Hot flush? Being plugged into an electrical socket is more like it. A power surge! And I want to harness that power. I want to say what I think – not the polite thing but the true thing.' Bev gestures outwards. 'Who cares about manners in a storm? Who gives a flying fuck? I want to *roar*! I want to take this "change" and make it mine – let it make me fierce and bold – a bloody force to be reckoned with.'

'I like the sound of that,' says Janet.

'Women of a certain age are meant to stay out of the way and be discreet, thoughtful, accommodating – which is another way of saying we should shut up.'

'Or pipe down,' Janet says with a small smile.

'Exactly! And I don't want to pipe down when everything in my body tells me that right now is when I should speak out. I don't want to get out of the way – I want to get *in* the way. Because I have all this feeling surging through me and I want to . . . harness it. I want to put it to good use. I want to protect the mums on my ward and I want to help other women too. We get information about menstruation, pregnancy and childbirth and all that is vital, but *still* there isn't enough about the menopause – and there's a lot of misinformation. My dinosaur of a GP actually sniggered when I said the words "hot flush". Janet, I swear I nearly smacked him.'

'Sounds like he had it coming.'

'I want to help women get the care they need, tell them they might not need sleeping pills and antidepressants – they might well need hormone patches. And I want bloody testosterone for free on the NHS because it's our hormone, too! Look.' Bev shimmies forward and tugs at the waistband of her trousers. She points to a translucent patch stuck on each hip bone. 'My hormones. I wear them like holsters, Jan, two guns, cocked and ready! Because do you know what? I don't just want an adventure; I want a fucking fight.'

18

The skies break, thunder so loud it seems to come from the belly of Whernside itself. After each lightning flash the darkness feels blacker, the night air colder.

'We need to try and work our muscles.' Janet shivers. 'Keep active, generate more heat.'

Bev's teeth chatter. 'You're not suggesting j-j-jumping j-j-jacks, are you?'

'Curl up as tight as you can – minimum surface area of your body exposed.' Bev obeys, and Janet does the same. 'Now clench all your muscles – fingers, toes, legs, everything – clench, then release. Clench again. Keep doing it until you feel yourself warming up.'

'I do feel a wee bit warmer,' Bev says after a while. She gives Janet a little dig with her elbow. 'Bet you're glad we splashed out on the superior deluxe room with the high-thread-count bedding, eh? What a storm, though! It just seemed to come on us all of a sudden.'

'You summoned it, didn't you?' Janet jokes, but then thinks, and why the hell not? Why couldn't the rage of a menopausal woman release the heavens? She blows into her hands, which she can't seem to get warm.

Bev moves closer and starts brusquely rubbing her hands

up and down Janet's arm, stimulating the blood flow. 'Let me take your pulse again.'

'For goodness' sake, I'm fine!' Janet thrusts her hands under her armpits, but Bev ignores her and swiftly retrieves a wrist.

'A bit elevated, but that's only to be expected out in the cold like this. Nothing to worry about for now.' Bev returns Janet's wrist and briefly feels her own pulse. 'Same here. Still firing on all cylinders!'

Janet studies her a moment and then says, 'You're a real trouper, aren't you?'

'Well, thanks very much, Janet.' Again that pleasure in Bev's voice, as if what Janet says matters. The thought itself warms her.

'To be honest,' Bev says, 'I'm worried about Eddie – all the things that must be going round in his poor head. I wish I had something better for your ankle. And JFC, I'd sell my soul right now for a hot-water bottle – or a bottle of whisky. But, I'm hanging in there. I suppose my training helps – in my job I can't afford to panic. Because when things go wrong in obstetrics . . . it can tear your heart to pieces.'

Next to her, Janet is still.

'But I'd never give it up,' Bev continues, 'despite the bad days, the shit pay, the heartbreak. However hard it gets, I'll keep putting on my uniform and going back to my ward. Because at the end of the day what I want most is to be there for them.'

Janet stares down at her hands, one cradled in the other. 'The babies.'

'No,' Bev says. 'Not the babies! Don't get me wrong,

I love the moment I first lay eyes on a newborn. Who wouldn't? Wee miracles. But it's not the babies that keep me coming back, it's the mums. They are so strong, so fierce! They take my breath away. So if you think I'm a trouper, I've learned everything I know about perseverance and strength from them. And you, of course.'

'Me?'

'You might think you're leaning on me with your twisted ankle, but believe me, I'm leaning on you just as hard. Like I said, we're in this together.'

Bev rubs her hands, hunches forward against the cold. Under the cover of the dark Janet stares at her, the midwife who loves her patients. Ever since that night Bev appeared glowing luminous at Janet's window, the woman has continued to surprise her: nipping to the charity shop and ending up driving across half the country, marching out of a restaurant with a handbag full of bread rolls and an unpaid bill, tirelessly searching for the hawk's-beard because Janet had said she would like to find it. Who is this woman who hoisted her honeymoon tablecloth halfway up a tree? Who strode off into the mist in her squelching shoes in search of safety. And bally well found it! For all her inexperience with the outdoors, Bev has found them pretty damn perfect shelter.

Bev is still sitting hunched forward, uncharacteristically quiet, lost in thought.

'All right there?'

Bev straightens up, pushes her hair back from her face. 'Yes . . . I was just thinking about my own mum. I never wanted kids myself, but when Mum died, which was just as I hit menopause . . . it wasn't that I started wanting kids, exactly, more that I realized that big parts of my life were over. I tried to explain it to Eddie – he said he understood – but it's different for men, isn't it? They can go on having kids for ever. But that's it for me. And even though I had made my decision and it was the right one, there was still a kind of grief in saying goodbye to the possibility. I think it was the sadness of losing Mum, really.'

'Were you with her? When she died?'

Bev shakes her head. 'No, she died in hospital. I'd visit every day and she used to call me when she couldn't sleep at night and we'd chat. She called that last night, sounded tired but OK. I told her about the fluffy cream cardie I'd bought her from Marks. She said Adelola – that was her favourite nurse – had just been over to see her and had dabbed some eau de cologne on her wrists. 4711. I could hear Mum was getting tired, so I said, "Why don't you just put your phone on the pillow and I'll read to you." I read *The Wind in the Willows* – same copy she used to read me when I was little. I could tell she'd fallen asleep because her breathing changed. After a while I put the phone on my pillow and lay there, listening to her breathing. Then I fell asleep' – Bev's voice falters – 'and when I woke up, she was gone.' Bev wipes her face on the sleeve of her jacket. 'I miss her every single day. I feel it here.' She presses her hand to her breastbone. 'It's like I've swallowed something, and it's lodged in my windpipe, and I can't get it to shift.'

Bev rummages in her pocket, pulls out Janet's hanky and dabs her eyes, blows her nose.

'I hope that Adelola stroked Mum's hair or held her hand. In those last moments, that person you love with all

197

your heart, you want to know that someone is there with them ... because ...' A sob catches in Bev's throat. 'Because ...'

'Because you can't bear to think of them dying alone,' Janet says quietly.

Silence.

'Did you lose someone?'

Janet opens her mouth. At first the words don't come; they are buried too deep.

And then:

'My Adam.'

When the midwife placed her swaddled baby in her arms, Janet unwrapped him like a gift, pressed his naked skin to her own, breathed him in, over and over till she was drunk with the smell of him. His sweet round face looked right up at her, not crying but curious, taking her in.

She remembers his eyebrows, such quizzical little brows. Any new experience – first taste of a spoonful of puréed carrot, the feel of grass under his bare feet, the sound of music playing – and the eyebrows would wiggle.

She didn't know how she would be, as a mother. She worried it would not come naturally to her; her own family had been so distant. But from the moment Adam arrived, everything made sense; she knew instinctively what he needed, understood his different sounds and cries. Sometimes at night she would feel the need to look in on him, put her hand on his tiny chest, but each time he reassured her with the warmth of his little body, the rise and fall of his breath.

She'd wake to his cry – five a.m. sharp every morning – and he'd lie there looking up at the zebra mobile on the ceiling, eyebrows going like the clappers, and then he would see her, smile and her heart would stop. She'd lift him up, hold him to her and take him back to her bed. He'd have his milk and she'd have her tea and they would watch the day start, see the way the raindrops would paint themselves on the window, listen to the wind in the trees. Just seeing leaves could make him smile.

'He lit up my whole life.'

Janet stops, lets a tear escape down the hollow of her cheek, reach her chin, then fall. She waits for the rest of the words to come.

'I bought him a set of pyjamas,' she murmurs, 'blue-and-white striped, like Cornish pottery. He looked so handsome. I put him to bed wearing them and in the morning, the moment I stepped into the room, I knew.' The stillness. The silence. 'I knew he had gone.' Janet's hands reach out, her fingers open and close on empty air. 'My son.'

Adam. Her boy, hers to take care of, to love, nurture. Five months they were together. One hundred and forty-eight days.

Janet exhales, empty. No more words. They are released to the night. Unconsciously her arms stretch out, holding nothing.

But through the darkness Bev's hand reaches out and takes Janet's. Holds it tight.

❧

'I always placed him on his back to sleep,' Janet says, 'just like they tell you to. His head wasn't covered.'

'You didn't do anything wrong, pet. You do know that,

don't you? SIDS isn't anyone's fault.' Bev's voice is calm, her words clear and certain. 'We can't pretend to understand it. We can only do what we can – bring them into the world, protect them and love them with our whole heart. That's all we can do.'

'But it *was* my fault,' Janet says, words falling out of her mouth like broken shards. 'He was my responsibility.'

Bev's hand presses into Janet's; safe, strong.

'What about Brian, did he look after you?'

'Brian left me for someone else before I even knew I was pregnant. So it was just the two of us. I was all he had. So it was my fault alone.'

'No, Janet. It wasn't your fault. You didn't do anything wrong. Your midwife must have told you that at the time?'

Janet shakes her head.

'No one came to see you afterwards?'

'I didn't let them in.' Janet's voice is a whisper.

She couldn't bear to see anybody, had shut them all out, the midwife, the doctor, her friends, everyone. She didn't want comfort, didn't deserve it. And what comfort could ever be given?

'They should have kept trying,' Bev says. 'I would have broken the bloody door down. I would have held you in my arms and told you that it wasn't your fault, told you until you believed me.'

Bev lets go of Janet's hand, puts her arms around her, and holds her close.

'It wasn't your fault, Janet. It wasn't your fault, love.'

19

Janet feels like she has been pulverized by an antique Victorian cast-iron garden lawn-roller that has gone back and forth over her entire body. Everything aches. Everything. Muscles, joints, ligaments that had never previously called attention to their existence now shriek their presence. At her ankle a constant throbbing sensation; a dirty bandage shows at the top of her boot. Next to her Bev is asleep, curled in a foetal position. She's been out for about half an hour. Janet decided it was safe to let her doze for a while since dawn isn't too far away and Bev seems to run hot. So Janet remains sentinel, alone with her thoughts.

Tentatively Janet holds out one of her hands and gently starts to massage it. Her hands are filthy and scarred but she focuses on easing the pain out of each joint, massaging her thumb into her palm, along the tip of each finger, until she feels the soreness start to ebb. Then she starts on the other hand, working in the same way, with the same care and attention. Light begins to seep into the little burrow. Janet moves her focus to her wrists, then her forearms, her elbows. She reaches up to knead the muscles in her neck and her shoulders. Her hands trace over her chest and stomach and under her oilskin her blanket of foliage crackles. She stretches forward and works on as much of her legs as she can reach, pressing to ease the tightness in her hamstrings, her quadriceps. When her fingers come into contact with her skin she is aware of its thin, crêpe-like texture, of the places where the flesh is soft and dappled in liver spots. But she also feels the definition of her muscles, honed from gardening, the shape of her biceps, deltoids, scapula. She tentatively charts the territory of her body, following an orienteering map of her own: her slope lines, her earth walls, her watercourses. Her body is an old map, worn and faded. But it still records a life lived. A body that has been loved. That has nurtured life, given birth. The map is still true.

A rustling, a skittering of paws and suddenly a whiskery snout pushes in under the tablecloth bivouac and nuzzles against Janet's face.

'Hello there, and where did you spring from?' The ears of the red setter are soft and curly and flop against her cheek. She scratches its velvet head and the dog gives her another nuzzle, looks ready to tell her all his news, when a man's voice calls from above.

'Hello? Anyone down there?'

The setter gives a happy bark and dashes back out of the burrow. Janet lurches unsteadily to her feet. The bracken is still warm from her body and she shapes it around Bev, cocooning her. She checks her temperature, her colour. All good.

'Hello? Everything OK?' The voice calls again. 'Do you need help?'

The rain has stopped and a silver dawn is unfolding. Janet limps to the muddy slope leading up from the shelter.

A curly-haired young man dressed in green waterproofs looks down anxiously.

The red setter bounces round Janet, eager to play.

'Percy, easy, boy!' the man says. 'Sorry. He's excited to see you. He knew you were down there. Here, please take my hand.'

The man scrambles down the slope towards Janet, reaches out and carefully helps her up. Her legs are pins and needles and pain flares from her ankle. Janet takes in his kind face, his concerned brown eyes, the russet of his stubble and thinks how true it is that people often resemble their dogs. The sky is sapphire and a pale thumbprint of moon is still visible. Half of Bev's tablecloth hangs valiantly from the silver birch, ravaged, but somehow in one piece. *Like us*, Janet thinks.

'Percy and I were out for our morning walk and I caught sight of this.' The man points to the tablecloth with his stick. 'Thought we'd better come over in case someone was in trouble. When we got close Percy must have got your scent. Don't tell me you've been out all night on your own?'

'Well, there are two of us, but yes, we did get stuck. My fault. We were looking for hawk's-beard and lost track of the time. I haven't been here in decades and the mist came down so fast I got completely disorientated.'

'Did your phone lose reception?'

'I don't have one.'

The young man looks completely stumped by this detail but recovers. 'Are you cold, hungry? I can give you my hoodie. I might have a packet of Werther's . . . Sorry, not much to offer – mostly biscuits for Percy.'

'We're OK.' Janet leans against the trunk of the birch. 'We decided it was better to hunker down for the night than risk going further in the wrong direction after we lost the light. I twisted my ankle; that didn't help.'

'Where were you heading? Dent?'

Janet nods.

'You're not too far off the path.' He points ahead to where the hill falls in a steep incline. 'See over there' – he gestures across to the west – 'that's the way down to Dent. I'll walk you back.' The man whistles to Percy, who is lapping noisily at a puddle. The dog bounds over, ears flapping.

'Thank you, but I can get us down. I'm tougher than I look. We'll be fine now that I can see where we are again.'

The young man takes convincing but finally relents.

'At least take this.' He hands Janet his hiking stick. 'And when you do get to Dent, the Fireside Cafe in the village opens early and does an excellent breakfast. I'm going to look for you on my way back home and if you're not there, I'm coming back up for you.'

Janet watches the man leave, Percy springing at his heels.

A chiffon of mist hovers over the distant fields and sunlight streams like bright shards of water, baptizing the new day. Everything looks rinsed clean, newly minted. Tree branches shimmering with raindrops reach upwards, outwards. To the east the peak of Whernside soars.

A gentle breeze ruffles Janet's hair and she breathes deep. *Petrichor*. Blood of the gods, immortality, life itself. Unbuttoning her oilskin, she sees how the layer of leaves under her coat has moulded to the shape of her body, a silver-green armour of bracken, protecting her organs, keeping her safe. She shrugs off the coat, gently brushes herself down and, ably assisted by the kind man's stick, makes her way to the edge of the stream. The water is high after the rainfall and the stream froths and gasps. Janet awkwardly bends, palms the icy water, and splashes it over her face, once, twice, three times. She washes away tracks of tears, the dirt and mud, runs her hand over the shape of her skull, her hair a silver cap, sleek and shining in the light.

Standing tall, she closes her eyes and pulls another long, deep draught of air into her body, feels it filling her lungs, oxygenating her blood. When bindweed invades a plant it gradually strangles the life with its arrow-shaped leaves until the host plant collapses under the weight of its usurper. Janet is vigilant about keeping bindweed at bay on her plot, but she has let it wrap itself around her heart, slowly strangling her with regret. Last night Janet had to stand her ground and survive. And she did. She feels tender like a bruised fruit, but there is something else, too – sweetness, possibility.

≈

Bev and Janet make their way slowly back towards Dent, small dots in the vast green of the landscape, under an ocean of sky. Behind them sunlight warms the trunk of the silver birch, catching the gleam of its bark and the slender filaments of Italian damask twirling from one of its branches. Later, birds will take advantage of those dancing threads, chattering excitedly as they gather materials to make their spring nests.

The women follow the path across Middleton Fell. Despite their difference in height and the muddy terrain, a natural rhythm develops between them, a shared tempo. It's a little offbeat, perhaps, definitely more experimental jazz than classical waltz, but a rhythm none the less. Mostly they walk in silence, lost in their own thoughts. From time to time Janet stops to point out the views, to make sure Bev sees Howgill Fells, drinks in the panorama of Dentdale. After the shame of getting them lost yesterday she is buoyed to be pathfinder once more.

'Here she is,' says Bev.

'Who?'

'The Janet who caught the fish and cooked it on the open fire. All the women you have been and all the others still to come.'

And for a brief moment Janet feels it again, that flicker of hope.

~

Leaving the open moorland behind, they make their way down Flinter Gill, a steep, rocky pathway leading back to the village. On their right a boisterous stream tumbles down flat steps of limestone through a wooded ravine. Yellow flag iris festoons their way.

'Janet! Look!'

And even before she sees it, Janet remembers: a majestic old-growth oak on the edge of the path. Erosion has exposed massive knotted lateral roots on one side of the trunk so that the tree stands, astonishingly, suspended on a twisted arch, making a gateway just big enough to walk through. Janet stops. She had forgotten the Wishing Tree.

'There's a sign!' Bev says, rushing towards the old wooden plaque. 'Listen to this, Janet: "To wish – circle the old tree. Its guardian spirit traditionally grants a wish to all who make their way clockwise three times through the twisted arch. Bad luck will surely befall those who go round the tree anticlockwise." A wishing tree! How lucky are we?'

Across the years Janet hears Nancy's voice. *Clockwise three times through the twisted arch. What's your wish, JP? Your wildest longing?*

Ducking down, Bev weaves her way through the knotted roots three times, her lips moving slightly as she makes her wish.

'Your turn!'

Come on, JP, what are you waiting for? Make a wish!

Janet lingers for a moment, leaning against the tree trunk, imagining the hundreds and thousands of wishes whispered into its roots. Flinter Gill was the end of her Three Peaks hike with Nancy. The end of them. Beyond the track lay the village, other people, real life. She longed to stay on the trail, out under the big sky, out with the soft-baaing sheep and the endless green where their love could remain unsullied by prejudice. When it came to it, she just didn't have the guts. Not even for Nancy. Back then Janet had wound her way around the roots without making a wish. But Nancy was attuned to her.

'What did you wish for, JP?' she pressed.

'Nothing. I have everything I want,' Janet answered.

But Nancy saw it on her face. Her voice was barely a whisper. 'Don't back out on me,' she said.

Janet couldn't bear to look at her.

'I'll give you everything, always. You know I will.'

And Janet did know. And she also knew that with Nancy it was all or nothing.

'I can't go back to how we were before,' said Nancy, 'pretend this never happened. You have to choose. Be brave, JP, fight for the life you want.'

Janet wanted to say, *I choose you*. But instead she said, 'I can't.'

Janet feels the rough bark of the tree under her hand. She is standing in the very place where Nancy confronted her, fought for her, tore the map from her hands, standing where she stood all those years ago, watching Nancy walk away from her, knowing with each step the value of what she was losing but unable to reach out and pull it back.

She could have chosen all. Instead, she chose nothing.

Janet exhales, leans the walking stick against the trunk and ducks down under the roots of the tree, holding on for support. Slowly, she circles clockwise three times, following her footsteps from years ago. But this time when she closes her eyes, her wish is right there, waiting for her. Even though it is all far too late and she has missed her chance, she makes it anyway.

∽

Back at the car park they change into dry things. As Janet pulls on a pair of Eddie's worn canvas trousers, she is grateful for Bev's Barnardo's bags. Until Bev hands her a chunky knitted orange poncho.

'But it's a perfect fit!' Bev exclaims, reaching up to pull it over Janet's head.

'There's no such thing as a perfectly fitted poncho.'

Bev doesn't fare much better herself, finally settling on a pair of yellow-and-brown tartan trousers and what she describes as a 'Bisto brown' polo neck.

'Looks perfect for a trip to the Highlands,' says Janet, 'in 1973.'

Bev laughs. 'My mum's auld claes. I still feel bad about telling you I was going to see Rona in Kirkcaldy. Neither of us has been there in over twenty years. I left when I was nineteen and moved down to London to do my midwifery training at Tommy's.'

'Consider yourself completely forgiven,' Janet says, 'though there is one thing I wanted to ask.'

'Go ahead.'

'Would you describe yourself as . . . a keen sportswoman?'

'What?'

'Do you like to run, cycle, play tennis?'

'You're pulling my leg, right?'

'It's just that your clothes – the joggers, the Aertex top, the cycling jacket . . .'

Janet's words are blotted out by Bev's belly laugh.

Janet tosses a wodge of poncho over her shoulder. 'What's so funny?'

Bev wipes her eyes. 'I wear them for the wicking, Janet. Breathable fabric. Every menopausal woman should have a wardrobe that wicks.'

The young man with the red setter didn't steer them wrong. At the Fireside Cafe they have a breakfast of champions: hot buttered toast, scrambled eggs, smoked bacon, and pots of fresh leaf tea.

Bev tells Janet about a surprise birthday party she is throwing for one of her nurses. She asks Janet's advice about the best flowering cherry to plant in memory of her mum. Janet sips the cup of tea Bev has poured for her, enjoying the perfect sugar-to-milk ratio. Janet orders extra toast because Bev might fancy just one more slice. Percy bounds up to the window and the young man waves at them from outside. Bev pops out and gives his walking stick back to him.

~

Turn around, sings Bonnie.

How different things look when you are travelling in the other direction, Janet thinks as she watches fields and villages flash by. At the speed Bev is driving, they will be back in no time. Just as she is settling into the journey, Bev takes a rogue right at the roundabout heading away from the motorway turn-off.

Janet sits up, peers at the signposts.

'I think we want to go that way.' She points in the opposite direction.

But Bev checks her GPS, nods affirmatively and carries on.

'Where are you taking us this time, woman? Land's End?' Janet jokes, but Bev's face is impassive as she indicates, takes the next left and then immediately turns right. Before Janet can object, they are parking up at Westmorland General Hospital.

'What the heck are we doing here?'

'Just thought we'd get a quick X-ray on that ankle.'

Janet keeps her seat belt firmly anchored.

'We've no way of knowing if it's just a bad sprain or if you've cracked a bone or broken it,' Bev goes on, somehow managing to maintain an authoritative air despite her questionable seventies attire. 'If you can't bear weight on it, you need an X-ray.'

'I'll be sure to have it looked at once I'm back home,' says Janet, who had no intention of doing any such thing.

'And I want someone to look at that cut and the goose egg where you knocked your head.'

'My head is fine!'

'Save your breath to cool your porridge, Janet. We're not shifting till you're seen.'

And despite all Janet's protestations – the hours they will have to wait, the germs they will expose themselves to in the waiting room – Bev is immovable. As Bev is the one with the car keys, Janet finally relents, but not without giving her orange poncho several sharp flounces as they make their way towards A & E.

Janet is proved correct on all counts – they do indeed have to wait hours to be seen and spend those hours in the company of various children with phlegmy coughs and a curdled-looking man who keeps bolting to the toilet. Her mood doesn't improve when the X-ray reveals no broken bones, making their detour, in her opinion, a complete waste of time. The doctor diagnoses a partial tear to the anterior talofibular ligament and she is made to wear a clunky black Velcro ankle brace and memorize and repeat the mnemonic RICE: Rest, Ice, Compression, Elevation. She is instructed to keep off her ankle for a full week. Though sympathetic, the doctor isn't worried about Janet's bump on the head. She cleans it up carefully and applies antiseptic cream. The only upside to the whole unnecessary palaver is that the doctor remarks on Janet's excellent blood pressure and overall state of health. The 'for your age' is implied. Still, Janet is buoyed by the positive appraisal. By the time they get back to the car it is too late in the day to make it all the way to Hastings, despite Janet's urging.

'Look,' says Bev, 'I know you want to get home, but I'm knackered and you're wrecked.'

They compromise on spending the night at a Premier Inn off the M6 near Crewe. Bev is kind, strict and professional as she oversees the RICE regime, timing the rounds of ice twenty minutes on, twenty minutes off. During Bev's endless chatty phone call to Eddie, Janet segues from dispirited to sulky to something bordering on insolent. She has a troubled night full of strange dreams and wakes up with fish hooks in the back of her throat.

❦

As they finally set off the next day, Janet's mood hangs heavy, made worse by the indignity of her leg brace. She feels tired and old and when a sign for a National Trust property flashes by, a deep sigh escapes her.

'What's up?' Bev says.

'I applied for a job with the National Trust,' Janet blurts.

'Oh, right?' Bev says, focusing on the road ahead.

'To be a tour guide.' Janet glances across at Bev. 'I thought I'd be rather good.'

'Nae doubt.' Bev nods as she overtakes another car.

'I didn't get it.' A beat. Janet tries to shrug it off but there is something of the confessional about Bev's car. She takes a breath, gets the rest out: 'And the thing is, it was . . . a *volunteer* position.' There is a strange relief in admitting it but, even so, her shoulders droop. Bev doesn't say anything for a moment, checks the rear-view mirror, changes lanes.

'I'm sorry it didn't work out, but do you know what? You don't have time for a job right now, Janet, volunteer or paid.' Bev takes her eyes off the road and looks at Janet, stern-faced. 'You've got to save your allotment.' She turns back to the road ahead but after a beat adds: 'And have you seen how much they charge for their honey!'

~

Bev offers to come in, help her get settled.

'Thanks, but no. If I can get down Whernside on this ankle, I can make it to my kitchen.' Janet chivvies her away. 'Especially in this damn orthopaedic boot you've got me in!'

Bev laughs. 'I see I'm still not forgiven. Speaking of forgiveness, if you're going to be obstinate about help, I'd best get back to Eddie. But listen, the boot isn't meant to encourage you to go gallivanting around on that ankle.

213

The doctor told you to stay off it for a week. Remember to—'

'Rest, Ice, Compress, Elevate! I know, I know!'

'Well, I'll be off, then. Goodnight, pet. You take care now!'

It's the silence that strikes Janet first. It has a different quality to the usual quiet of her house. Thick and heavy, it is punctured now and then by a creaking floorboard, a leaky tap. No more power ballads droning on – that's a relief! She moves through her kitchen, rattles her cupboards, clanks the kettle against the tap. Was it always this deadly quiet? Janet puts on the radio, fiddles with the dial but can't settle on anything. She switches it off, lets the silence seep back in. Her mint-green teacup sits alone on the shelf. She takes it down. She puts it back. Instead, she chooses the Doulton, upturned on the draining board.

Funny, she thinks as she hobbles about making the tea, it feels as if she has been away for ages but it's only been three nights. The past and present have collided, sending her thoughts scattering wildly like billiard balls in a break shot. She shivers, sinks on to a chair at her kitchen table and wraps her arms around herself. She remembers the comforting feel of Bev's arms. The kettle whistles on the hob but Janet remains at the table, her lips moving softly.

It wasn't your fault.

'It wasn't my fault,' she says, testing the words. After a moment she repeats them once more, trying to believe. Is it possible that Bev is right? After all, she is a midwife, an expert. *It wasn't your fault.* The kettle whistles on; warm clouds of steam billow softly across the kitchen.

By the time Janet limps to the sink to refill the kettle, which has boiled dry, it is dark outside. When will she see Bev again? She would like to take her to the allotments, show Bev around her plot. Maybe even introduce her to Patrice. But would she be interested? She nearly got Bev killed, after all. And anyway, Bev said she wouldn't 'bother her' once they were back in Hastings. Promised, in fact. After all those awful things she said to Bev, Janet wouldn't blame her. Bev has Eddie, endless grateful mums who name their daughters after her, nurses she throws parties for. Rona in ruddy Croydon.

Janet returns the empty kettle to the hob. She's lost the will to make tea now, to sit and drink it alone in her kitchen. She places the Doulton in the cupboard next to her mint-green teacup. Tomorrow she will return to her allotment, tend her plants. On her plot she is needed. For now, at least.

20

All plans of heading to the allotment are put paid to when Janet wakes in the night with a full-blown cold. Her head hurts, her bones ache and she's congested. She moans, rolls over and falls back into a groggy sleep. A few hours later, she manages to crawl downstairs in search of a clean hanky and something to soothe her raging throat. In the kitchen the radio is still singing away chirpily – she had turned it back on last night to take the edge off the silence, forgotten to switch it off. She had found a new station. The sound cheers her. Searching her pantry for a clove of fresh garlic and a knob of ginger, she finds nothing but a tin of sardines and a wonky-eyed potato. If she could get to her plot she could pinch a sprig of fresh mint, gather some stems of fragrant lemon thyme, a handful of oregano, and make herself a healing concoction to soothe her throat and relieve her congestion. In the end she resorts to a faded packet of past-sell-by Beechams Powders unearthed from the back of the medicine cabinet. She upends the packet of powder into the Doulton, mixes it with hot water and takes the dubious beverage back to bed.

As the long hours creep by, Janet finds herself wondering what Bev is doing. She hopes she doesn't get sick, too.

Should she call? But she doesn't have her number. She used to go out of her way to avoid the woman but now all she wants is for Bev to pop round with one of her ruddy note-lets. She'd happily hobble down to the community centre for the local murder mystery if Bev invited her now. Because things had shifted out there in the dark on the hillside.

Janet had hoped for some word from Glynis, but it's radio silence there, too. As evening draws in, she wonders if the whole trip was a wild goose chase.

Janet is lying in bed contemplating whether or not she can be bothered to bake the potato for dinner when some-one knocks at the door. Despite her ankle, she manages to get down the stairs at an admirable pace and there, silhou-etted in the glass panel in the middle of her front door, is that radiant glow of green. Janet raises her arms in a little cheer before opening the door.

'I thought you might need a couple of things,' Bev says, plumping a packed grocery bag on the kitchen table. 'It's just a few essentials—' She looks over at the radio, arches a brow. 'Gloria Gaynor, Janet?'

'That's Radio Three for you – too bloody eclectic for their own good.' Janet swiftly limps across to the radio and smacks the off button to hide the evidence that she is tuned in to Smooth Radio. 'Thank you for the shopping – you shouldn't have gone to any trouble.' Bev looks shattered.

'No trouble, just picked up some bits and pieces for you when I was shopping for Eddie and me. Oh, and there's a jumbo box of paracetamol and a jar of Schwartz lemon-grass flakes in there, too – I looked online and apparently lemongrass is one of your medicinal plants; it's supposed to be good for the immune system. I thought it might help your ankle to heal more quickly,' Bev adds informatively. 'But it sounds like you've got a stinking cold now. Let's hope lemongrass is good for that, too.'

'Lemongrass is an excellent antioxidant as well as an antifungal.'

'Aye, but it's not as good as a tot of whisky, is it?' Bev winks. 'Right. You look after yourself – I'll be by tomorrow to see how you are.'

After Bev leaves, Janet takes her time unpacking the shopping. 'Deliciously Ella Hazelnut Bites'? *My word!* 'Chilli and Lemon *Lentil* Chips'. Who knew you could chip a lentil? There is also a thick slab of a jolly-sounding 'Cornish Cruncher' cheese, a punnet of fresh raspberries and a tub of Greek yoghurt, as well as a large box of Yorkshire Gold teabags and some pink Jazz apples. Janet's cupboards haven't looked quite so full, or quite so *interesting*, for some time!

And, as it turns out, Bev is right about the Schwartz desiccated lemongrass – it does have excellent health benefits, because every time Janet catches sight of the little green-topped jar sitting on her bedside table she feels decidedly better.

The next day brings no news from Glynis, but Bev appears with enough home-made chicken soup to feed a land army. The next day she turns up with a perfectly cooked fish pie, followed on the next by a Thai green curry, and then an asparagus risotto. Janet plays it cool, of course, but she looks forward to the visits all day. She always has the kettle boiled and the Doulton and the mint-green cup out in preparation, whether Bev has time for a cup of tea or not. She won't make that mistake again. Usually Bev doesn't stay long – she is back at work and busy with her own life, and even though she relishes the visits, Janet can't quite silence the voice in her head that says Bev only comes round because she feels sorry for her.

By Friday Janet is feeling much recovered and when she hears that knock at the door she is already smiling as she hops gingerly up the hallway. But when she opens the door, she does not see the familiar face of Bev but instead a sandy-haired, round-faced man holding a Pyrex dish with a tin-foil cover. Eddie.

'I made an artichoke lasagne for dinner tonight,' Eddie says, carrying the dish through to the kitchen. 'Bev thought you might like some. She says you need to keep your strength up. She got called to cover a shift.'

Janet feels a wave of disappointment as she takes the dish. She tries to look grateful but the voice in her head sets up a chant: *meals on wheels, meals on wheels*. Perhaps after all Bev's visits are about medical concern, nothing else. And now she is delegating the chore to Eddie.

Janet thanks Eddie, and is about to show him out when he says, 'It's nice to finally meet the famous Janet. You've really given Bev a lift.' He smiles. 'She's been so blue since she lost her mum and, well, other stuff she's going through. Now it's *Janet this, Janet that*. She's got her spirit back.'

Janet beams, hugs the warm lasagne to her. *Janet this. Janet that.*

'Sounds like you saved Bev's life out there in the Dales. Thank God you know all that survival stuff. I shudder to think what might have happened.'

'We saved each other.'

The lasagne is delicious.

~

It is now more than a week since Janet met with Glynis and she still hasn't heard back. Should she call? Or would that irritate Glynis? On the positive front, at least Janet's health is greatly improved, in part due to the nourishing and delicious home cooking. Despite her promise to Bev to rest until she is fully recovered, Janet can't wait a moment more. She needs to get back to the allotment *now* and neither a head cold and sprained ankle nor the wrath of Bev can stop her.

Janet feels a prickle of anxiety as she fills her flask, packs her Bath Olivers and gingerly laces her boots. Do people still think she's responsible for the knotweed? Will Patrice be happy to see her? She remembers the careful way Patrice wiped the sea-blue cup for her, wished she had stayed that day, not stormed off. Janet unhooks her gardening apron, strokes the familiar roughness of its fabric. She has no idea what might have transpired with the Council over the last few days. She has thought about calling Patrice a few times but just hasn't felt up to the task. Janet slips her trusty gardening apron over her head, wraps the tabs firmly around her waist and ties them in a secure double knot. That's better. She lightly runs a hand over the familiar bodies of the tools in her pocket and feels their reassuring weight. Then, straightening her shoulders, she heads out.

The bed rest has at least helped the swelling in her ankle to go down and, despite the indignity of the brace, it makes getting around less painful. She refuses to wear it to the allotment, but does take a stick. Now that she's finally on her way, she feels a nervous flutter in her stomach. She tries to steady her nerves by going over the chores that will require her attention. Rigorous bindweed patrol, of course. Her trellises will need tidying; stems untethered by the wind will have to be retied. What else? Make sure slugs and snails aren't feasting on her plants, see how her little valerian seeds are doing – this is the first year she is starting them off in containers and though they are under cover she wants to make sure they aren't waterlogged.

Thinking about the jobs in hand helps calm her jitters and by the time Janet arrives at Seaview she smiles as she breathes in the salty smell of the sea, takes in the bursts of new growth everywhere. All around, on every branch, stem and stalk, she sees shoots and leaves furiously pushing their way forward. Cherry trees barely in bud a few days ago are plump with blossom. The privet hedge that runs along the perimeter fence of the allotments seems to have doubled in size and vibrates with the sound of house-proud sparrows, territorially swooping in and out.

No sign of Patrice at her plot and the door of her shed is closed. Her sturdy garden spade stands upright in the soil where she must have left it. The wood of the handle is faded from use, from the warmth and press of her hands upon it.

Patrice's immediate neighbour, Sanjay, is working on his greenhouse, carefully stacking glass panels in a pile. Janet thought he had finished constructing it several days ago. And come to think of it, isn't he usually at the bookshop at this time of day? He looks different, a slump to his shoulders, a downcast turn to his mouth.

Janet passes the shed that once had the embroidered *I do like to be beside the seaside* curtains strung in the window. The glass is bare; the curtains have gone. Janet peers inside and sees that the tools have been packed up and removed. All that remains is a piece of torn sacking lying on the floor. Janet quickens her pace as much as her ankle will allow, feels that prickling sensation on her skin again.

When she passes Ken's plot she stops. Ken isn't there but something is different. Janet tilts her head, trying to work out what's missing, like that game people used to play with objects on a tray, when something is removed and you have to guess what. What is it? Then it hits her. Ken and Brenda's faded blue rockers.

Janet remembers the first day she arrived at Seaview, seeing Ken and Brenda sitting side by side on those rockers eating their lunch together. She had noticed the rhythm of their chairs, tilting backwards and forwards in time with each other. She remembers the companionable quiet between Ken and Brenda as they enjoyed their sandwiches, a silence as warm and rich as a bed of freshly tilled earth. The only trace of the blue rockers, of the people who tended this patch for decades, are the places where the grass lies yellowed, flattened.

Janet's pulse quickens as she continues to her own plot. When she arrives, she can't quite believe what she sees. Her grass borders have been gently trimmed and, what's more, the clippings have been put on her compost heap. Janet inspects them and sees that they haven't just been tipped there helter-skelter, leaving them to form a wet green sludge; instead, they have been well mixed with dry straw, exactly as Janet herself does. Her gaze travels around her plot, takes in her trellis plants, all standing neat and tidy, every stem firmly secured. She bends down, inspects her beds. Not a snail or slug, nor a single tendril of bindweed. Her seedling trays are balanced at an angle to drain excess water. Sparkling outside her shed, her ribbed galvanized-steel bucket has not only been returned but has been so vigorously buffed it shines like a trophy.

Who did this? Surely not the Power Ballads? The Steer Manures?

'Janet! I was getting worried – I've never known you to miss a day, much less more than a week!'

Lakshmi stands on the path with an armful of colourful posters.

'You haven't, by any chance, been looking after my plot, have you?' Janet ducks her head.

'Sorry, no, I've barely been here, to be honest. The last few days I've been going into every shop and business in town trying to get a petition signed. We've got loads of names!'

'Good for you,' says Janet.

'I just hope it will help. The mood has been a bit grim.'

'Why? What's happened?' Janet steels herself.

'Nothing definitive yet, but poor Patrice has been at the Council every day, petitioning for meetings, trying to get more information, trying to find a way to at least delay things so we can put up a better fight. They keep fobbing her off, giving her email addresses to write to and phone numbers to ring – she calls, she emails and never hears back. When she's not stalking Pete Marsh at the Council, she's on the phone with the National Allotment Society trying to organize some legal help.'

'Where is she now?'

'She's finally got a meeting with Marsh this morning. She wore him down.'

'He sounds like a complete twit,' says Janet.

'Patrice says he makes a great show of caring about Seaview but her other sources on the Council say he's the one who's hell-bent on getting us closed down. Says we're a health and safety threat.'

'As if paving over green space isn't a threat to the health of the community.'

'I know! What's so threatening to health and safety about people growing flowers and vegetables, supporting the local ecosystem?'

'It's a ruse. Marsh is in it for the money.'

Lakshmi's eyes widen. 'What do you know? Anything we can prove?'

'Not yet.'

'The Council are moving so fast I'm afraid we're going to run out of time before we can mount a solid defence. We've been advised to remove belongings – lift out plants if we can find places for them. Can you imagine? Some people have already given up – put their names down on waiting lists for other allotments. Most of us haven't a hope in hell of getting another plot near our homes. With work and the kids, I can't make it over here as much as I'd like, let alone trek out to an allotment miles away. If Seaview goes, that's my gardening finished.'

'Are you packing up, too?'

'Me? No way!' Lakshmi gestures to her bundle of posters. 'My whole shed – actually, my whole plot – is going to become one huge protest! SAVE SEAVIEW!' She smiles at Janet. 'We have to do what we can, don't we? It's like what Patrice always says, we have to keep the faith.'

Keep the faith. Janet nods slowly. Yes.

~

Janet works on her plot. If she can't bring down her foe today, she can at least tend her friends. It feels good to be back amongst her plants, their shapes and familiar scents. Her body responds to their needs without thinking but though she keeps busy, she is flooded with a sense of foreboding. The machinations of Pete Marsh, *hell-bent on getting us closed*, the force of the Council bearing down, people already being frightened off. Not Janet – she will stay till the end. The seeds in the tray have grown into tiny seedlings ready to be planted out. Janet prepares the soil and carefully beds them in, replacing the cloche in case of a late spring frost. She puts in another couple of hours but, with her head cold still lurking in her system, she tires easily and eventually calls it a day.

On her way past Ken's plot, Janet is relieved to see him kneeling on the grass, harvesting asparagus.

'You aren't leaving, are you?' she blurts.

Ken straightens up. 'Leaving?'

'Your rockers are gone.' She points to the faded yellow marks in the grass.

'Ah.' He nods slowly, wipes his hands on his shorts, takes a breath. 'It was time; seeing Brenda's empty chair every day just made me lonelier, if you know what I mean.'

Janet does.

'And it wouldn't look right with just mine sitting there,

225

so I got my granddaughter to come and pick them up. But I'm not going anywhere. This plot has been in my family since the war. I'm buggered if I'm going to give up without a fight! If they think they are going to get their hands on my first earlies, they've got another think coming. I'm harvesting these' – he gestures to the pile of asparagus – 'for Patrice's refugee caff.'

Ken pulls a wrinkled hanky from his pocket, mops a line of sweat from his brow. Narrowing his eyes, he points across the allotments.

'Are those cranes getting closer?'

Janet looks over at the giant metal contraptions, watches their crank and shift as they shunt back and forth, burying the bowling green under heavy concrete blocks.

They do seem closer.

Ken sucks his teeth. 'Did the same to the old lido. I used to swim there as a lad. You should have seen it – beautiful, like one of those Greek amphi-things, largest lido in Europe. It's a Lidl now.'

'I've seen photos,' says Janet. 'Unforgiveable town planning.'

'Do you know what they called this bit of the coast in the war? Doodlebug Alley. We were slap-bang in the middle of the Jerrys' route to London and they threw everything they had at this town. Even Hitler couldn't destroy the lido, but Hastings Council?' Ken makes a slicing motion across his throat with the trowel. 'Gone, just like that, and for what? Another shopping centre, another blooming car park.'

'A shameful lack of vision combined with simple, grubby greed.'

226

Ken shakes his head. 'They've taken all of it, the cricket pitch, everything.'

He stretches his arm out and traces the perimeter of Seaview. 'This is the last big parcel of land left in the whole town. It's the one thing those beggars haven't turned into a block of fancy housing or a bloody Aldi. It's a crime, if you ask me,' says Ken, returning to his asparagus. 'It's a bloody crime.'

Janet couldn't have put it better herself.

21

Despite everything, when Janet walks Bev to the allotments the next day, she feels hopeful. Not only did Bev accept the invitation to come to Seaview, but a cryptic postcard arrived in Janet's morning post. On the front of the card was a charming picture of Peter Rabbit in Mr McGregor's vegetable patch. *Greetings from the Lakes!* On the reverse of the postcard the words: *You're on to something. Watch your back. More soon.* Janet has the card in her pocket and decides to show it to Bev as they walk together.

'Watch your back?' Bev says. 'I don't like the sound of that. What are you up to, Janet?'

Janet brushes her fears away. 'I've discovered some suspicious-looking links between Pete Marsh at the Council and a toady property developer called Bringley. I think they've seized other allotments through a combination of false pretexts and illegal backhanders. Think about it – where in the UK can you find generous swathes of land right in town centres? Allotments are an obvious target if you're low enough to go for them.'

'If there's big money involved, I especially don't like the sound of *watch your back*.'

Janet pockets the card again. 'Ah, but I've got Glynis on side.'

'You've got me too.' Bev punches a fist into the flat of her hand. 'Like I said on the fell, I'm ready for a fight!'

Janet smiles. She can't wait to show Bev her plot. Also, surely Patrice will be back today?

'Hey, not so fast on that foot, please!' Bev says as Janet speeds up.

Janet slows the pace and takes in her surroundings. Usually she just stalks ahead, eyes trained on the pavement, but today she notices the light sparkling on the water, not to mention a rather nice cake shop she hasn't spotted before.

'Fancy a bun and a takeaway coffee?'

'Janet, there will never come a time when I'll say no to a bun and coffee.'

'You seem to know everyone,' says Janet as yet another passer-by waves at Bev.

'*Intimately.*' Bev laughs and Janet joins in.

But as they turn down the path to Seaview their laughter is silenced.

The entire perimeter of the allotments has been cordoned off with biohazard tape. An officious sign has been erected by Hastings Council, referring to the presence of 'hazardous materials' on the site and forbidding all access by any unauthorized persons. The sign concludes in shouty red print that anybody breaking the rules could *FACE CRIMINAL PROCEEDINGS.*

Janet quickly scans the faces of the distressed and angry gardeners clumped at the gate until she spots Patrice, standing slightly to the side, her phone pressed against her ear, expression tense. Patrice looks up and when she sees Janet her face lifts for a moment, until her smile – is she pleased to see her? – is wiped away by whoever she is talking to.

'We haven't had a response to our petition yet ...' Patrice says, her voice raised. '... On what grounds? ... This isn't enough notice! ... What about people's private property?'

Janet feels the blood drain from her face. It's all happening too fast.

Patrice shoves the phone in her pocket, nods quickly at Janet and turns towards the gardeners.

An uneasy quiet falls.

'Folks. I'm gutted to tell you this' – Patrice steadies her voice – 'but the Council motion has passed. They are repossessing the land.'

Mickey bellows, 'What right do they have?'

'At the end of the day, the Council owns the land,' Patrice says wearily.

'But they're our allotments!' cries Sanjay.

'We have rights!' Lakshmi shouts.

'We do,' Patrice agrees, 'but the Council are maintaining that the knotweed is a threat to public health and safety. They've deemed Seaview unfit for purpose.'

'What about our stuff – all my tools!'

'My Royal Horticultural Society bench!' cries Felicity bloody Kendal. 'It cost a fortune!'

Patrice holds up her hands. 'We've been ordered to stay off the site until the knotweed has been eradicated by professionals so that it doesn't spread any further. After that, they say we can come back to remove ...'

'What the . . .?' Lakshmi points across the allotments.

Two bulldozers, hunched like army tanks, lurch towards them. The allotmenteers watch in horror as the machines reach the wildflower corridor, lower their enormous blades and noisily start ripping up the land. Gardeners momentarily stare transfixed as the wild grasses, the dog violets and the bluebells are torn up, and then roar into life in a cacophony of anger, panic and disbelief.

'Stop them!'

'This can't be legal!'

'Call the Council!'

'They can't do this; they have no right!'

'Call the NSALG!'

'What about the badgers? The hedgehogs?'

'Call the RSPCA!'

'What about the hedgerows?'

'Call DEFRA!'

'What about my gooseberries?'

'Call the police!'

Janet doesn't join the clamour, barely hears it. Instead, she reaches into the pocket of her oilskin and her hand closes round her Huntsman penknife. She flicks open the blade, grabs the black-and-yellow biohazard tape and slices it apart. Striding through it, she heads straight towards the bulldozers.

Enough of being ignored.

Her pulse pounds in her ears. *This time you're going to bally well fight for what you want!* Enough of being a coward, enough of letting what's most important just go. *Enough, Enough, Enough* sounds with each footstep as she walks towards the bulldozers. She doesn't feel the pain in her ankle, the congestion in her chest. She feels only adrenaline and the force of her blood powering through her body, propelling her forward. She is close enough now to see the mangled bodies of the lesser celandine, the primroses, the daisies. She can make out the crushed faces of the delicate white ramsons, the sweet star of Bethlehem. Pollinators flap in a panic for their lives: bees, ladybirds, butterflies, shield bugs, hoverflies. Janet keeps on walking. She doesn't see the bulldozers' rollers battering on their track chains, pulverizing everything in their path. As the bulldozers' engines roar, it is Bev's voice Janet hears: *Who cares about manners in a storm? Who gives a flying fuck!* And as she gets closer still, Janet sees Nancy staring at her from behind the tumult of the waterfall. *This is your power, your force.*

She feels it now – not her fear, not her cowardice, but her force. Finally. And what a force it is, women's anger, she thinks as she closes in.

Janet stops, holds her ground. The blades slice forward blindly, razing everything in their paths. This is not the way to eradicate an invasive species. This is the way to spread it. That was all just a pretext. The bulldozers, however, are frighteningly real. Janet stands tall, resolute as the hulking machines plough towards her. Mud churns, engines roar; they are almost upon her now.

A commotion, a flash of green and suddenly Bev is there at her side, grabbing her arm with one hand, waving her high-vis jacket above her head with the other. Silence falls as the drivers cut the engines and the bulldozers shudder to a halt.

'What the fuck?' one of the drivers shouts angrily, disembarking from his cabin and striding towards them.

He is interrupted by an almighty roar.

'*DO NOT* swear at us!' Bev thunders.

The other driver joins him, waves his finger angrily.

'Lady, you're not allowed . . .'

Bev brings the thunder again. '*DO NOT* tell us what we are allowed to do. And *DO NOT* point your finger at us!'

Atta girl, Janet thinks and watches Bev stare the man down till his hand drops to his side.

'This is public land.' Janet's voice is steely. 'We have every right to be here. We're not leaving. If you want to flatten these allotments, you'll have to flatten me.'

There is noise . . . a cheer? She turns and catches her breath.

Standing behind her is an army of gardeners. Patrice is at the front, her eyes fixed on Janet. Lakshmi stands next to Patrice; then Ken, smiling, teary-eyed. Checked Shirt is there, Rosa too, Sanjay pumping his arms skyward. They are all there.

And right beside Janet is Bev.

Eyes fixed on the drivers, Bev says, 'Pay close attention to my friend Janet. This is a woman who knows everything there is to know about plants, including untraceable poisons. This is a woman who knows how to track down your darkest secrets. This is a woman who knows how to stand her ground and survive come hell or high water. I wouldn't take her on, mate.'

The drivers look at each other and shrug. One driver leans back against his bulldozer, takes out a pouch of tobacco and starts rolling a cigarette. The other turns away, pulls out his phone. It won't be long before word gets back to Marsh and his cronies and they retaliate. But right now, Janet can't entirely focus on any of that. *My friend Janet*, Bev said, as if it was the most ordinary thing in the world.

Gardeners raise their voices in another cheer.

'We're all with you!'

'Yes, what should we do?'

As she looks at the band of gardeners, Janet realizes they are talking to *her*. They are looking at *her*. Indeed, Patrice is looking at her so intently Janet can barely take in the others. But they are all there, supporting her – even the Power Ballads and the Steer Manures. All of them, trusting her, waiting for her direction. She suddenly realizes it's not just about saving the allotments; it's about saving the allotmenteers. Plants. And their people. She has to get it right. Janet hesitates. She has got it so wrong before.

Bev leans in. 'I think your troops are awaiting instruction.'

Janet falters. She'll say the wrong thing, do the wrong thing. She looks back at Bev, shakes her head doubtfully.

Under her breath, Bev whispers, 'Janet, you're odd as socks but you're a force to be reckoned with. Blast them with it.'

And Janet knows what they must do. She looks to Patrice's face in the crowd. Meets her gaze, holds it.

'We need to keep the faith,' Janet says. 'We have to believe in each other and in our plants. Plants are the original settlers. They were here first. Plants are the greatest force of life on the planet; we depend on them for the food that we eat, the air we breathe, for shelter, for medicine, for warmth. Life itself. This land is theirs and no one is taking it without a fight.' Gardeners nod their heads in agreement, united.

'Plants stand their ground in all weathers,' says Janet, 'and so must we.'

There is a silence. A robin trills a full-throated whistle.

'If we want to keep these allotments, we've got to fight for them. PROTEST AND SURVIVE,' Janet's voice rises to a shout.

'Like Greenham!' Patrice cries.

'Or Occupy,' says Lakshmi.

'If they want to raze Seaview, they'll have to go through all of us!' Rosa shouts, linking arms with Ken.

'Too right!' Ken calls out.

Other gardeners who have just arrived start to break through the cordon and join them. Some, including Felicity bloody Kendal and Mickey, hover at a distance.

'Let's do what we did at Greenham!' Patrice says, throwing her arms outwards.

'Weren't they all lesbians?' FbK wrinkles her nose.

'Make a human chain!' shouts Patrice.

'What good will that do?' jeers Mickey.

Patrice is already humming 'Chant Down Greenham', her eyes shining.

An awkward semicircle forms between the bulldozers and the rest of the allotments. Everyone is looking at Janet.

'Spread out,' she commands, 'occupy as much space as possible.'

The semicircle morphs into a messy oblong as people pull in different directions.

'We look pathetic!' someone says, and Janet has to agree. They need something to anchor them, like the canes securing her plants. They need something to help them hold their ground. Tools!

'Go to your sheds,' Janet instructs. 'Grab whatever large tools you have – spades, rakes, hoes – get as many as you can and bring them back here.'

Gardeners sprint across the allotments, returning with armfuls of tools. Ken grabs a border fork and suddenly looks ready to clobber any invader.

'Our arms aren't instruments of violence,' Janet says, 'they are tools of cultivation. They represent who we are: strong, resilient gardeners who will protect the life we tend and nurture. Our protest is peaceful, our eyes on the future!'

She sees Bev hoist a spade skywards, her face strong, fierce. Standing her ground indeed.

One by one gardeners raise their tools to the sky.

Mickey and a couple of his cronies watch them, arms akimbo, smirking.

'A few spades and a load of OAPs,' Mickey says. 'They'll be quaking in their boots.'

But no one listens to Mickey; in fact, no one hears him because another voice breaks through, deep, slightly tremulous but resonant. Patrice, head thrown back, is singing.

'We shall not, we shall not be moved
We shall not, we shall not be moved

*Just like a tree that's standing by the waterside
We shall not be moved.'*

For a moment Janet almost forgets where she is, so caught up is she in the sound of Patrice's voice, but then other singers join in – Lakshmi, Rosa. Something about holding spades and rakes seems to give everyone a sense of purpose and the anthem gains force.

'*Just like a tree that's standing by the waterside,*' Janet hears Bev sing out lustily, '*We shall not be moved.*'

Janet shuts her eyes for a moment and listens to the music. It isn't Rachmaninov, that's for sure. The melody is iffy and Ken is wildly off pitch. And yet, when she opens her eyes and looks around, she sees a land army, united.

Janet takes a breath, grips the hoe in her hand and joins in.

'*Just like a tree that's standing by the waterside . . .*'

22

As the day progresses, word of the protest spreads and to the delight of the gardeners new recruits arrive thick and fast. Lakshmi and her twin girls bring poster board, spray-paint and markers. Soon a selection of handmade signs flutter across the allotments like flags:

Save Seaview! Stop Capitalist Gentrification! Defend Green Spaces!

The social media crew, also led by Lakshmi, circulates news of the demonstration along with accompanying photos of the protesters. Phones soon start to chirp with messages of support.

Janet admires how quickly Bev integrates herself into the allotment community. She feels a sense of pride that Bev, *her friend*, is so personable. It also makes her more aware of her own social inadequacy.

'How the heck do you do it?' she asks after watching Bev chatting away to another group of gardeners. 'You already know everyone's names!'

Bev shrugs. 'Och, they're a friendly crowd.'

'It doesn't come naturally to me,' Janet says, and toes a tuft of grass with her boot.

Bev considers for a moment.

'You can't be a good midwife without being able to connect with people quickly. It comes easier to some, sure, but it's also a skill you can develop, like anything else. You have to work at it.'

Janet shrugs.

Bev goes on, 'You let people see a different side of you today and look how they responded – they were all happy to follow your lead.'

A loud roar reverberates across the allotments and Sanjay starts waving his rake back and forth and pointing. 'Look! The bulldozers are going! We won!'

A huge cheer goes up and gardeners wave signs and tools in the air triumphantly as they watch the bulldozers retreat. Only Janet seems untouched by the jubilation sweeping Seaview.

'What is it, Janet? What are you thinking?' Bev asks.

'The real bun fight hasn't even started. This land is worth millions. Marsh isn't going to be put off. He'll strike again. It's just a matter of how and when. We need a more solid defence. By which I mean we need an *offence*.'

'OK, but for now, take the win! Look how you've galvanized everyone!'

It is true, Janet has connected with more people today than she has in the seven years since she got her plot. In fact, it seems that the only person she hasn't had time to chat with is Patrice, who is constantly surrounded by dozens of people or being interviewed by Lakshmi for social media posts.

Patrice is also busy sharing a litany of protest songs, and soon many allotmenteers, including Rosa, Ken and Sanjay, are fluent in 'We are Gentle Angry Women (Singing for Our

Lives)' followed by 'The Women's Army is Marching'. Whilst the singing and sign-making creates a convivial mood, party-like after the departure of the bulldozers, Janet knows that if they are really going to stand their ground the protesters will have to keep vigil through the night. As dusk falls many gardeners make their excuses, promising to return in the morning, but a few diehards volunteer to continue the occupation overnight. Sanjay suggests that they move their line of defence eastwards to encompass the pizza oven and be handier to the compost toilet. Patrice champions the idea.

'The warmer we are, the better fed we are and the more fun we have, the longer we can hold out,' she declares. 'At Greenham there was always singing and dancing and plenty of hot meals to keep us warm.'

Patrice makes a few phone calls to her friends at the cafe to organize food whilst Lakshmi contacts a small envoy via social media to bring blankets and sleeping bags. Rosa phones her husband and instructs him to get her home-made pepper pot soup and rhubarb crumble out of the freezer and bring them over.

Calor gas stoves are collected from sheds and groups of gardeners huddle round the dancing blue flames, chatting, drinking tea. As the evening progresses, teas and coffees are replaced by bottles of wine and flasks of whisky, and more singing.

When Bev heads off, she makes Janet promise not to stay out all night.

'You're still recovering from a nasty cold and the temperature is going to drop tonight. I expect to see the light in your bedroom window on by nine p.m. at the latest.'

'Message received,' says Janet, affronted and pleased in equal measure by her curfew and the idea of someone looking for a light in her window.

'Janet?' Patrice walks towards her.

Janet is suddenly tongue-tied.

'Thank you for this.' Patrice gestures out to the little camps of protesters dotted over the allotments.

'I hope it makes a difference.'

'It already has. It's lifted people's spirits. And it's so good to have you back; I was getting worried something had happened to you! Come join us.'

Janet looks over to the band of gardeners grouped around Patrice's camping stove and nods.

'I can't remember the last time I stayed out all night,' Patrice says, as the two of them join the group. 'Must have been Greenham, 2000. I was one of the last protesters to leave. I wear that as a badge of honour!'

Janet glances across the campfire at Patrice. She can easily picture her at Greenham, keeping the women's spirits up, leading them in song with her remarkable voice.

'My kids love to camp in the back garden, in the summer,' says Lakshmi. 'I get the tent out, their pillows and blankets and teddies, and they think it's super fun. Funny, it never occurs to me to join them!'

Janet studies the moonlit faces around her. Lakshmi and Sanjay are young, thirty-something, but many of them are middle-aged or older. Rosa and Patrice are probably in their mid-sixties and Ken must be well into his eighties. Today all these people stood their ground together with her. She feels a glimmer of pride to be part of the circle.

'We're getting a lorry load of likes on Twitter,' Lakshmi

says, head bent over the glow of her screen. 'Especially this picture of you, Janet!' She hands Janet her phone.

'What picture?'

'I hope you don't mind me posting it – look how popular it is, though. See how many likes you have!'

'So many what?' Janet peers at the screen. What exactly is she supposed to be looking at?

'Here, see this little heart icon? See how many likes there are beside it – five hundred and twenty-eight.'

Beneath the heart, Janet sees yellow smiling faces, rainbows and more hearts in different colours. Do people not use actual language any more?

'You've been retweeted, *loads*!'

'Is that good?' It certainly isn't something Janet has ever aspired to.

'It's fab! It all helps raise the profile of our cause.'

Janet peers at the tiny screen, looking at an image of a woman marching directly into the path of bulldozers. She doesn't recognize herself. Her shoulders are thrown back, head lifted, the silver of her hair gleaming like a medieval knight's helmet. In contrast to the old family photo, Janet's whole face is visible, her jaw firm, eyes blazing, chin jutting forward. Good grief, was she really that close to the bulldozer blades? Is it really her? She brings the phone closer. Yes, her mouth, her eyes, her hands clenched in fists. *You're a force to be reckoned with*. Janet feels a thump of pleasure as she hands the phone back to Lakshmi. She catches Patrice looking at her and feels her cheeks hotplate. Amazing how much heat those Calor stoves put out.

'Do you think this will change things?' Sanjay asks as he

helps Rosa distribute steaming bowls of soup and then settles himself between Janet and Ken. 'I mean, all respect to you, Patrice, but Greenham never got the bomb banned despite all those years of protest.'

'RAF Greenham is closed. The cruise missiles are gone. The fences are down. I'd call that a pretty good result from a group of unarmed women camping out,' says Patrice, 'even if we didn't achieve world peace. *Yet.*'

People spontaneously burst into applause, which Patrice acknowledges with a gracious nod.

'The point is we're taking a stand,' Lakshmi says. 'Everyone has been so gloomy since we first heard the news from the Council. But now look at us!' She holds up the picture of Janet and the bulldozers. 'We're crushing it! I'll take solidarity over despair any day! And look at the support coming from the community.'

'Our voices count,' Patrice says. 'I don't regret one day at Greenham. Like the wise man said, "Even if I knew that tomorrow the world would go to pieces, I would still plant my apple tree."'

'David Attenborough?' Ken asks, tucking into his soup.

'I believe it was Martin Luther,' says Patrice. 'Though I'm sure David Attenborough would agree. This pepper pot soup is amazing, Rosa, thank you! Reminds me of my mum's cooking. And the crumble smells delicious – I have to save room.'

'All grown right here at Seaview,' Rosa says proudly. 'The callaloo and okra in the soup, the rhubarb. I grew it all from seed.'

As people tuck into their supper, Janet thinks of Rosa planting those seeds in her plot, tending them over the weeks and months and finally harvesting them. And now they are not only being eaten, but shared. The thought satisfies her as fully as the food itself.

'Blimey, that's hotter than the hob of hell.' Ken wipes sweat from his brow with his hanky. 'That'll keep me warm tonight! Makes you think, doesn't it, about all the food people have grown right here on this one patch of land.' Ken gives his face another dab then watches the glowing flames of the Calor stove. 'The Allotment Army – that's what they called us during the war. And you know what? It really felt like we were part of the fight, out in all weathers digging for victory as hard as we could. I was so proud to be a part of it, even though I was just a kid, picking caterpillars off cabbages and digging up spuds. We were keeping our families and the country alive, putting food on our tables.'

'Our cafe depends on produce from the plots at Seaview,' says Checked Shirt, whose name turns out to be Anya. 'You should see the queues at lunchtime. For some of our refugees and unhoused people, it's their only meal of the day.'

'Whatever happens to Seaview, we're going to keep the cafe going,' Patrice pledges.

'I remember the day one of the fishermen spotted a Belgian steam tug out at Fairlight,' Ken says. 'It was right at the start of the war. The boat was full of refugees, old men, women and kiddies. A few of the children were younger than me and I was only a lad. They'd come all the way from Belgium on that battered excuse for a boat. They told us they saw Antwerp go up in flames behind them as they left – imagine that! Their homes on fire, everything they'd ever known gone. We gave them baskets of carrots, potatoes, cabbage – rhubarb, too, come to think of it. Made them as welcome as we could.' He shrugs. 'It's the least we can do, isn't it? Extend a helping hand to people in need.'

'It is.' Patrice passes Ken a steaming mug of tea and Janet notices how she gives his arm a quick squeeze.

Ken cradles the mug in his hands, still staring at the flicker of the stove.

'I remember Mum saying that working on her plot during the war kept her from losing her mind. All she heard on the wireless day in, day out was death and destruction, and every night she listened to the sound of doodlebugs dropping on Hastings. Planting seeds in the ground and watching them grow felt like the only sane thing in a world gone mad, she said.'

There's a murmur of agreement and the group falls silent, save for the scraping of spoons against bowls, the chinking of cups, the hiss of the flames.

'I think I know what your mother meant,' Sanjay says quietly after a moment. 'For me, it's the simple things. Sometimes I feel so powerless in the face of world events, you know? I watch the news and feel such a sense of hopelessness. But on my plot, I can *do* something positive, cultivate things.'

'You did a lovely job restoring that old greenhouse,' Patrice says.

A man with a Saint George's Cross tattoo who Janet doesn't remember seeing before pipes up next. 'My granny's garden in Eastbourne was full of camellias. They're the first thing I planted when I got my plot here. The smell reminds me of her.'

'My plot gives me space to just *be*,' Lakshmi sighs. 'There is literally not a single space in our house that's mine – not a room or cupboard or even a bookshelf. My girls have more private space than I do. But my plot here, it's just for me. I can do whatever I want, plant anything, arrange my tools the way I like them – not how my husband thinks is most logical. And I can come back the next day knowing all my things will be just as I left them, that my watering can has not disappeared into my daughter's bedroom to be draped in tinsel to stand in as the carriage in "Cinderella"!'

Everyone laughs.

'Don't get me wrong,' she says, 'I love my family. But when I come here, I feel such a sense of . . .'

'Peace?' Patrice offers, and Lakshmi considers.

'More like independence,' Lakshmi says after a moment. 'Even when it is pouring with rain I can sit in my shed, drink a cup of tea and think with no one tugging at me or shouting for me. I can just be me for an hour or two.'

Patrice lifts her battered enamel kettle off the stove and pours water into a large teapot. She slowly circles a spoon in the pot.

'What about you, Janet?' she asks gently.

Janet feels herself instinctively pulling back into the shadows. Giving instructions is one thing, sharing personal stories is quite another. But she invokes Bev's words: *it's a skill you can develop . . . you let people see a different side of you today*. She clears her throat and says, a little gruffly, 'There's something about planting seeds, seeing them take root and grow that gives me a sense of anticipation, a feeling of hope.'

Around her, gardeners nod in agreement.

'I feel the same as you,' she hears Rosa say. As Rosa starts to unspool her story, Janet feels her body relax. She has become part of 'we'.

Her plot has been her little life raft, giving her something to hold on to. Now she feels its dimensions shift and expand. There are others here alongside her. It feels more like the deck of an ocean liner.

She just prays they all survive the icebergs ahead.

23

Despite Glynis's instructions not to telephone unless it's an emergency, Janet, impatient as a mayfly at dusk, has broken down and left two messages – suitably cryptic, of course – but hasn't heard any more from her. Though increasingly anxious, as she arrives at the allotments the next morning she is cheered by a robust and fresh-looking group of protesters already in place, relieving the night-shift stalwarts.

'Janet,' calls Lakshmi, bustling over and putting a warm hand on her shoulder. 'We're trending on social media. As of this morning #saveseaview has over a thousand followers! And the *Hastings Independent* is promising to do a feature today! Pensioners camping out to save their potatoes turns out to be total catnip to the press! A local radio station is sending out a reporter to do roving-mic interviews, so we'll definitely want a vox pop from you, Janet – you're our poster girl. Oh, and get this! I've heard that *South East Today* might get a TV crew over from Brighton this afternoon to highlight the protest on the evening news tonight! Can you believe it?'

Before Janet can answer, Lakshmi bounds off to the gate to update the next arrival.

Passing Patrice's plot, Janet lingers for a moment looking

at the clutter of chairs, the upturned crates and buckets still grouped in a circle from last night. The shape of the Calor gas stove is pressed into the grass like a full moon.

~

At lunchtime Janet takes a break from the protest to put in half an hour on her plot. Her Russian sage, which is starting to lean, needs attention. Janet pulls her ball of jute twine from her apron pocket, grabs a bundle of medium-length sticks from her shed and sets to work. It is only when she fumbles with the knot for the third time that she realizes how anxious she is.

By the time Bev arrives, face flushed, eyes bright, each one of Janet's plants shows to its best advantage. Janet wipes a line of perspiration from her forehead and surveys them proudly.

'I couldn't wait to get here today! It feels great to be in the fight!' Bev says. 'What can I do?'

Bev has something of the fell night about her, but with less anger, more exhilaration.

'I know you have other battles to fight,' Janet says.

'I do. But right now, I am supporting my friend in hers,' Bev says simply.

My friend, there it is again, like a bee landing on a flower – so mundane and so exquisite.

'And it's not *not* my fight. I can't tell you how many of the new mums have told me about the stress relief gardening gives them – how it helps them with postpartum depression, and anxiety. I've already drafted a letter to our local MP about it! And guess what, Janet . . . I've got the printer at work cranking out flyers about menopause well-being. When we've saved Seaview, you can help me change women's healthcare in East Sussex – how does that sound?'

'If we can save Seaview, I'll fight for whatever the hell you want.'

Janet is still waiting for Bev to admire her freshly titivated plot. But Bev is looking back over her shoulder.

'When I was coming up from the gate, I saw a lady protesting who looks at least ninety. She can't weigh more than a tin of beans, but she's down there holding a huge sign that says *Mother Earth Shall Not Be Moved!* Isn't that great? And when I asked her which plot was hers, she said she doesn't have a plot! She just comes here to chat to people. I had to stop myself from "doing a Mum" and throwing my arms around her.'

Bev beams at Janet. 'Right, we've been delayed by bulldozers and biohazard tape, but will you finally do me the honour of showing me your plot? I've been admiring quite a few on my way in. They make me think of the little worlds you catch a glimpse of for a moment walking down the street in the evenings when people have turned on their lights but haven't closed their curtains.'

'You make it sound like *Rear Window*.' Janet wipes damp palms on her apron. What does her plot reveal about her? She had planned to lead Bev round, pointing everything out, giving its genus, describing its healing properties. Instead, she stands rooted, watching Bev make her own way. Bev is like a child searching for treasure at the bottom of the garden.

'I didn't know what to expect,' she says when she has

finally explored every bed, 'but it feels unexpectedly familiar.'

'I can assure you my plot is nothing like the others!'

'No, I mean, familiar to *me* – it's a bit like being at work.'

Janet frowns.

A pair of sparrows chatter to each other self-importantly then flutter off in search of food.

'Look.' Bev points at Janet's row of cloches, their bodies protectively arched over trays of seedlings. 'These are like our little NICU incubators, and here' – she points to a line of lolly sticks stuck into the earth – 'every patient tagged and dated—'

'So I know when I planted them . . .'

'All tucked in with cotton wool!'

'Keeping them warm,' Janet says. Perhaps it did look as if she were performing some kind of horticultural obstetrics. She shifts uncomfortably.

Bev nods happily. 'I mean, if you had a choice, this is where you'd want to come, isn't it? If I was one of those' – she points to a row of sorrel – 'I'd be really chuffed if this was where I ended up. You'd know you were getting the best possible care: flannel on the forehead, lavender on the pulse points, ice chips to suck – the absolute best care.'

Janet looks up. 'So . . . you like it?'

Bev turns to her. 'It's perfect. I mean, look at these!' She points to Janet's intricate Russian sage lattices. 'They're like wee crutches! Aren't you clever?' She tilts her head to one side. 'It must be hard.'

'Fiddly more than hard. Really you just have to have the patience to—'

'I mean, hard to face losing all this. When you care for something this much, it hurts.'

'Yes.'

'Well, I'll tell you one thing, we'd better bloody well make sure that git Marsh doesn't get his hands on your allotment.' Bev takes out her phone. 'Which reminds me: Lakshmi has roped me in to help with the social media and I wondered, can I film you?'

Janet's response is direct and immediate.

'Heck, no!'

'You'd be great!'

'I'd be hopeless.'

'You won't.'

'I will.'

Bev folds her arms, stares at Janet.

Janet folds her arms, stares back.

An impasse.

The sound of singing floats up from the protesters. Patrice must be back.

'We'll face them with refusals
We'll face them with song
We'll blockade their bases, sit silent and strong . . .'

Bev tries again. 'I think you could really connect with people.'

'I haven't connected with people for years,' Janet shoots back.

'You connected with me,' Bev says.

Janet uncrosses her arms, reties her gardening apron, then eventually says:

'Go on, then.'

Bev sets up the shot with Janet in the foreground, her plants behind her. Bev presses record, mouths, 'Go.'

Janet stands stiffer than a bamboo cane, staring fiercely ahead.

Bev hits pause. 'What's wrong?'

'What should I say?'

Bev smiles encouragingly. 'Why don't you tell us who you are and then say something about your plot.'

Janet nods.

Bev lifts her phone again. 'And . . . Go!'

Iron-faced, Janet guns the words at the camera: 'I AM JANET PIMM. THIS IS MY PLOT.'

Bev lowers the phone. 'That was good, but . . . could you maybe try and look a bit more *relaxed*?'

'How can I relax when you are pointing that thing at me?' Janet gestures crossly to the phone.

'Imagine you're talking to me.'

'I *am* talking to you!'

Janet shifts awkwardly, deadheads a couple of nearby flowers. Bev tries again.

'Just tell me about your plants, why you planted them, why they are important to you.'

Janet furrows her brow, thumps one hand inside the other.

'Can't you just ask someone else?'

'Listen, imagine you are taking a group of friends round your plot – just me and Patrice, for example – and you're pointing out all the things that you've planted and telling us about them.'

Janet's face clears. 'Oh, you mean like a *tour*?'

'Aye! Exactly like a—'

Janet holds up her hand, flutters her eyes closed and tilts her head. When she opens her eyes, her face is transformed. She looks directly at Bev behind the phone.

'Hello,' she says, her gaze open, her voice warm. 'Welcome to JP's Tours! I'm Janet Pimm and this is my allotment.'

And she's off, leading the way along her beds of basil, spearmint, marjoram, pointing out fine details so that Bev can come in for close-ups. She makes visible endless hues of green and shares fascinating snippets about herbal remedies. She explains how the tiny herb eyebright makes an excellent tea, that the Greeks believed it could restore lost vision. She describes how the bowl-like structure of the evening primrose means that it functions like a satellite dish, receiving and amplifying sounds. 'Like little ears, really,' she says. 'In fact, when the primrose hears the buzzing of a bee, she sweetens her nectar with extra sugar! Brava, yes? Indeed, brava!'

There is something for everyone and every so often Janet turns and makes eye contact – not effusive but attentively keeping her audience with her.

'At twilight,' she says, as if she is reading a bedtime story, 'the garden needs time for itself, time to settle. Plants have their own circadian rhythms; some get up early whilst some do the night shift. Some put in a full day, like the anemone, who works an industrious eight a.m. to six p.m. – though on a dull day you might have to give them a poke; they can be fair-weather friends! The dandelion is the teenager of the plant world – opens at ten a.m. and shuts shop again at noon, hence their name: go-to-bed-at-noon! Evening primrose is a night owl and red flax is an early bird.

'Plants can work magic. Did you know that *Dictamnus fraxinella* exudes such a cloud of oil on a warm night that you can make a lantern from it? Or that *Silphium laciniatum* has leaves that point north and south so rigidly you can use it as a compass? Or that poor old *Caesalpinia pluviosa* is always weeping?'

Janet smiles at the camera, imagines her little flock following her on her tour. 'I hope I'm not putting you off with the Latin names? Noble though they are, sometimes the common name of a plant can be even more beguiling. For example: weasel's snout, poor man's treacle, sauce alone – is there a better name for wild garlic? Here's another: water blinks – doesn't that sound like a plant you would like to pass the time of day with? I know I would! Slender hare's-ear, sneezeweed, stinking goosefoot – you know that fellow is going to pong! Herb twopence, ploughman's spikenard – excellent for lung complaints, by the way! Great leopard's-bane and the garden becomes a jungle, true lover's knot and kiss-me-quick and now it's a spot for romance!'

Janet hunkers down in her herb bed, her hands cupping a plume of basil.

'Plants know we're here,' she says, suddenly whispering. Bev draws closer. 'They can feel us. So don't be shy – reach out, touch them.' She stretches her hand towards the camera lens of the phone. 'But handle with care! The *Mimosa pudica* is so sensitive that too much handling can make the dear little thing collapse from shock.'

255

Janet straightens up and makes her way to her rosemary bush. Gently she curls her hand around one of its outstretched branches, breathing in its scent. The silvery grey of its needles matches her hair.

The rosemary is for Adam, of course, for remembrance. Rosemary was the first thing she planted on her plot. It is always with her, keeping her company, evergreen.

'Plants can help us heal,' Janet says quietly. She gestures out towards the sprawl of verdant plots and Bev pans slowly round. 'In the nineteen-forties, volunteer gardeners worked on this very allotment, digging for victory for all that they were worth. During the war, allotments just like this one provided one-fifth of the nation's food. These plots saved lives.'

Janet takes a step closer and looks directly into the camera lens. She opens her mouth. No words come out. Bev holds steady, waits. From the hawthorn, noisy sparrows chatter. A light breeze moves across the allotments. Janet takes a breath.

'We say that we look after our gardens, that we tend our plants, but the plain truth of it is – our gardens look after us. We all have a finite time on earth, some of us only the briefest moment. I have come to realize over the years that we have to make the most of this fleeting moment we share right now, together, on this green planet.'

Janet exhales slowly. Bev is staring at her, eyes full. 'I think that's about all I've got . . . Unless you'd like a tour of Mickey's hairy gooseberry balls?'

24

The following day the protesters wake to lidded skies that promise a downpour. There is an unfortunate morning rush hour at the compost toilet, which leads to several people going home to freshen up, but not always returning. Showers fall steadily all afternoon. The throngs of supporters from the community who lined the allotment fence the day before are thin on the ground and the *South East Today* TV news crew fails to materialize. Inside the gates, the number of allotmenteers currently occupying the site is down by half. As the remaining gardeners prepare for another night of occupation, many look haggard, and spirits are markedly lower.

Patrice, however, is blooming. Nipping home briefly for a wash and brush-up (and to get the six-person tent from her garage), she comes back sporting a bright-red bandana, which is tied jauntily around her neck. Under her white shirt she wears a faded T-shirt with the slogan: *The power of the people is stronger than the people in power.* When Janet catches sight of her she instantly imagines a young Patrice, protesting at Greenham, full of energy and passion, fighting for what's right. The bandana definitely suits her. She's as resplendent as a red horse chestnut tree in candle.

The forecast predicts a chilly night and Lily Barton, ninety-three with a bad hip but a powerful community spirit, has offered to donate a trunk full of blankets if someone can come and pick them up.

'I'll go,' Bev volunteers. 'Come with me, Janet. We can pick up the blankets and stop off at home for a minute to grab some more provisions.'

'Fine.' Janet is keen to check if Glynis has been in touch. There is no flashing green light on the answering machine in the hallway and no letter or card on the mat. She decides she can't wait around any longer and phones Glynis again. Still no answer. Has Glynis abandoned her? She leaves a message, using loosely veiled references to Flopsy, Mopsy and Cotton-tail, updating Glynis on the state of play at Seaview and asking her to get in touch as soon as she can. She can barely conceal the tension in her voice.

Janet refills her Thermos and, instead of packing two biscuits in her Lakeland 'Biscuits for One' snack container, rakishly stuffs the whole packet of Bath Olivers into her pocket.

On the way back, the car wedged with blankets and home-made quilts, Bev stops alongside the Hastings Council building and glares up at it with the intensity of a dentist studying an X-ray of a cracked molar.

'Musing on the sublime beauty of brutalist architecture or plotting a break-in?'

'Neither.' Bev's eyes are luminous headlights in the dark evening. 'My brain's been spinning since our adventure, and do you know what I think?'

'I feel sure you are about to tell me.'

'I think attention should be paid. Bollocks to the government for ignoring the needs of menopausal women and for not seeing to it that *all* GPs get proper training about something that *half the population goes through*!'

'Good point.'

'And bollocks to Pete Marsh bulldozing over everyone to line his own pockets. And bollocks to anyone who doesn't see or listen to or value women of a certain age! Or any bloody age, come to think of it!'

She turns to Janet, eyes blazing. 'Ever since that night in the storm, Janet, I've been thinking, if I'm going through the bloody change, I am going to embrace it. Leverage it. I'm going to do things differently.' And with that, Bev grabs her handbag, propels herself out of the car, then heads towards the Council building.

Janet follows, eyebrows tilted in expectation.

Bev stands scrutinizing the grey concrete wall, lips pursed.

'What do you have in mind?' Janet says. 'Are we making Molotov cocktails to lob over the parapets? Do you have a quart of Navy rum in that handbag? Should I start foraging for glass bottles?'

'Dear God in Govan, no!' says Bev. She unclips her bag, withdraws a large handkerchief and proceeds to tie it tightly over her nose and mouth. 'Sounds like you know how to make one, though!' Her wide eyes stare at Janet over the top of her mask and her voice is slightly muffled.

She dips into the handbag again and presents Janet with another handkerchief. 'Pop this on.'

'Are we going to hold up a stagecoach?'

Suddenly Janet feels something cold and metallic pressed into her hand. Looking down, she sees a tin canister with a parakeet-green lid. She peers at it. *Highly Flammable.*

'Spray paint!' Bev announces. 'I swiped a couple of cans from the sign-making group. Green for you. And this for me.' Bev pulls out a matching canister with a florid purple lid and starts vigorously shaking it up and down. The mixing ball inside the can makes a satisfying rattling sound.

'Suffragette colours,' says Janet, nodding at the green and purple. 'So, your idea is . . .?'

'Remember the other day in that traffic jam outside Tunbridge Wells? That wall covered with graffiti? You said something about if people were going to graffiti a "big canvas", why the heck didn't they actually say something worthwhile.'

It does sound rather like her.

'Well, now's your chance.' Bev's eyes gleam as she gives the can another vigorous shake and flips off the lid.

Janet looks around. The street is quiet, dark, but someone could come round the corner at any moment.

'Much as I applaud your spirit, I feel I should point out that graffiti is considered an act of criminal damage. You can get an unlimited fine.'

'*Unlimited* fine!' repeats Bev. 'Wow. I didn't know that.' She gives her can another shake, puts her finger on the trigger, and takes aim.

'The way I see it,' says Bev, 'they're the ones committing acts of criminal damage.'

'The Council?'

Bev shrugs. 'Everyone in power who doesn't actually know or care a damn about the people they're supposed to be representing. We pay our taxes, obey the rules, generally do the right thing whilst they break their own laws left, right and centre! I think it's high time we sent them a message, don't you? Loud and clear.' Bev raises her voice, 'And basically BOLLOCKS to anyone who tries to stop us! I'm embracing the change, Janet, watch me!'

There is a whoosh, a fiery smell and a sudden streak of purple hits the wall.

Bev gives a little shudder. 'Now that feels *good*! Try it, Janet!'

Janet unholsters her tin. There is a hiss, a fiery smell and a stroke of green crosses over Bev's purple: a kiss, a target, the cross hairs of a rifle.

Janet feels a surge of excitement, considers for a moment, then takes aim, fires again.

Majorana hortensis, she writes in huge sprawling letters, *anti-inflammatory and antioxidant. Beneficial to hormonal health, especially for women.*

'What does marjoram look like?' Bev's eyes sparkle.

'Tiny ovate leaves, round and glossy on a longish stem.'

Paint shoots from Bev's can and hits the wall, creating a fair illustration.

'Brava!' Janet nods approvingly and sets to work on sharing another gem. *Salvia officinalis*, her green paint twirls on the wall, *used since ancient times for warding off evil and boosting female energy.* She instructs the illustrator: 'Two-lipped flowers in whorls, forming simple racemes.'

Bev frowns. 'And another word for *racemes* is . . .?'

'Basically, little branched spikes with purple flowers and

261

a green stem.' Janet sprays a curve of green; Bev adds the purple flowers. It's a bit out of proportion, but close enough.

She raises her can again but freezes. A car's engine rumbles; the prongs of its headlamps veer towards them like a couple of searchlights. Grabbing Bev's arm, she pulls her into the shadows.

'Press yourself flat against the wall! Don't move!' Janet hisses as the car roars past, leaving the street dark and silent once more.

Janet's heart castanets in her chest. 'Let's speed this up and get out of here before we get caught!'

'Right, then. Next!' Bev commands.

Oenothera biennis, writes Janet, *relieves PMS symptoms, minimizes breast pain, reduces hot flushes*. 'Lanceolate . . . I mean lance-shaped leaves in a tight rosette; four bi-lobed petals.'

'Bring it on!' Bev cries.

Clitoria ternatea, writes Janet, *memory-enhancing, antidepressant and aphrodisiac*. 'I'll leave you to work that one out.'

'Now you're talking!' shouts Bev, and gives a wolf whistle. 'Haven't got any of that knocking about on your plot, have you, Janet?'

Janet stands back to admire their work.

The wall pulsates with words and images, alive with medicinal plants. Really rather magnificent.

'We should sign it!' Bev cries, raising her can again. 'Tagging. Like real graffiti artists!'

'I'll just remind you of the unlimited fine.'

'Something a wee bit incognito, then.' A crease of a frown ripples across Bev's forehead as she considers.

Suddenly her eyes widen. 'Got it!' And with a quick shake of the can, she takes aim once more and flourishes a signature. She turns to Janet. 'Well, what do you think?'

'*The Invisible Women's Club*,' Janet reads, and gives a slow smile.

'Perfect, right? Woo – I'm a bit dizzy.' Bev steadies herself against the wall. 'We should probably get away from the fumes.'

'And the crime scene!'

Bev takes a moment to add '#saveseaview' before nipping back to the car. She turns on the headlamps, lighting up the wall. 'Wow,' she breathes, a reverent hush to her voice. 'It looks like a stained-glass window in a church.'

'Really?' Janet retorts. 'Because I have yet to see a church window featuring detailed depictions of *Clitoria*.'

Beside her, low vibrations shudder, like the rumbling of the Underground. Janet turns to see Bev shaking with laughter.

'Aye, neither have I,' Bev gasps. 'But now you mention it, I'd bloody well like to!'

Janet feels her own body start to judder and as the women peel away from the scene of their crime, the car reverberates with laughter. *Roar*, thinks Janet. Isn't that what people say? Because that is exactly what this feels like, a wild, full-bodied roar from her very depths. The revolutionary call of female laughter. And what does it sound like? Like a peal of bells. Bells ringing out across the land.

Suddenly it hits Janet. She can't afford to wait for Glynis any more.

'If we want to save Seaview, we need to be like our friend *Clitoria*; we need to self-pollinate.'

Bev glances across at her. 'Which means what exactly?'

'It means we have to prove Pete Marsh planted the knotweed. People always make a mistake. We just have to find it.'

'Righty-o.' The car zips along the dark streets. 'So how will we do that, then?'

'Well, it rather looks as if we're going to have to break in to his house.'

25

Early next morning the bulldozers roll back on to Seaview and destroy the whole of the wildflower corridor, leaving a battlefield of shorn and broken bodies in their wake. But a greater shock hits the gardeners as the bulldozers blindly plough through plots 4 and 5. Vegetables and flowers are pulverized and an ancient apple tree that has stood as long as anyone can remember is uprooted and lies on the ground, its felled branches still holding their brand-new spring leaves. Patrice does her best to comfort Hamid, who has lost his entire crop of vegetables, and Gillian and Daisy, the two sisters who have worked their plot for the past decade and whose lilac and butter-yellow tulips had just started to open. The mood on the allotments plummets. Half the protesters put down their signs and instead start to clear out their greenhouses and sheds, dig up their perennials in earnest. The singing stops.

Janet knows they have run out of time. She needs to strike now.

❧

'Right,' Janet says, panting a little as she and Bev walk up the steep hill to Chillington Court. 'According to today's schedule for Council proceedings, Marsh is chairing a town hall meeting this afternoon, due to start in . . .' She checks her watch. 'Six minutes. Given the agenda, it should take a good hour.'

'What's on the agenda?'

'Car parks and dog mess,' Janet explains. 'No two things more guaranteed to get the British populace aerated. Might even overrun if we're lucky. But we should err on the side of caution and try to get this done and dusted in half an hour or less.'

Janet pulls a piece of paper from her pocket, unfolds it, quickly peruses her notes.

'The security system was installed when the housing complex was built, but it's a pretty standard edition. I don't think it will cause us any problems.'

Bev stops. 'Security system?'

Janet links Bev's arm, propels her forward. 'I bet he hasn't even set it. Wants a new place with all the bells and whistles but can't be bothered to read the instructions. Probably doesn't think anyone would have the audacity to break in. I had a look at the sales particulars of the properties and there is a segregated pedestrian gate; it's a CSG 10700 hinged automatic so there will be a code . . .'

'Which we have?'

'Which we don't have, but that won't be a problem.'

'JFC, you're confident. My heart's going like the clappers.'

'We're different. You've got people skills. Think of it as biodiversity. The more diverse the system, the stronger it is.'

'I'm not sure that "people skills" are at the top of the list for cat burglars, but thanks.' Bev takes a breath and picks up the pace. 'I know I said I was all about embracing change, but my stomach seems to have been taken over by an Olympic gymnast who is giving it her all on the vault – she's just done a round of flic-flac with a half-turn!'

'Nerves keep your senses sharp.' Janet peers at Bev, frowns. 'I see you're not wearing your trademark chlorophyll.'

'My what? Oh, my high-vis. Well, no, I thought I should try and dress the part, so I went for all black. In fact, I also brought these.' Bev pulls two pairs of taupe tights from her bag and hands a pair to Janet.

'Exactly what would you like me to do with these?' Janet asks.

Bev glances around cautiously and then says in a loud whisper, 'I thought we would put them over our heads.'

'Over our *heads*?' Janet looks askance. 'Why on earth would we do that?'

'To disguise ourselves,' Bev hisses.

Janet barks a laugh. 'We don't need disguises – we've got our superpower.'

'Our superpower?'

'Invisible women, remember? Come on!'

As they approach the electronic pedestrian gates to Chillington Court, Janet slows her pace. She bends, re-laces her boot and folds up the hem of her trouser legs to reveal a compression bandage around her calf.

'Oh no – is your ankle hurting again?'

Janet doesn't answer, but leans on Bev and limps

awkwardly towards the gate. A man in a bike helmet is on his way out and holds the gate open for the old lady and her helper.

As he pushes off on his bike, Janet lets go of Bev, stands tall and forges ahead.

'Always full of surprises,' Bev says.

'That Tubigrip came in handy, and, after all' – Janet winks – 'I got it from a medical professional!'

Chillington Court is comprised of soulless identical houses, all with imposing porticoed doors on streets named after birds of prey. They pass along Harrier and take a sharp right on to Falcon before reaching Marsh's street, Condor.

Finding where Marsh lives had been relatively simple. Patrice had mentioned that he was in the new development built over the old rec. Janet could probably have worked it out for herself with just a cursory glance at the insipid, lifeless construction that is Chillington Court: remote-controlled garages, ugly-as-sin gravel driveways and anaemic paint-jobs. Finding the actual street Marsh lives on proved trickier, but she got there eventually through a spot of estate-agent-website cross-referencing of properties taken off the market around the time Marsh took up his position on Hastings Council. Two properties in Chillington Court had sold, one on Harrier, the other on Condor. Harrier had gone for 5k over asking and had a beech tree in the garden; Condor had gone for 20k under and was pure 'blush' patio. What she doesn't know and hasn't shared with Bev is that she still isn't sure of the house number, the crucial detail the estate agent left out of the particulars. There are only four houses on Condor, so that's good. Unfortunately, they are all identical in shape, colour and design. It's impossible to know from the estate agent's photo which is Marsh's.

The first house on Condor has a wheelchair ramp outside the front door, the last one a swing set in the garden, so that narrows things, but the middle two are a matching pair: faux-wood blinds, gravelled driveways, unspeakable topiary. It could be either. Janet looks from one to the other.

'Everything OK?' Bev stands beside her.

'Which one, which one . . .' Janet takes a breath, clenches her jaw, and follows her gut.

'Walk with confidence,' she mutters to Bev.

Bev obeys and as they reach what Janet hopes to hell is Marsh's front door, Janet rootles in her pocket as if for a key, pulls out a hairpin, slips it into the lock and applies gentle pressure whilst sending up a quick prayer.

Both pressure and prayer are answered as the lock clicks and the door opens.

'JFC!' Bev exclaims. 'How did . . .?'

Janet taps the side of her nose and Bev's hand flies to her mouth.

'Did they teach you this at GCHQ?' Bev's lips move behind her fingers, her eyes perfect circles.

'Need-to-know basis,' Janet says, slipping the hairpin back in her pocket, relishing the rare chance to be a woman of mystery. No need to bore Bev with the various YouTube videos she had watched into the early hours last night or the number of hairgrips she ruined as she practised on her own front door. Thankfully she has quite a collection of grips, as they have proved remarkably handy over the years for training her star jasmine.

She pokes her head through the doorway, checks the alarm system. Not armed. Thank heck for that. What looks like a change-of-address letter from the NHS lies on the doormat. Pete Marsh's name is on it – she got the right house. Phew! There are only so many break-ins she can tackle in one afternoon.

'Coming?' Janet stands inside Marsh's hallway looking as if she is inviting Bev in for tea.

'Remember, fast and forensic,' Janet instructs as she closes the front door. 'We'll start upstairs, take one room at a time, cover as much ground as carefully and quickly as we can. Search the places you least expect to find things – including the most obvious places.'

'Like the sock drawer? Eddie always hides my birthday present in his sock drawer.'

'Sock drawer, wardrobe, bathroom cabinet. Everything. Look for anything that could be even remotely connected to Seaview, to Bringley's, any property portfolios, even Council stuff, because if he's keeping it at home rather than at work there will be a reason.'

'My life of crime is about to reach its zenith,' Bev says, as she follows Janet up the taupe-carpeted stairs. 'Liquorice wheels down my pants pale in comparison!'

Marsh is aggressively neat. His shirts, perfectly laundered, hang obediently on metal hangers alongside shark-grey suits. His underwear drawer is full of mathematically folded boxers and spheres of socks. Shoes stand side by side in officious rows.

Bev searches Marsh's jacket and trouser pockets but comes away empty-handed.

'If someone wanted to trace my movements it would be so easy. Every time I pull on a pair of trousers or my coat, even my uniform, there's a receipt or a bus ticket or shopping list in the pocket! Not so our Pete.'

Janet looks through the chest of drawers, under the mattress. A Kindle lies on his bedside table. Janet takes a cursory glance – the complete œuvre of Jeffrey Archer. Figures.

Bev appears from the en suite bathroom. 'Is he married?'

Janet is hunched on the floor, peering under the bed. 'Divorced.'

'Girlfriend?'

Janet looks up. 'Could be, why?' She ducks back down to continue her hunt.

'Well, it's just that I found this in the clothes hamper.'

Janet pushes herself up again. A white bra dangles from Bev's outstretched hand.

'Bev! We're looking for property portfolios, Council folders, paperwork connected to Seaview or property developers – who cares about the underwear!'

Bev does, it seems, as she is still examining the bra.

'The thing is, it looks like one of mine – a bit worse for wear, but you keep it because it's a comfy fit. But would a woman leave an old bra like this in her new boyfriend's clothes hamper?'

Perhaps Bev has a point, but they need to keep moving. Janet glances at her watch, fast and forensic.

They shift their search to the guest room, which is even more minimalist.

'There's still a price tag on this.' Bev points to a bedside lamp. 'Marsh isn't just tidy, it's like he lives in a showroom – apart from the dirty laundry.'

'Enough about the laundry!'

'If you were breaking into my house, you'd need a pneumatic drill to work through all the layers of our stuff. Neither Eddie nor I are particularly tidy. And I've still got so many of Mum's bits and bobs.' She sits on the bed and picks up one of Marsh's perfectly pristine pillows, turns it over. 'Doesn't look like he's ever used this room. So no guests or visitors. It's funny, isn't it, what your home says about you?'

Working quickly, Janet opens a chest of drawers – every single drawer is empty. Curious. Then again, what would someone think if they broke into her house and saw all her things in boxes, her bare cupboards, her unused spare room? A life half lived?

Bev is right. Marsh's house is more like a showroom than a real home, or not a showroom exactly, more like . . .

'It's like a *set*,' Bev declares, staring round, 'a theatre set, like the shows down at the community centre.'

Yes, that's exactly what Marsh's place feels like. A facade, a pretence. What the heck is he hiding?

'We need to search downstairs.' Janet heads towards the landing, but when she turns, Bev is still sitting on the bed, her hands in her lap.

'You know, Janet, our trip got me thinking about a lot of things, particularly about how I want to spend my time going forward.'

Janet looks at her watch. Right now she would like Bev to spend her time helping her search the rest of Marsh's house.

Bev sits back, crosses her legs.

'Do you remember me saying that there are rooms in my head Eddie will never enter?'

Janet would like to say that there are rooms in Marsh's house that she is keen to enter swiftly. Instead she says, 'Yes.'

'Well, since I've been back I've been asking myself: is that Eddie's fault or mine? If I don't want to let him in, that's one thing, but if I do . . .'

'You need to *open some doors*?' says Janet, pointedly.

'Exactly! So we've talked a lot, more than we have in a long while, about us, about what we both want. I've said I want a proper date night once a week.'

'What did Eddie say?'

'Totally up for it. Loves the idea. I think when I was away, when he didn't know where I was, it really frightened him. You can forget what you have sometimes, can't you? And if you lose sight of what's most important, you risk losing it altogether.'

Janet leans in the doorway. She has suffered two great losses in her life – her true love and her beloved boy. And whilst losing Adam was, according to Bev, beyond her control, there are no two ways around the fact that losing Nancy was entirely her own fault. Cowardly. Futile. Self-destructive. Maybe that's why she's let herself drift, why she's kept herself at arm's length all these years; she didn't think she deserved love.

'Our place isn't swish like this,' Bev goes on, gazing about the bedroom, 'but it's like us, Eddie and me: what you see is what you get. One of the reasons I fell for Eddie – apart from the sex – is that he's so honest. Dependable, like that aspidistra, remember? That might not sound romantic, but I think it's what I love most about him. It's good to be reminded.'

Janet turns back towards the stairs.

'What about you, Janet? Has there been anyone special since . . . Brian?'

'Can we have this heart-to-heart another time, please? We need to crack on here before Marsh comes home!'

'Anyone at the allotments caught your eye?' Bev presses on.

'I'm going down,' Janet snaps. But she hovers on the stair.

'The thing is,' Bev says, 'I thought at my age it was probably too late to make a new best friend, but it turned out it wasn't. So, following that line of thinking, it's never too late to fall in love, is it?' Bev holds the moment then pushes herself up. 'I'm just going to have a nosey through the medicine cabinet and I'll be right down.'

Downstairs, Janet opens the door to a liver-coloured room she imagines Marsh calls his 'den'. One wall is given over to a gigantic plasma TV; a giant leather couch stretches in front of it. Janet makes for Marsh's desk at the far end of the room, where cream folders are stacked in a neat pile. She rifles through them systematically. All seem above board: minutes, planning applications, policy documents. All rather blah de blah.

What on earth was Bev doing, going on about someone *special*? Probably a bout of nerves, an adrenaline rush. What were her words? *It's never too late to fall in love, is it*? Janet tries to focus on the documents in her hands.

A noise outside startles her. Janet freezes. A man's voice.

It's too early for Marsh to be back. Someone talking on their phone? Her heart thumps against her chest. The voice fades. Probably the next-door neighbour. Still, it takes a moment for her heart to find its regular rhythm. *Focus, Pimm.*

She rifles through the files once more, her fingers shaking slightly. There is nothing interesting here – though she is curious about the unusual amount of hard copy. Most people store everything on their computers nowadays, don't they? Janet once worked with an archivist who told her it was impossible to get rid of digital data entirely. Despite the reassuring crunch as you drag a file to the waste-bin icon and click delete, digital artefacts always leave a trace. If you have the right tools, the right know-how, practically anything can be recovered. *It's actually very hard to disappear*, he said. Not if you're a seventy-two-year-old woman, Janet thinks.

Janet spots a paper shredder crouched under the desk. She hunkers down, gasping at the assault to her knees and ankle but determined to find the smoking gun that will save Seaview. But the shredder is empty apart from a few curls of paper.

A noise from upstairs. Janet straightens up, calls out, 'All right up there?'

'Yes. Sorry,' Bev shouts down. Janet glances at the time. They should get out soon, just to be cautious. She rifles through the rest of the folders but finds nothing of note.

French windows lead out from the den to a paved 'garden', completely covered with patio stone to stifle any natural growth. Janet shudders. A path follows along the side of the house back round to the front door. Nothing worth searching out here – Marsh has probably never even been outside.

Where next? The garage. Accessed from a door inside the den, the garage is suspiciously pristine. A metal filing cabinet glints like a knife in the corner. Strange place to keep one's filing. Why isn't it in the den with the rest of his office things? She tugs a drawer. Locked. Slipping a hand into her pocket, Janet pulls out another hairgrip. She pushes it in as far as it can go, turns it clockwise and then counter-clockwise a couple of times. Nothing.

'Come on, you blighter,' she mutters, and tries once more, turns the grip clockwise again, slower this time, and breathes out as she feels it slide into place. She jiggles it back and forth to release the locking mechanism. One, two, three, four, five . . . and it gives. Huzzah! A standard five-pin lock, then, nothing too tricky. Turning the hairpin clockwise once again, she hears the locking mechanism collapse, a sound as comforting as hot water filling a teapot. The drawer slides open, revealing a flotilla of cream folders. She withdraws one and leafs through. Bumph to do with Chillington Court: grounds maintenance fees, electric bills, gas, water . . . And then she sees it: none of these documents are addressed to Pete Marsh. The house isn't in his name. Is he subletting? The addressee seems to be an organization or corporation. Not Bringley's, but Kandox Holdings. Could they be connected?

She strokes her chin. 'I wonder . . .'

She opens another folder and finds property details on a £2.2 million house in Marbella. *Hola!* Janet has often regretted studying German instead of one of the Romance languages. But she is in luck because these details are in English.

> 7 bedrooms, 6 bathrooms, lounge + dining room, kitchen, games room, laundry room, office, wine cellar, 4-car garage, exterior swimming pool. Andalusian patio with orange trees, garden with fruit trees (orange, lemon, kiwi, grapefruit, mandarin, tomato).

'A tomato plant isn't a fruit tree, you twits!' Janet says under her breath. Six bathrooms! Whatever next!

Another sound from outside. Just a car. But Janet is edgy now. Don't get distracted; always keep your eye on your exit strategy. She needs to get Bev's phone, photograph these documents, then get the heck out. They clearly need to find out more about Kandox Holdings. Is Marsh planning on purchasing this palatial property? It would make sense of the Chillington house's transient feel. This vapid new-build is just a stepping stone to a bloody great mansion in Spain. And where will he be getting the money from to finance such a purchase? A nice deal with Bringley's as he offers up Seaview Allotments' prime seaside real estate? It would fit, but it's speculative. She needs more, something concrete.

The kitchen is the last room left and Janet doesn't hold out a lot of hope. She goes through cupboards, shelves, drawers. Looks in the oven. The fridge is one of those giant American models speeding up global warming. Inside, the usual suspects: eggs, milk, a packet of bacon. There is also a bottle of 'buttery' Chardonnay – good God, where is the man's self-respect? She is just opening the salad crisper when Bev appears, red-faced, fringe damp against her forehead.

'All right?'

'Yes, sorry, I'm having another power surge . . .'

'Here.' Janet hands her the Chardonnay.

'Oh, thanks. Um . . . perhaps after we finish, though . . .'

'Not to drink! To cool down.'

Bev clamps the wine bottle under each of her armpits in quick succession. 'That's better.'

'Give me your phone, Bev. I need to photograph some papers.'

'What did you find?'

Janet suddenly puts a finger over her lips 'Shh . . . What was that?'

'I didn't hear anything. Hold on, I'll take a peek.' Bev returns the wine to Janet and darts off to the hallway. Moments later she is back, her face bright crimson. 'JFC!' she gasps. 'It's Marsh! He's on the, on the . . .' She desperately searches for the word.

'On the *what*?' Janet chivvies.

'On the . . .' Panic lights Bev's eyes. She starts to mime a long oblong shape.

'What on earth is that? A rolling pin?'

Bev shakes her head.

A crunch of gravel.

On the driveway.

Janet stands immobilized, her mouth as dry as a bag of fuller's earth, as Pete Marsh puts his key in the lock.

*

Several things happen in quick succession. Janet shoves the wine back in the fridge, grabs something from the crisper and pulls Bev out of the kitchen, into the den. Pushing Bev behind the leather sofa, she drops down beside her.

Time behind the sofa moves excruciatingly slowly. Have they been here a minute or an hour? Water drips off Bev like a monkey brush vine after a rainstorm in the Amazon. They hear the fridge door opening, wine being uncorked, a glugging noise. Bev points to her armpit with horror. The door to the den opens and Pete Marsh comes in.

The flat-screen TV bursts into life. Marsh channel-hops from *Antiques Roadshow* to a nature programme to a football match. Football wins. At least the sound of the crowd might help cover the sound of Bev's panicked breathing.

How are they going to get out of this?

A microwave pings and Marsh returns to the kitchen, buying them a moment of time.

Bev shoves her phone into Janet's hand.

'Get the photos,' she hisses, eyes wild, face glossy with sweat. 'I'll be your wing woman.'

'How?'

'I'm the people person, remember.'

Before Janet can respond, Bev scuttles across to the French windows, slowly slides them open and slips out, disappearing round the side of the house just as Marsh returns, a plate in one hand, glass of wine in the other. He sits on the sofa, facing the screen.

His phone rings.

'Hey, babe! No, just in. Gonna watch the game.' He aims the remote, turns down the volume. 'Nah, those tossers

279

can't find their way out of a paper bag – postponed till next week . . . I wouldn't call it a protest, just a lot of OAPs and middle-aged frumps having a strop. I've called in a couple of favours – it'll be over soon. I should be able to fly over at the weekend and then we can celebrate—'

The doorbell rings.

'Babe, gotta go. What? . . . Sure, I'll grab some from the duty-free shop at the airport. You too. Bye.'

Marsh gets up, goes out to the hallway.

Janet bolts across to the internal door to the garage, slips in and pulls open the filing cabinet. She can hear Marsh opening his front door.

There is a menacing pause and then Janet hears Bev's voice.

'Well, hello there!' Bev stutters. 'I'm . . . I'm from . . . from . . .'

Janet steels her jaw, her hands, fists, every toe clenched. *Come on, Bev, you can do it, you can do it.*

A rustle of papers. A silence. Then the sound of a throat clearing, and Bev's voice calm and controlled: 'I'm Bev Bytheway from the East Sussex Consortium for Women's Menstrual Health. Your name has been passed on to me as someone in our community who is extremely committed to women's menstrual health.'

Janet gives a sudden snort of laughter. Claps her hand over her mouth.

'Mental health?' she hears Marsh reply. No doubt he has slapped his friendly councillor-about-town smile on.

'Men*strual*!' Bev clarifies.

'Oh . . . and *my* name came up?' Janet picks up a shift in register in Marsh's voice.

280

Quickly laying out the documents on the garage floor – the Spanish house particulars, anything with Kandox on it – Janet holds the phone to her face. Where is the view-finder? How is she supposed to take a photo with this thing?

'Yes!' Bev is saying. 'And we are all very grateful for your support, Councillor Marsh. We are campaigning for an end to the tampon tax, which I am sure you feel as strongly about as we do, flexi working days for women during heavy flow . . .'

Janet can imagine Marsh reeling his smile in.

'. . . and, of course, mandatory menstrual awareness training for all GPs.' Bev is in her stride now.

Where the heck is the button? Janet's fingers skate over the surface of Bev's phone. Something happens and the screen is filled with her own face, glaring down; she skitters her fingers again and now she seems to be capturing slow-motion video of herself. What's wrong with a good old-fashioned Nikon?

'Right.' Marsh's voice is brisk and businesslike now; he wants to get rid of Bev. 'If you'd like to leave your literature, I'll take a look. I'm afraid I'm a bit busy right now, so if you'll excuse me . . .'

Time is running out; sweat slicks across Janet's lip, her heart quickens. Bev isn't going to be able to distract him much longer.

'We're also campaigning for more comprehensive HRT treatment on the NHS,' Bev soldiers on.

'Oh?' Marsh is sounding prickly now, eager to get away.

'Hormone replacement therapy. Do you know that three in every five women are negatively affected at work as a result of the menopause? And that one million women in the UK leave their jobs every year as a result of menopausal symptoms that could easily have been treated?'

'Listen—'

'Did you know that women eligible for senior management roles often leave work at the peak of their careers due to menopausal complications? When they could have simply been prescribed HRT? Did you know *that*?'

Janet finally figures out how to work the camera and rapidly documents the papers, almost spilling them on the floor as she puts them back in the drawer, heart hammering in her chest. Janet pushes the drawer closed and shudders a sigh of relief as she hears the lock automatically click back into place.

'Hormone replacement therapy,' Bev continues undaunted, 'is made from yams now, thank Christ! They gave women in my mum's generation the urine of pregnant horses! I mean, how would you like it if a doctor prescribed *you* pregnant horse piss to take *orally*?'

Janet would pay good money to see the expression on Marsh's face right now. She slips carefully out through the French windows and bolts round the side of the house.

Ducking down behind an extremely unattractive wodge of artificial hedging, Janet peers through the 'branches', ready to come to Bev's rescue if needs be. Bev is still parked on Marsh's doorstep, chatting away with all the verve and commitment of a Jehovah's Witness.

Come on, woman! Get out of there! She gives the branches a rustle, calls a low birdlike 'woo woo'.

'Now HRT is mostly transdermal. Anyway, I know you're a busy man, so to conclude,' Bev starts to wrap up, 'we're looking for bright young things to redesign the sanitary bins in the public lavatories on the prom – talk about square peg in a round hole, right? Who isn't sick of banging their legs on one of those sticky bins? And so tricky to open to put the used ST or tampon in! So do let us know if you've got any ideas there. On behalf of fifty-one per cent of the population, I thank you so much for your commitment to menstrual health!'

Bev crushes a wodge of her home-made flyers into Marsh's hand and leaves him standing in his doorway looking like he has his arm in the business end of a birthing cow.

As soon as he closes his door, Janet and Bev half limp, half speed-walk in silence to the gates of Chillington Court and back out on to the streets of Hastings. It isn't until they are halfway down the hill that they slow their pace and look at each other.

Bev is electric. 'Oh my stars! I think my heart is going to beat its way out of my chest.' She clutches Janet's arm. 'Did you get the photos?'

'I did.' Janet turns to face her. 'You were magnificent! Magnificent!' She erupts with laughter. ' "How would you like it if a doctor prescribed *you* pregnant horse piss?" '

'I'm on fire!' Bev says. 'Help ma kilt, I could really take to a life of crime. Vigilante midwife, fighting for the common woman . . . Do you think we've got enough to stop him?'

Janet runs her hand along her jaw. 'I don't know. We need to get these photos to Glynis. She might be able to use them. She was adamant about old-school post but we just haven't the time, we have to risk it – can you text them to her if I give you her number?'

Bev nods, her fingers already moving over her phone screen. 'I'll upload them to Dropbox and then send her a link with a coded message. Something about Flopsy?'

'Good. And I think you might be on to something with the mystery woman. But we've got to hurry – Marsh was talking about calling in some favours and I didn't like the sound of it. These bastards obviously play dirty.'

Janet's stomach contracts.

They need to get back to the allotments.

26

Police cars flank the gates of Seaview and shock-faced supporters watch as an officer with a loudhailer orders everyone occupying the site to 'LEAVE NOW OR YOU WILL BE ARRESTED.'

Janet grabs Bev's wrist, motions to her to backtrack up the road.

'We can't leave them!' Bev looks at the protesters, holding their signs, blankets draped round their shoulders, worry scored across their faces.

'We're not leaving,' Janet hisses, 'we're going in through the gap in the fence further up. It comes out just beyond the compost heap. Come on!'

Crouching low, the women make their way around the perimeter fence until they come to the gap. They push their way through branches of privet and, for the second time that day, break in. Staying close to the ground, Janet and Bev sidle round the back of the compost heap.

'Janet!' a loud whisper.

They turn to see Patrice coming towards them.

'I thought I saw you!' Her face is lined with fatigue, her bandana skew-whiff, but her chestnut eyes shine with a fierce light.

'The police got here about ten minutes ago, threatening to arrest everyone who doesn't clear off. Two more bulldozers have arrived.'

Janet thinks of Marsh, the 'favours' he was pulling in.

'Arrest them for what exactly?' Janet asks.

'Trespassing.' Patrice roughly runs a hand through her hair.

'This is still public land – you can't trespass on public land,' says Janet.

'I know, but the police are calling it a biohazard zone and they're being really aggressive.'

Janet hesitates; she doesn't want to upset Patrice, but she doesn't want to keep secrets from her any more. Patrice is the Allotment Chair; she deserves their respect. She's earned it.

'I found this' – Janet takes a small freezer bag out of her pocket – 'in Marsh's possession earlier today.'

Bev peers at the contents. 'You took his asparagus?'

'It's not asparagus,' says Patrice, studying it. 'It's knotweed – rhizome and shoots!'

Janet turns to Patrice. 'Look, you probably don't want to know where I got this . . .'

'I probably don't.' Patrice looks at Janet. 'But go ahead and tell me. I'm not doing this by the book any more. They certainly aren't. Fight fire with fire.'

'I found it in Marsh's salad crisper – never mind how I came to be in his house. Knotweed is gynodioecious, correct?'

'Yup.' Patrice nods. 'Doesn't germinate outside of Japan.'

'And for the non-gardeners here,' Bev says, 'gynodio-whatsit means?'

'Gynodio*ecious*,' says Janet. 'Comprising both female and hermaphrodite variants.'

'Both of which are needed in order to reproduce, in the usual manner,' Patrice adds.

'But only the female variant was imported to the UK,' Janet says.

'So there's no seed dispersal,' Patrice adds.

'But knotweed *does* spread through rhizome fragments, stems and crown,' Janet says, rattling her bag.

Bev holds up her hands. 'Bottom line – can we go to the police with that?'

'I don't think so,' says Janet. 'We'd have to explain where we got it . . . and how.'

'But maybe it's enough to convince a few of the other councillors that Marsh sabotaged the allotments so he could sell off the land?' Patrice says. 'If we can win some of them over . . .?'

The megaphone barks, 'THIS IS YOUR FINAL WARNING: LEAVE NOW OR YOU WILL BE ARRESTED.'

The women look at each other.

'Protest and survive?' Patrice asks.

Janet and Bev don't miss a beat.

'Protest and survive!' they cry in unison.

∾

'This is public land!' Patrice shouts at the police. 'It belongs to everyone!'

'YOU ARE TRESPASSING IN A BIOHAZARD ZONE. THIS IS YOUR FINAL WARNING.'

'This is a national disgrace!' Ken shouts to the officer

with the megaphone. 'What kind of a country is this if you can't even stage a peaceful protest to protect your vegetable patch? Not the one my dad fought for, that's for sure.'

An officer makes a show of taking out a pair of handcuffs, standing ready. The gardeners confer. Wearily, they start to put down their signs, pick up their belongings and make their way to the gate.

Lakshmi comes over to Patrice.

'I can't afford to get arrested,' she says. 'I have to think of my girls.' She shakes her phone in her hand. 'But I'm going to post the hell out of this; it will be all over Twitter and Insta! Speaking of which, #saveseaview is blowing up on social media! We're connecting with some great allies out there. And look at this pic my sister Sangita sent.' Lakshmi turns the screen of her phone towards Janet and Bev. 'Horticultural graffiti right there on the Council's wall! Done by some group called the Invisible Women. Heard of them?'

'They sound rather daring,' says Janet, poker-faced.

Bev, pink-cheeked, nods her agreement. 'Braw lassies.'

'I know, right?' says Lakshmi. 'I'd become a member of that club for sure!' She wishes them luck and makes her way to the crestfallen troop of gardeners who file out of the gate amidst cries of support from well-wishers.

Only Patrice, Janet and Bev remain inside the biohazard tape boundary.

'Come along now, ladies,' the officer calls, putting down his loudhailer. 'Off you go.'

'Never could abide that term,' Janet mutters. '*Ladies*. Sounds like a public convenience.'

'Me neither,' Patrice says. 'And do you know what? I'd rather be a public *inconvenience*.'

The officer jingles a set of handcuffs. 'Tick tock.'

Patrice turns to Janet and Bev. 'You don't have to come with me, but I have to do this.' Patrice starts walking, slowly and steadily, towards the officers at the gate.

'That's right,' the officer says. 'And you two ladies, come along now. Follow your friend.'

Janet and Bev stand their ground and watch Patrice near the gate.

'Poor Patrice,' Bev says. 'This must be killing her.'

But Janet smiles, because she sees the glint of a key in Patrice's hand. Another member of 'the club' in action? Suddenly Patrice darts left, seizes the wheelbarrow lock-up chain, wraps it around her torso and chains herself to the equipment shed.

'She's pulling a suffragette!' Janet rushes forward as fast as her tender ankle will allow.

'Wait for me!' Bev cries.

Patrice wraps the chain taut around the tangle of their three bodies, locks the padlock and throws the key into a nearby compost heap.

From the other side of the perimeter fence phones snap and flash.

'No photos!' an officer shouts at the crowd, but few take any notice. Lakshmi has commandeered another phone from somewhere and is simultaneously filming the crowd with one phone and talking animatedly into another.

'I need a camera crew down here NOW,' she shouts.

The two officers retreat to their car to confer with each other. One makes a call, whilst the other rummages in the boot.

'Bugger,' Patrice says, watching the officer stride back

towards them with a pair of bolt cutters. 'This calls for a Greenham move. Let's make our voices heard in the time-honoured tradition of women speaking truth to power! I'll kick us off.' She thinks for a moment and then smiles. 'This was always one of my favourites – feels appropriate:

> *'They can't forbid me to think*
> *And they can't forbid my tears to flow*
> *And they can't shut my mouth when I sing.'*

Patrice's voice soars over the shouts of the officers, spills across the allotments. Janet hears voices joining in, Rosa from the other side of the gate, Sanjay and Ken putting their practice with Patrice to good use:

> *'They can forbid nearly everything*
> *But they can't forbid me to think*
> *And they can't forbid the flowers to grow.'*

A loud cheer goes up from the crowd.

The officer approaches and grasps the chain forcibly.

'Your turn, Janet,' says Patrice.

For a moment Janet's mind is blank. She is damn well going to sing something; she won't let Patrice down. But what? And then it comes to her. A song from the compilation CD Bev kept playing on their road trip. Thanks to Smooth Radio, Janet now knows all the words:

'Oh no, not I, I will survive.'

She looks across at Bev, whose brows are raised in happy surprise.

'A wee power ballad, Janet?'

Why not!

'*Oh, as long as I know how to love, I know I'll stay alive.*'

Bev joins in, swiftly followed by Patrice, and the trio performs a soaring and spirited rendition of Gloria Gaynor's 'I Will Survive' as the police officer starts to cut the chain.

'Brilliant,' shouts Lakshmi, now filming with two phones.

'Encore!' the crowd bellows.

'Go floppy,' Patrice hisses as the bolt cutter severs the chain in two. The three women slump to the ground, heavy and flaccid as sacks of compost left out in the rain. The officers wrangle the women's wrists into plastic zip-tie handcuffs.

'Come on now, ladies, stand up. Time to go.'

'If you want us out, you'll have to carry us out,' Patrice retorts.

'Better take the big one first, Trowler,' the officer says, reaching for Bev.

'Aw, in the name of the wee man!' Bev cries indignantly as one of the men grabs her under the knees and the other threads his arms under her armpits. They groan a little as they lift her from the ground.

'Are you sure you wouldn't rather walk to the car, lady?'

'Protest and survive!' shouts Bev.

'This is undignified. Come on, love, act your age!' he says.

'Believe me,' Bev snaps back, 'I *am* acting my age!'

The policemen make their way slowly and awkwardly through the gates and to the car with the slack body of Bev. A growing crowd of allotmenteers and their supporters video and photograph the spectacle, calling out encouragement to Bev whilst booing the policemen.

'We'll get much better publicity this way,' Patrice says to Janet. 'Makes the police look bad – like they're using undue brute force on harmless "ladies" of a certain age.'

'Like the iconic image of Mrs Pankhurst being carried away from the gates of Buckingham Palace by a beefy police inspector,' says Janet.

'Exactly,' Patrice says.

'Patrice,' says Janet suddenly, her words coming out in a rush, 'I always meant to compliment you on your wasabi. They can be devilishly difficult to cultivate from seed but yours are rather lush.'

Patrice gives a deep smile of pleasure. 'That means a lot coming from you.' She holds Janet's gaze for a moment. 'I confess, I do like a challenge. And some spice.' She gives a wink, lifts her cuffed hands to her neck, straightens her bandana. 'Your plot really stands out from the crowd; it's actually my— Watch out! Here we go . . .'

The sweaty, red-faced officers grab Patrice and huff and puff with the effort of carrying her limp body to the squad car. By the time they get to the gates a TV crew is set up. Janet watches Patrice make an impassioned statement to the camera as the officers try to bundle her into the police car. Pride fills her chest.

'Oh, fabby, the TV crew did arrive!'

Janet turns to see Felicity bloody Kendal by her side.

'Where on earth did you spring from?'

'I just popped through the back gate – a friend of mine who works in media in Brighton tipped me off that *South East Today* were finally on their way. I just threw on the first thing I could lay hands on' – Felicity flutters a Chelsea Flower Show frock – 'and rushed down. I'd better go and talk to them – they'll need someone clean and well spoken to interview.'

'Right. Before you do that, would you mind just grabbing those secateurs and snipping this off for me?' Janet holds up her wrists. 'I'm afraid I got myself all muddled up in the sweet-pea ties.'

FbK picks up the secateurs. 'You certainly are in a muddle. I can't imagine how you did this. I never bother with sweet peas – too fiddly.'

'Oi, there's another one!' an officer shouts.

'She's cutting her loose!'

Both officers run towards Felicity, who freezes, drops the secateurs, serpentines round some raised beds and runs straight towards the TV cameras. The officers tackle her and bundle her, screaming, into the car.

Janet, still handcuffed, allows herself a little chuckle as she awaits her turn to be carried off the site under the full gaze of over a hundred smartphone cameras and a TV crew.

27

The custody officer, Sergeant Brownstone, a freckled-faced man with pendulous earlobes, informs the women of their rights.

'You have the right to legal advice,' he says.

'Our lawyer will definitely be advising us,' says Patrice. 'I texted her from the squad car.'

'Tell him,' Felicity pleads, 'that I have nothing to do with whatever you were up to!'

Janet smiles warmly at her comrade-in-arms, her sister suffragette. 'Oh, Felicity, you diehard – trying to get back on to the outside to lead the troops!'

'Clever!' says Patrice. 'Don't worry, Feliss – Lakshmi will take charge whilst we're in the clink.'

Felicity shrieks, 'Don't call me that! Officer, I am not with these women! You can't arrest me! My husband and I sponsored the police charity fundraiser last year!'

Sergeant Brownstone plods on. 'You have the right to tell someone where you are.'

'I think everyone has a pretty good idea,' says Bev. 'Did you see the size of the crowd filming them carrying us off the allotments? Lakshmi should have loads of great footage for all her social media feeds. We might make it on to the TV news! Eddie won't believe his eyes!'

'You have the right to medical help if you're feeling ill,' Brownstone continues.

'I do have rather a dodgy ankle,' says Janet, casting a quick glance round the police station. 'You don't have any gin, do you? Purely for pain-relief purposes.'

Sergeant Brownstone is not amused.

They are each allowed a phone call. Patrice calls the lawyer for the National Society of Allotment and Leisure Gardeners, Bev calls Eddie and Janet rings Glynis but the line is engaged. Janet tries not to feel let down by Glynis. Perhaps she expected too much. After all, who is Janet to Glynis? Just an acquaintance. Someone she worked with years ago. Maybe Glynis thinks she's going a bit dotty, wanting to play spy games.

'And now, ladies,' Sergeant Brownstone announces, and Patrice catches Janet's eye, 'you will be held in the detention suite until you are questioned and then charged or released.'

'I'd like my own suite!' Felicity bloody Kendal announces, as if she is booking a room at Claridge's. 'As I've clearly stated, I'm not with the others.'

The women surrender their personal possessions, which takes FbK considerably longer than the rest of them.

'I am most certainly not giving you my jewellery unless you can assure me it's going into a proper safe – this is twenty-four carat.'

A very young-looking officer leads them to the 'suite', which, despite its posh-sounding moniker, is a soulless whitewashed room with two flat bench-cum-bed structures along the walls cushioned with blue pads, a metal WC and a handbasin.

'I suppose this is why they call it a suite,' Janet says, motioning to the facilities. She sits down on one of the benches next to Bev.

'How long are we going to be here?' Felicity screeches.

Patrice settles herself on the other bench, pushes up her shirtsleeves, folds her arms. 'Unless things have changed since the last time I was in, they've got a maximum of twenty-four hours before they have to charge us or release us. The clock starts the moment the custody officer states we are being held, so' – she checks her watch – 'twenty-three hours and forty-five minutes, give or take.'

FbK gawks at Patrice open-mouthed. 'Since *the last time*. Are you saying that you have been here *before*?' She looks round the room, her face dripping with disgust.

'No. I've never been *here* before.'

FbK clutches her throat.

'Not in this lock-up. But I've been arrested loads of times. Let me see . . .' She leans back cosily and reels off previous arrests on her fingers as if counting trips to the garden centre. 'There was Reclaim the Night, of course – that was a good one! Then Equal Pay; both of those were up in London. I'm telling you, Feliss, the cells up there aren't a patch on this.' Patrice gestures round the room appreciatively. 'In Westminster we were fifteen to a cell and the loo was a bucket in the corner.'

Felicity leans weakly against the wall as Patrice continues with her litany.

'There was Greenham, of course. I was in and out of that police station like a fiddler's elbow.'

296

'I demand you get me out of here immediately!' Felicity shouts at the surveillance camera positioned in the ceiling.

'But on the bright side,' Patrice goes on, a twinkle in her eye, 'if we're in for the full twenty-four hours, we get two light snacks and a main meal – so perhaps think of it a bit like a long-haul flight to Australia.'

Felicity slumps to the ground in a heap of chiffon, head in her hands.

'I remember a gang of us got arrested on a real fire-cracker Labour Union march in Paris,' Patrice continues. 'That police station gave us *chocolat chaud* in the morning. Delicious. Cells full of smoke – then, everyone smoked like chimneys. Very atmospheric.'

'You can't beat the smell of French tobacco,' Janet says. 'Gauloises, blue packet.'

'Gitanes Brunes,' Patrice says, and nods accommodatingly. 'Each to her own.'

'The French even protest with style,' Janet says.

'*Bien sûr*.' Patrice smiles.

Bev turns to Janet. 'Do you think Marsh is the one who set the police on us?'

'I wouldn't be surprised.'

Bev lowers her voice. 'Do you think they could charge us for breaking and entering?'

'Don't forget criminal damage – the graffiti,' Janet reminds her.

Bev breathes out a long exhalation. '*Clitoria ternatea!*'

'And then there's the restaurant in Windermere. I believe it's called a "dine and dash".'

'Or, in our case, a drink and slink,' Bev says with a laugh. 'We might be in for life!'

'Our criminal behaviour is certainly snowballing,' Janet agrees.

'I always thought allotments were these easy-going places where people pottered around in old cardigans growing marrows. How wrong was I?'

'You've no idea the lengths some gardeners will go to for their crops.'

'I'll tell you something, Janet, I'm bloody glad I picked you up at the bus stop that day!'

'Me too,' says Janet.

How long ago it all seems, Janet thinks, Bev giving her the lift to Windermere, the two of them checking in to The Laurels, the ridiculous waiter at Ascotts. So much has happened so fast. And so much has changed. Including Janet. She thinks of the photo Lakshmi took of her storming towards the bulldozers, how she hardly recognized herself, jaw firm, eyes blazing. The thrill of firing green paint on to the Council's wall, the self-confidence she had breaking in to Marsh's house. And yet just weeks ago she was invisible, even to herself.

But never to Bev. Bev had seen her from the start. A plant can languish in a dark corner, but pay it a little attention, move it a couple of inches into the light and it can be transformed. In some ways it takes so little to change everything. Bev has helped deliver Janet back to herself.

'There is one thing I regret,' Bev says after a while.

Janet raises a brow.

'I really wanted to find the northern hawk's-beard for you.'

'You tried ruddy hard. And I'm sorry I was so rude to you.'

'Och, you were just upset.'

'I was rude. No excuses. The dandelion does indeed share many similarities with the northern hawk's-beard. It was an easy mistake. I'm sorry.'

Bev gives her hand a quick squeeze. 'Thanks, Janet. When we get out of here, let's go back and have another look for it. What do you say?'

Janet smiles, squeezes Bev's hand back. But she knows that the hawk's-beard was never what she was really searching for out on the fell. Part of her had always longed to go back, be braver, do things differently, even though that was impossible. She can't change the past. But she is learning to forgive herself, do things differently in the future. *All the women you have been and all the others still to come.*

She glances over at Patrice, who is leaning against the wall, her eyes closed. Her shirt is muddied, sleeves pushed back, her strong arms folded across her chest. Janet looks down at the palms of her own hands and notices how faint the scars from the rue are now.

~

Sergeant Brownstone is aware of a growing thrum of noise from outside the police station. Tired from the night shift, he is looking forward to clocking off soon and getting breakfast followed by a hot shower and a kip. The noise outside swells and when he opens the door of Hastings police station he has to stop himself from swearing out loud. The crowd surges forward, waving signs: *Beet the Corporate Slugs! Don't be Mean, be Green! Hostile Takeover!* A chap at the front in khaki shorts and jumper waves his fist defiantly. As well as the angry protesters, several members of the local press and the *South East Today* news crew are visible, flashing cameras and thrusting microphones forward.

'Any comment on the wrongful arrest of local allotmenteers?' a flame-haired reporter from the *Hastings Observer* asks.

'Are the police investigating the allegations that Hastings borough councillors are being blackmailed by property developers?'

Sergeant Brownstone holds out his hands in a placatory position and takes a step back. He needs reinforcements; this crowd is too big to handle on his own. Where is his relief? Constable Trowler should be in by now. Trowler nicked the damn women in the first place. Let him sort this mess out. But right now, Sergeant Brownstone has to play the hand dealt him. It is a bad hand, and it's about to get worse as suddenly the crowd parts and two women walk smartly up the steps of the police station.

One of them, a tall Black woman in an elegant suit and heels, gives Sergeant Brownstone a firm handshake. 'I'm Kelly Scott, the legal representative for Seaview Allotments, engaged by Patrice Winston. This is Lakshmi Banerjee, Acting Chair for Seaview whilst Ms Winston is detained. You are currently holding my clients over allegations of trespass on a biohazard site?'

'Correct.'

'I am here to inform you that is a legally bogus claim. The land is public and Seaview has not actually been declared a biohazard by the county – though someone certainly seems to have gone a bit mad with a roll of black-and-yellow tape. So you need to release these women. Now.'

'We were told . . .'

'I don't know who falsely instigated this arrest, but anyone can purchase biohazard tape on Amazon – maybe your officers should put their energies into investigating *that*.'

When the four women appear on the steps of the police station, looking somewhat worse for wear from their night in the cell, a huge cheer goes up from the crowd. Felicity, reunited with her possessions, quickly applies a slick of frosted lipstick and allows herself to be swooped upon by a hungry pack of local press.

'I have always believed with my whole heart,' she gushes, 'that we, the so-called "little people", must fight for what is ours, whatever sacrifices it may take. Think of the plucky women at Greenham, think of those brave suffragettes – what I did was really no more than following in their dainty but noble footsteps.'

Janet, Bev and Patrice stare at her.

'I imagine,' Janet says, 'that this is the first time Felicity bloody Kendal has ever aligned herself with the "little people".'

Patrice snorts a laugh. 'Won't be the last, though. She is going to milk this one for all it's—'

'Bev!' Patrice is interrupted by Eddie, who bounds up the steps two at a time and throws his arms around Bev.

Right behind him are Checked Shirt Anya, Rosa and Ken, who rush over to Patrice. Janet stands alone for a moment, then catches sight of Lakshmi coming towards her and smiles broadly. But Lakshmi's face is drawn, the corners of her mouth downturned.

She reaches out to Janet, takes her hands. 'I'm so sorry, we tried so hard, but we couldn't stop them . . .'

'Couldn't stop what?' Patrice says, coming over to join them.

'What's happened?' Bev is at Janet's side.

'Janet's plot.' Lakshmi's voice breaks. 'They bulldozed it.'

∼

It wasn't enough, Janet thinks as she takes in the torn-up roots, the churned earth, the pulverized bodies of her plants. Finding the transplanted knotweed, the trip to the Lakes, Glynis, breaking in to Marsh's house, getting arrested . . . in the end, none of it was enough. All those days digging, tending, planting, all for nothing. All that life gone – her lady's mantle, her thyme, her sweet marjoram, all destroyed. They've won again, those greedy men in suits, just like they did all those years ago back in GCHQ. They have eviscerated everything she's worked for.

Janet sinks to her knees in the debris of macerated leaves and roots and buries her hands deep in the soil. In the far corner her rosemary bush lies on its side, toppled. Its broken branches continue to scent the air as its roots weep sap.

'They won't get away with this,' Lakshmi says, snapping pictures of the devastation. 'I'm posting this right now, along with the other plots they destroyed. Our followers will be up in arms!'

But Janet barely takes in her words. It's over. Her delicate-petalled evening primrose, her spearmint, her soft-leafed sage – all gone.

Bev hunkers down, puts an arm around her. 'We can get it back to rights, Janet. Tell me what to do.'

'We'll all help,' Patrice says fiercely. 'We can replant it just as it was.'

Janet knows they are trying to make her feel better, but all she feels is tired, literally worn out; now that her plants have gone, it is as if she has been uprooted with them. She pushes her fingers deeper into the soil.

As she moves her hands in the earth something grazes the side of her thumb, a piece of rock churned up by the blades of the bulldozer. But when she looks closer she sees it is shards of wood and glass from her home-made cloche. Like everything else, it has been destroyed. Janet slowly starts to gather the fragments, doesn't want a night-time prowling fox or badger to cut their paw. And it is then that she sees it. A tiny shoot poking up through the soil. One of the seedlings she had bedded in the other day. No bigger than a whisker, but its tiny roots are holding on. Holding tight to its future.

And her own words flood back to her – about gardening being a sort of time travel, about having faith in the future.

After a forest fire destroys everything in its path, scorching the land, leaving it black and charred, fireweed appears almost overnight, its soft, downy blanket covering the damaged ground. Foxglove and bracken quickly follow. New growth is stimulated. Life prevails as it does right here in this small seedling boldly pushing its shoulders above ground, holding on, believing in its immense capacity for life. Janet smiles softly, stretches her hands out, hovers them just above the dark earth, feeling its energy, its force. What lies before her isn't barren wasteland. It is a fresh start. A new life.

∼

As they walk back home together, Bev stops to check her phone, which is pinging incessantly.

'JFC, look at this one, Janet,' she says, pointing to a photo of Janet stoically being carried off the site by the burly policemen.

Lakshmi has been as good as her word and Twitter and Instagram are flooded with dramatic images of the protest, the arrest of the women and the decimation of Janet's plot.

'She's done a fab job.' Bev goes on scrolling through the images. 'There are loads of pictures and so many . . . Oh!' Bev stops in the street, clamps her hand to her mouth.

'Everything all right?' Janet asks.

But Bev seems to have lost the power of speech and just stares down at her phone, wide-eyed.

'For heck's sake, what is it?'

Finally, hand trembling, Bev holds the screen to Janet.

'You've gone viral!'

28

Janet buttons her shirt after an invigorating hot shower. Life, she thinks, has a way of offering a turn in the road just when you are least expecting it.

Her story has exploded. Followers who relished the video tour of Janet's plot had been outraged at images of Janet being carried off in handcuffs. The anger turned to delight when they saw the photos of the women triumphant on the steps of the police station. But since Lakshmi posted the images of Janet's decimated plot, Twitter and Instagram have gone wild. People not only care about the plight of Seaview but feel a personal connection to Janet and her plants. Hashtags like #mimosapudicahavefeelingstoo and #theeveningprimroseislistening proliferate, and not only that but the posts seem to be spurring on a slew of actions and protests across the country: *No Dig on our Land! Green Rights!*

Gone viral? Janet ponders the term as she towels her hair dry. It's true she has caught sight of a couple of reporters lurking on her street – perhaps she really will have to get net curtains after all. Such a fuss. Hardly Profumo, or being hounded by the paparazzi, but still, *gone viral*. Extraordinary.

A loud knock at the door. Too early for Bev.

A reporter?

But it isn't Bev or the press.

Standing on Janet's doorstep in a dove-grey trouser suit, sporting a pair of shoes that remind Janet of two Viennese whirls, is Glynis.

'Well, haven't you been making a name for yourself, Pimm?' Glynis says. 'It's always the quiet ones – isn't that what they told us? May I come in?'

Glynis sits at her table sipping Golden Tippy Assam as if it is a perfectly normal occurrence.

'Moving?' Glynis eyes the boxes of crockery and linens still scattered around.

'Just sorting some things out,' Janet says.

'Right. Apologies for not returning your calls. Douglas ended up in the ICU. He pulled through, determined old bugger that he is.'

Janet notices the slightest clench in Glynis's jaw.

'We're staying with his sister in London for a few days – they're running some tests on him at Guy's, might be able to get him in on a clinical trial. Thought I'd take the opportunity to nip down here. I didn't forget about you, Pimm; Giulia has been on the case.' Glynis unzips a sleek navy leather briefcase, takes out a dossier and slides it across Janet's kitchen table. 'It's all here – bank statements, property holdings, travel logs.'

Janet fans the documents across the table like a winning poker hand and whistles low and long.

'So, Marsh *is* working for Bringley's. I knew it.'

'Hand in glove. Giulia was having a little trouble finding

a way into the paper trail until you advised me to look into the ex-wife – the old *cherchez la femme*.'

'My friend Bev worked that one out,' Janet says with a touch of pride.

'As soon as we established that Marsh and his ex-wife, Victoria DeVere, were still thick as thieves, we had the thread and it was just a matter of pulling it. She owns hundreds of thousands of pounds' worth of stock in Bringley's. They were playing the long game – got divorced to sever the legal conflict of interest, but retained all the assets in her name. The pair of them have been easyJetting back and forth from Gatwick to Málaga like they're commuting on the Piccadilly Line. The Seaview deal was going to be his *coup de grâce*. Once he pushed through the sale of the allotment land to Bringley's, he was going to join her in Marbella for good.'

The Seaview deal. Janet takes a sip of tea, trying to wash away the sour taste in her mouth. 'Rotter,' she mutters.

Glynis nods in agreement. 'He took a risk planting the knotweed. Either he was getting cocky or he was in a big hurry to get his hands on the cash. You were spot on about Kandox, by the way – the entity picking up the tab for Marsh's house. It's one of Bringley's many shell companies.'

Glynis gathers up the papers, stacks them neatly and slips them back into her folder.

'It took Giulia some time to run down all the Russian dolls of their money laundering but now we can see the wider scheme. They've been targeting allotments and children's playgrounds in AONBs and seaside towns across the country for the last several years. They use a combination of bribes and blackmail to get local officials on board, then they swoop in to steal public land for massive private profit.'

'Pure evil,' says Janet.

Glynis tucks the folder into her briefcase, stands up. 'Despicable. But that ends now. They met their match in Janet Pimm.'

'And her friends,' adds Janet, blushing ever so slightly.

Glynis carefully smooths the lapels of her perfectly tailored jacket.

'Indeed. I hear the Invisible Women's Club are rather a force to be reckoned with.' She looks directly at Janet. 'When you plan your next coup, count me in.'

If Bev were here, she would hug Glynis.

Janet shakes her hand. Firmly.

'I can't thank you – and Giulia – enough.'

'When Douglas was in the hospital, I would have gone up the walls without this excellent puzzle to work on. So, thank *you*.' Glynis narrows her eyes. 'I knew Napier was a fool to get rid of you. You were so damn clever.' She gives a wry smile. 'Looking back, I'm sure that is exactly why he got you transferred. He knew you were so sharp you could cut him.'

'Perhaps.' But it doesn't seem to matter so much any more. Janet has spent too much time thinking about the past.

Glynis taps her briefcase. 'Right. Giulia has alerted the UK Financial Intelligence Unit to Bringley's shady business practices. We'll leave them to take it from here. I've got a car waiting outside, so I must dash, but I'll run this dossier over to the Detective Superintendent of East Sussex before

I head back to London. She can deal with Marsh. But if you want to have a quick chat with your foe before they come for him, I left Marsh's number under my teacup. Because this time, justice has been well and truly done. This time you got the bastards, Pimm, and you should have your moment. So long.'

Even after Glynis has disappeared from sight, Janet can still hear the sweet clip of her Viennese heels.

Janet takes the time to pour herself a fresh cup of loose-leaf Assam before she makes the call.

Marsh's voice exudes confidence with a hint of impatience.

'Pete Marsh?' says Janet.

'Yup.'

She sees him in that ugly liver-coloured den, so smug.

'Mr Marsh, I'm in possession of travel records and bank statements establishing that you and your ex-wife, Victoria DeVere, are conspiring in criminal activities including tax evasion and insider trading.'

'Who is this?'

'Undeclared income, hidden offshore accounts . . .'

'What the—'

'. . . the bribery and blackmail of local councillors in Hastings, Lancaster and Worcestershire . . .'

'Rubbish.'

'. . . and let's not forget the Wildlife and Countryside Act 1981, section one hundred and fourteen; the knot-weed you've been spreading around the country clearly violates that law.'

'I'm hanging up right now.'

'I wouldn't be surprised if you keep knotweed rhizomes in the fridge. Next to your buttery Chardonnay.'

A pause. 'Who the fuck is this?'

'I'm a representative, speaking on behalf of "OAPs and middle-aged frumps". And our message to you is: get those bulldozers off our allotments *now* or we're going to wikileak you to hell and back.'

29

Crowds flock to Seaview. Patrice was right to pull out all the stops. It is a perfect May day for a fete; the sun is out in all its glory in an embarrassingly blue sky. Gardeners proudly display the actual fruits of their labour, along with flowers and vegetables, on trestle tables. Sanjay's asparagus focaccia are going like hot cakes and there is a queue for Rosa's home-made rhubarb crumble. Ken, selling his spring cabbage, proclaims to all the customers that every penny they make will support local refugees. Brenda would be proud to know their plot is still going strong.

Felicity's trestle table is covered in a red-and-white-checked tablecloth heaped with a gleaming selection of glass jars of apricot jam and preserved plums, all with attractive gingham-patterned lids.

'Home-made jams,' she trills.

'Is it just me . . .' Bev whispers to Janet as they pass, 'or do those look exactly like Bonne Maman with the labels steamed off?'

Janet nods. 'Never mind the fact that British apricots and plums won't be ripe for at least another couple of months.'

'Janet,' Felicity calls, 'do take a pot of my apricot jam – take two! No charge!'

'She's changed her tune,' Bev remarks as they walk on.

'Oh yes.' Janet arcs her brow. 'FbK has become quite the fan since I *went viral*.'

Bev links her arm through Janet's. 'You should be proud.'

'I'm not sure winning the approval of FbK is something to write home about.'

'You continue to inspire me, just like the very first time I saw you striding down the street.'

'Don't be silly.' Janet's cheeks pink.

'You marched right up to those bulldozers! You broke into Marsh's house! You got arrested for your green activism . . .'

'So did you.'

'I would never have survived that night in the storm without you,' Bev says.

'Without me, you would never have been out in the storm.'

'And you might like to know that you have also inspired me in the purchase of a two-person tent. I've just booked Eddie and me in for a week's hiking and camping in North Norfolk this summer!'

Janet is astounded, but attempts to sound neutral. 'Is Eddie . . . pleased?'

'He will be when I tell him. It will be good for us, an adventure. A real change. Out in nature, sleeping under the stars. Start flat was my thinking – that's why Norfolk – then next year, who knows, we might even give those Three Peaks a go!'

Good grief!

'Right, Janet, if I'm going to help you with your plot you'll have to give me a lesson or two.'

'Teach you!' Yes indeed! They will begin with the essentials of mulching and compost, of course, and then . . .

'Thought we might start with a wee bit of topiary . . .' Bev says.

Janet blanches.

Bev nods. 'Aye, a dove or maybe a nice duck would show off your plot really well. What do you think?'

'A duck,' Janet says faintly, but she sees the corner of Bev's mouth twitch and then her companion gives a snort of laughter.

'I had you there for a moment!' Bev says, wiping her eyes. 'You should have seen your face. But seriously, I'd love you to teach me – if you have time, of course.'

It's true that Janet's schedule is rather busy, what with the invitations to give talks and workshops, be interviewed and pose for photo shoots. In recent exciting news, a nearby National Trust garden has been in touch inviting her to give a series of masterclasses on medicinal plants. Perhaps their honey is rather on the pricey side, but after all, it *is* organic. And delicious. The Steer Manures – or rather, Nick and Mary – have offered to help Janet with her replanting and presented her with a smart new garden fork. They are setting to with a redesign of the raised beds in their plot, and have asked Janet's advice.

But despite all the 'likes', and the 'tweets' and offers and kindnesses, Janet still feels an ache that no comfrey poultice or sage tea can calm. Because, splendid as all this is, it isn't what she longs for. She wished for it that day walking clockwise round the old oak tree, whispering into its wild roots.

Love.

~

The fete is drawing to a close. A group of gardeners and guests lounge by the pizza oven, drinking wine, laughing, lingering to watch the sun set. As she leaves, Bev announces that she has finally decided what kind of plant she would be: '*Clitoria ternatea*, nae doot.' Bev is going to meet Eddie for a date night at Bella Vista on the prom, but she is coming for her first gardening lesson tomorrow after work. Janet has decided that she will leave part of her plot to rewild, but there will still be medicinal herb beds, of course. No rue this time, though. Janet has given Bev the recipe for the tonic she concocted out on the fell, which Bev has already posted to her new menopause blog.

Janet thinks again about what plant she would be as she walks towards her plot. Her ankle is fully recovered now, hardly a twinge. Remarkable how the body continues to heal despite ageing, steadfastly believing in its own renewal.

Janet stops in her tracks. '*Selaginella lepidophylla!*' she declares loudly, startling two crooning pigeons. Of course! The desert fern that lives for years in a semi-desiccated state, dried fronds curled in on themselves, a brown husk. But deep inside, the fern holds tightly to the possibility of another life. And when the rare burst of desert rainfall patters down on its parched body, its bowed fronds open out, arch backwards and reveal an oasis of green inside. A beating heart that was there all the time, just waiting for its moment. Yes, *Selaginella lepidophylla*. That's her plant.

The silvery, crystal song of a robin carries on the air. Janet smiles. She has always loved robins, how fiercely they protect their territory, defend what is theirs. But as she listens, she realizes it's not a bird after all. It's the sound of someone whistling, weaving the robin's dusk call into a smoky jazz riff. Good whistlers are so rare these days. She listens until the last sweet note hovers in the air and is gone.

Rounding the corner, she sees Patrice, in a crisp white shirt, a red bandana at her throat, standing on Janet's plot almost as if she were waiting for her.

'Patrice.'

'Janet.'

A beat.

'Thank you for taking care of my plot when I was away.'

Patrice holds her gaze. 'My pleasure.'

Music wafts across the allotments; Sanjay must have brought his guitar and people have started to sing. The sky is stroked lilac and orange.

'I was just thinking about your plants,' Patrice says, her eyes still fixed on Janet's, 'and that you must have a very strong heart.' A smile plays at the corners of her mouth.

'My heart?' It is certainly going like the clappers right now.

'The linden, the motherwort, not to mention the borage and the lemon balm,' Patrice continues, gesturing to the places in Janet's plot where those plants once flourished.

'I'm not sure I follow . . .'

'Every single one of them is a heart plant, right? Not to mention your hawthorn.'

And suddenly it hits her. Nearly every one of her plants was associated in some way with protecting or strengthening or repairing the heart. Is that what she has been doing all along? Seeding a plot to help mend her broken heart?

'And then there's your coriander, of course,' Patrice goes on, still with that smile teasing at her lips.

'Excellent for digestive health,' Janet says quickly, feeling her stomach flip.

'Is that right?' Patrice says. 'Hmmm. Because I was thinking more about how it's associated with desire . . . or, to be more specific' – Patrice raises a slow brow – 'lust.'

Lust? Really? Whatever next! But now that Janet thinks about it, her bed of coriander *had* been particularly fulsome this year – the thick froth of its succulent leaves, the wild green of its scent.

Janet opens her mouth to say something, but her words don't seem to be behaving at all. Where have they gone? And at that exact moment, a light gust of wind blows over the Channel and sends a flurry of waves eagerly jostling to the shore. The breeze continues its breathy way towards Seaview Allotments, buffeting across the grass pathways to Janet's plot, where it whips up a tiny leaf fragment, dancing it in the air.

Patrice blinks rapidly, pulls a handkerchief from her shirt pocket and presses it to her face.

'I seem to have something in my eye.'

'Shall I take a look?'

'How kind . . .' says Patrice, removing the hanky and stepping nearer to Janet.

Janet looks intently into Patrice's eyes. 'I don't see anything.' A catch in her throat, her voice barely a whisper.

'You don't?' Patrice says and, reaching her strong arms out towards Janet, she pulls her close. 'Do you think you might take another look?'

And then Janet does see something in Patrice's eye.

A reflection of herself.

And it happens, at long last.

A moment . . . a look . . . mouths moving close . . . then closer still.

Credits

Quotes on pages 95 and 316 from the film *Brief Encounter*, directed by David Lean, written by Noël Coward, Anthony Havelock-Allan, David Lean and Ronald Neame.

Lyrics on pages 97, 98, 135 and 210 from 'Total Eclipse of the Heart' by Bonnie Tyler, written by Jim Steinman.

Lyrics on page 290 from 'Silos Song', written by Rebecca Johnson and the women of Greenham.

Lyrics on pages 290 and 291 from 'I Will Survive' by Gloria Gaynor, written by Freddie Perren and Dino Fekaris.

Acknowledgements

Thank you to the endlessly brilliant Judith Murray, who I'm honoured to call my agent. Thank you to Kate Rizzo for all your great work. Thank you to Sally Oliver and all at Greene & Heaton.

Deep gratitude to the incredible team at Transworld. To Sally Williamson, my fantastic editor, for your expert guidance and your unwavering faith in *Invisible Women*. To the extraordinary Alison Barrow. Thank you so much, Hayley Barnes and Lara Stevenson. Thank you, Eleanor Updegraff for your attentive copy edit. Thank you, Marianne Issa El-Khoury for the gorgeous cover design.

Thanks also to Kristina Arnold for your support of *Lost Property* and *The Invisible Women's Club*.

Special thanks to friends and fellow writers: Ericka Waller for your generous reading and spot-on generative feedback; Lou Kuenzler for your astute advice and expertise; Kate Anthony for your excellent support and for believing in Janet Pimm's story from the get-go (and viewing many versions!); Jo Franklin, Sarah Tarlow and Christine Paris Johnstone for reading early drafts.

Thank you, beloved book coop, Jane Sillars, Debbie Kilbride and Jen Harvie. Thank you, Ali McArdle for the wisdom and beauty of your friendship. Thank you, Claudia Barton for the sparkly stuff. Thank you, Gretchen Schiller for your sweet constancy. Thank you, to my wonderful families – Mum and Dad, the PJs, the Hills and the Restas. And most of all, thank you, Leslie Hill. For everything. For your endless editing, dramaturgy and inspiration. For your incredible work and insight, tirelessly and expertly given. Thank you for your unfaltering faith in this book and in me. I could not have done it without you.

Thank you to all the sterling folk who have added their time, voices and knowledge to highlighting issues around women's health and the menopause.

Thank you to gardeners and green activists everywhere and, in particular, to my fellow allotmenteers at Marina Allotments in St Leonards on Sea.

Thank you, dear bloggers for all that you do to spread the word about the books you love. And thank you, dear reader for your generous time and attention which means so very much.

With thanks to everyone at Transworld for bringing
The Invisible Women's Club to publication.

Editorial
Sally Williamson
Katrina Whone
Vivien Thompson
Judith Welsh
Lara Stevenson

Copy editor
Eleanor Updegraff

Publicity
Alison Barrow
Hayley Barnes
Chloë Rose

Marketing
Julia Teece
Sophie MacVeigh

Production
Phil Evans
Cat Hillerton

Sales
Tom Chicken
Deirdre O'Connell
Emily Harvey
Louise Blakemore
Phoebe Llanwarne

Design
Marianne Issa El-Khoury

Contracts
Rebecca Smith

Operations
Alexandra Cutts

Q&A for *The Invisible Women's Club*

Q: Janet's love for her allotment is a huge part of her life. What do you think the power of nature is and why do you think this is so important to Janet?

A: I think, perhaps now more than ever, we are aware of the power of nature and its precarity, how vital it is to protect our extraordinary green planet.

A couple of years ago I made a performance called *Wild Longings*. A site-specific theatre piece which included a locally foraged feast, it sought to make audiences aware of human caused environmental damage whilst celebrating biodiversity. As part of my research, I worked with botanists at the Carnegie Institute. One day I asked the Director of the Centre, botanist Sue Rhee, what it was that had drawn her to spend her life studying plants. Without taking a beat she replied,

'I love plants for their patience. I love them for their ability to stand their ground and fight for survival whatever comes at them.'

In the book I give that beautiful sentiment to Janet. I associate that patient stoicism, that sense of holding on, with the female experience. Allotments, gardens – these are places where women often toil unseen, in private. Places where they can be powerful, where they can take up residence. Places where they can be themselves. Gardens provide a feeling of belonging, safety even. That is why her plot is so important to Janet. It gives her a place to be herself, where her loneliness is not so acute. Her plants give her a sense of purpose and let her express her deep need to tend and care and nurture. And to love.

Women have a particular relationship with plants that is both practical and poetic; they garden to provide food and nourishment and they garden to create something beautiful. There is a will and a want to nurture, to not only bring life into the world but to protect and tend it. In gardens as well as in allotments women are growers, artists, providers and care takers.

Virginia Woolf called for a room of one's own, necessary for women to create, to thrive. This may well be a study or writing nook. But it might also be the garden, the greenhouse, the allotment, or as it was for Woolf at Monk's House, the garden shed.

Q: The allotment community come together to stand up against authority and capitalism in the form of a very selfish council member – were there any particular real-life protests that motivated you to write about this?

A: Yes, for some time I have been aware of several cases wherein allotment land has been seized by local council and property developers. Happily there have also been a few success stories, such as the two year campaign by the stalwart gardeners from Farm Terrace allotment who fought to stop their allotment being turned into a car park.

Even more than that, at the time of writing I was increasingly aware of, and worried by, new government policy around policing dissent and curbing the right for public protest which led to the 2023 Public Order Act. I wanted to show the power of peaceful community action around green issues.

Q: The intergenerational friendship between Janet and Bev is at the heart of *The Invisible Women's Club*. What inspired you to write this and is there anyone from your own life who you drew on when creating the individual characters?

A: From the outset with *The Invisible Women's Club,* I wanted to write about female friendship. Specifically, I wanted to write about new friendships that are forged later in life. I was curious – why is it that as we age, we tend to stay committed to the long-established friendships we have made over the years but don't necessarily feel like we have as many opportunities to make new friends? What keeps us back? Fear? Shyness? What factors might stand in the way? Family? Work? Time? I wanted to explore what the challenges might be and what it's possible to discover in a later-in-life friendship, both in another and in oneself. I also wanted to look at the possibilities of intergenerational friendships. Many treasured friendships, including several of my own, are with people whose ages differ by decades, a factor which can enrich the relationship. I was keen to discover the levels of experience, maturity and confidence intergenerational friendships reveal and how these aspects shift and alter between friends and over time.

One of the things I love about intergenerational friendships is how they allow you to shapeshift and swap preconceived or expected roles and behaviours. I value the wisdom of my friends in their seventies, I love how they model aging, how they break the rules and make their own, what great advice they give based on their own lived experiences. But I also love the moments when *they* are the ones who exhibit the vim and verve, who try new things, take risks, who are raucous and wild. In *The Invisible Women's Club* Janet is old enough to be Bev's mother but it is Bev who takes on the more maternal role, allowing Janet to be vulnerable. Both women enable each other's sense of mischief, almost acting as the 'straight woman' to allow the other to misbehave.

Janet was a product of my imagination, she announced herself very clearly from the get go in her gardening apron with its assortment of tools and was not to be ignored! For Bev, I was inspired by my Mum. Like Bev, Mum was a midwife, who went above and beyond in her patient care, as so many of our NHS staff do. Mum hails from Thurso in Scotland and like Bev has a great spirit and sense of humour.

I was writing this book during the bleak winter lockdown and in the midst of my own perimenopause and really wanted to have a Bev around! I wanted her positive spirit and her cheeky humour. I wanted that for my readers and for myself. It was a joy to write her, and a joy to think about my Mum.

Q: Which character do you identify the most with in the story, and why?

A: This is a great question and reminds me of an email from a lovely reader who wrote that she was more of a Janet than a Bev (ironically her name was Bev!). I identify with both Janet and Bev. I know Janet can come across as a bit spiky at the start but my hope is that once the reader learns why – how lonely she is, how heavily her past weighs on her – they forgive her and also see her being brave and kind. Bev is a born carer but with a great sense of humour and of justice. Together, like so many good friendships, they bring out the best in each other.

I have to say I am also rather fond of Patrice, and I wouldn't mind Glynis's savvy and her sartorial style!

Q: Why do you think women can so often feel invisible at a certain age, and what made you want to highlight this issue?

A: I think a lot of young women feel (often uncomfortably) hyper visible. At middle age, there is pivot to invisibility, and that invisibility is not just feeling unseen but also unheard.

Many of us feel that somewhere between our forties and turning fifty, people stop seeing us. People push past us in queues, shop assistants ignore us, we start getting the table by the toilets in the restaurant, and then our order doesn't get taken as promptly. We might be able to take these daily rebuffs on the chin but things take a different, darker turn when we shift to the work place, and see how consistently middle aged women are looked over for promotion. And if you have been out of the workplace for some reason – family, health, redundancy – as a middle aged woman it is almost impossible get back in, whereas for a man the fifties is seen as your professional prime.

A lot of this feeling of invisibility is directly connected with the perimenopause and menopause, as if visibility is somehow connected with fertility. During and beyond perimenopause a lot of women feel an anger that can be hard to express. In writing the character of Bev I wanted to create a relatable character who struggles with these feelings of anger, often unable to articulate them to herself, let alone anyone else. Bev has a voice, a strong powerful voice but feels silenced. Ultimately it is Bev's relationship with Janet that enables her to vocalise the rage she is feeling and then act upon it as a force for good.

Age renders women invisible but friendship can make us feel seen. Janet is almost immobilised with loneliness but her attempts to find friendship backfire and she feels unlovable and invisible. The irony is that the person who has seen her from the start is Bev. Bev sees Janet for the woman she is. She sees aspects of Janet that Janet herself has lost sight of. Midwife Bev helps deliver Janet back to herself. I think we often seek friendships that in some way complete us. By our friends we are truly seen. They remind us of who we were and have faith in who we can become.

Q: One of the messages in this novel is that women can find their voice at any stage of life. What advice would you give to anyone who feels they might have lost theirs and wants to find it once more?

A: Women *have* a voice but are often unheard, ignored, interrupted.

For me *The Invisible Women's Club* celebrates brave, bold, tenacious women who fight for each other and for what they believe in. It lauds the wit and wisdom of older women, their friendships, their voices and the power of their laughter. I love the activism of older women, whether its celebrity octogenarians like Jane Fonda still marching, still protesting, or the older lesbian visibility of Miriam Margolyes out and proud on the front of *Vogue*. I love the generation of women who are currently speaking out about gender based ageism, about lack of menopause training and treatment.

Humour is such an integral part of female friendships. There is nothing that cements a friendship more than those laugh-till-you-cry moments. By the time Janet and Bev get theirs they have well and truly earned it, having, amongst other things, survived a night in the wild, shared secrets of grief and betrayal and broken the law by covering the walls of Hastings Council with menopause-themed graffiti. I love the raucousness of female friendships and think there is something revolutionary about women's laughter.

So my advice, dearest reader, is to find your role models, to hold on tight to your friends and make new and unexpected ones and to believe fully and absolutely in yourself, in your right to speak and in your right to be heard.

And keep that revolutionary laughter flowing!

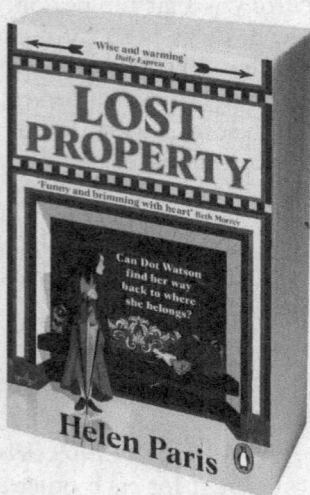

'Wise and warming' Daily Express

LOST PROPERTY

'Funny and brimming with heart' Beth Morrey

Can Dot Watson find her way back to where she belongs?

Helen Paris

One lost purse. One lost woman.
A chance encounter that changes everything.

Dot Watson has lost her way. Wracked with guilt and
struggling with grief, she has tucked herself away in the
London Transport Lost Property office, finding solace
in the process of cataloguing misplaced things. It's
not glamorous or exciting, but it's solitary – just
the way Dot likes it.

That is, until elderly Mr Appleby walks
through the door in search of his late wife's purse
and Dot immediately feels a connection to him.
Determined to help, she sets off on an extraordinary
journey, one that could lead Dot to reclaim her life and
find where she truly belongs . . .